I0819575

MAN OF MY DREAMS

ALSO BY OLIVIA WORLEY

ADULT

So Happy Together

YOUNG ADULT

People to Follow

The Debutantes

Final Cut

MAN OF MY DREAMS

A NOVEL

OLIVIA WORLEY

MINOTAUR BOOKS
NEW YORK

This is a work of fiction. All of the names, characters, organizations, places, and events portrayed in this work are either products of the author's imagination or used fictitiously.

First published in the United States by Minotaur Books,
an imprint of St. Martin's Publishing Group

EU Representative: Macmillan Publishers Ireland Ltd, 1st Floor,
The Liffey Trust Centre, 117–126 Sheriff Street Upper, Dublin 1, D01 YC43

Printed in the United States of America. For information, address
St. Martin's Publishing Group, 120 Broadway, New York, NY 10271.

www.minotaurbooks.com

Designed by Devan Norman

The Library of Congress Cataloging-in-Publication Data
is available upon request.

ISBN 978-1-250-37233-8 (hardcover)
ISBN 978-1-250-37234-5 (ebook)

First Edition: 2026

10 9 8 7 6 5 4 3 2 1

FOR THE READERS, THE WRITERS,

AND ALL THE BOOK LOVERS—

THANK YOU FOR GIVING MY STORIES A CHANCE

PART ONE

MEET-CUTE

NOW

YOU ARE MY FAVORITE GHOST. I see you everywhere: a flash of hair on a busy street, that fool's-gold catch in the sun. A familiar laugh reaches into my marrow, and it springs to my lips like a childhood song, a curse.

You.

But it never is. A head turns, or the light changes, and then the illusion is gone. Still, I can't escape you.

I find you today at the window—front and center, you'll be glad to know. A stack of your candy-pink books entices readers inside: *Haunt Me Then* by Ivy Harcourt, right beside a poster with your author photo: honey-blond waves, baby-blue eyes, and cherry-lipstick grin. It's an advertisement for your launch event, which happened a week ago, but evidently, they're not ready to let go of you yet.

I know the feeling.

Suddenly eager to see your signed copies, your name scrawled in ink, I step up to the bookstore entrance and reach for the door, and that's when it happens: the scratch at the base of my spine, the undeniable tingle that signals the truth to my body before I see it myself.

You, standing inside the bookstore, chewing your lip as you browse the stacks. I wait for the mirage to fade like always, but this time, you're real.

Here, close enough that I could touch you. I want to press my hand to the glass, to let my breath fog it with all the unasked questions: *Do you feel me? Do you know?*

Does it terrify you?

The temptation is so strong that I almost let it carry me away, let myself push through the door and call your name. But not yet. You're a writer, so you know the value of building tension—those little threads weaving until they become something new and surprising but wholly beautiful.

Soon.

I step back from the door, the fire in my blood receding to a dull, quiet sizzle. It never goes away, that feeling. The anger, the need. It will be necessary, too, in the coming weeks—fuel for what I have planned.

For now, though, I let it simmer. I leave you behind.

A smile cracks on my lips as I slip back onto the street, just another one of your readers disappearing into the crowd.

1

HE'S STANDING IN THE ROMANCE section—new releases—and it hits me with the force of a subway car plowing into the station: If my life were a rom-com, this is how it would start. Bathed in gentle spring light through the bookstore windows, the handsome stranger browses, pushing back tousled brown hair. He's wearing a Kate Bush T-shirt—the album cover for *The Kick Inside*, as soft and worn-looking as the identical one that hangs in my closet, a college thrift-shop find that practically begged me to take it home.

But what really captures my attention—the string plucked in my heart, buzzing with the quiet hum of fate—is the book in his hand: *Haunt Me Then* by Ivy Harcourt, the story I know like I know the way home.

"That's my book." The words slip out, and he looks up at me, brown eyes locking on mine. A bolt of heat zips down my spine, my cheeks no doubt flushing as pink as the cover.

"Sorry." I let out a laugh—nervous, breathless. "I mean, I wrote it."

He looks down at the book and then back up at me. A small, sweet smile curves on his lips, making me sizzle inside like butter on a hot pan. "No way."

Now I can't fight my ridiculous grin. "I had my launch party here last week."

"That's so cool." He opens the book to the first page, my signature looping beneath the title. "Congrats."

That sweet-puppy smile is still on his lips, so distracting that it takes me a moment too long to realize how this looks. *Oh no.*

"I promise I don't usually go lurking in my own book's section, like, waiting for someone to pick it up," I rush to explain—laughing a little too loudly to compensate for my burning cheeks. "Although you're the first guy I've ever seen with it, which"—I tuck my hair behind my ear, shamelessly flirting now—"is a definite point in your favor."

His smile fades. "Oh. Actually, I grabbed this for my—"

"Babe, look. I found this in the Used section for eight bucks." A petite, curvy woman rushes up to him with another bestselling romance in her hand, stopping when she sees me. Her eyes widen, darting from me to the book. "Wait, you look so familiar. Are you . . ."

"Hi," I say, flooded with white-hot humiliation as I understand what's happening here. "I'm Ivy. Um . . ." I give a little *ta-da* gesture. "I wrote the book."

"No way!" She gapes. "I'm literally *so* excited to read it. I've seen it everywhere, and my friends have been raving. Wait, would you sign it?"

"It's already signed," the guy cuts in.

"Oh." She laughs, bumping his hip with her own. "You officially win boyfriend of the year." She turns to me. "Wait, did he make you sign this for me? Oh my god, I'm so—"

"No, it's okay!" The overly bright ring to my own voice makes me want to wince. "I signed all the stock when I did my launch event here."

"Wow." The girl gives another stunned look at the cover. "This is so unbelievably cool, thank you!"

My cheeks burn with a mix of gratitude for the compliment and humiliation at my own misreading of the situation.

"Thank *you*." I take a step back, bumping into a rotating display of vintage mass-market paperbacks that nearly topples over. My heart thuds as I catch it. "Well, I hope you enjoy! I have to go, but it was so nice to meet you . . . ?"

I trail off, realizing I didn't even ask for their names. Not only have I just hit on this girl's boyfriend, but I'm also rude.

"Shara," she says. "And this is Dave."

He gives a small, awkward wave.

"Shara and Dave. Really great to meet you." I'm about to turn and flee when Shara speaks again.

"I already can't wait for the next one! Do we get to hear more about it anytime soon?"

She's clutching the book to her chest with a playfully conspiratorial smile. Dread winds its way through my bloodstream.

"As soon as I can," I tell her with a little wink.

I don't think I've ever winked in my entire life. Shara, bless her, doesn't call me out on the winking or the full-body sweat that is definitely shining on my skin.

"We'll be looking forward to it," she says, squeezing Dave's arm.

I wave goodbye, turn, and make a break for it.

By the time I remember the rotating display, it's too late. It crashes to the ground in a spectacular rain of shirtless men and heaving women, pages fluttering—loud enough that every head in the bookstore snaps in my direction.

"Shit," I blurt. Instantly, I reach down to haul the display up, but a bookseller stops me. Maggie, one of the people who worked my launch event.

"That's okay." She gives me a kind smile. "We've got it."

I watch in humiliated horror as another bookseller comes to help her fix my mess. I do my best to grab the fallen books, but I don't really know where they go on the shelf, and eventually, I realize I'm doing more harm than good. With another round of profuse apologies and thanks to the booksellers, I make my escape.

From one of the covers on the floor, a bare-chested Fabio looks up at me with his signature smolder, like we all should have seen this coming.

It's not until I'm two blocks down Broadway that I see the pure, ridiculous irony here: The reason I came to the bookstore in the first place was to distract myself from my last romantic disaster.

The walk light on the corner flashes orange, and I stop, a dry laugh bubbling out of me.

Two days ago, my debut novel surpassed all my wildest dreams by hitting the *New York Times* list as an instant bestseller. When my editor called with the news, I burst into tears and immediately called Aunt Mia, who cried joyfully along with me. That night, Dani organized a celebratory dinner with all our friends in the city, and we did everything we were supposed to: fell into squealing hugs, spent way too much money on fancy dessert, and cried some more.

And the whole time, in the back of my brain, I kept hoping that Xander would text me.

"Don't even think about it," Dani said when she caught me staring at my phone, her best-friend telepathy sharp as ever. "He's not worth it, Ives."

She was right. Deep in my bones, I know that no man who cheats on me deserves even one iota of my attention. He didn't even come clean—if I hadn't stumbled across those texts with some girl named Cat, a whole month's worth of raunchy banter and plans to meet up, I probably never would have known.

The worst part is, I miss him anyway. I may have been the one to break up with Xander, but he barely even fought it, and now, three weeks later, I still find myself wondering how someone who was so important to me for six months—my longest relationship in years, as sad as that is—could have cared about me so little.

Maybe I just need to accept that the only happily-ever-after in my future is fictional.

The walk light changes, but still, I don't move. The crowd surges ahead without me, spilling over with the excitement of a warm Friday afternoon. It's my favorite kind of spring day in New York: bright, buttery sun with cool shade to cut the heat, flowers blooming in store displays and bouquet armfuls. Tote bags and books, lemonade and picnic blankets. It feels like everyone is in love—with the weather, with the city, with each other.

And I am *not* going to waste it moping over a shaggy-haired poet. With a renewed buzz of energy, I shove my phone into my pocket, veer away from the subway station that would take me home, and turn instead toward Washington Square Park.

I'm nearly there when my phone buzzes with an incoming call. When I see the name on the screen, my stomach twists.

"Hi, Laura!" I answer, putting on a bright, casual tone.

"Ivy! How's my newest bestseller?"

My agent doesn't sound like she's about to drop disastrous news on me, and I let out a small breath. Most publishing professionals thrive on email, but Laura is old-school. I know this, and still, every time she calls me out of the blue, I can't fight the instinctive response that Laura dubs Gen Z phone panic, even if, at twenty-six, I'm not entirely sure that I qualify.

"Good," I say, trying even harder to mean it. "Loving this weather. How about you?"

"Oh, you know." I can picture her wry, hand-waving expression. "Dreading the three-month period when everyone decides it's fine to wear flip-flops in New York."

I chuckle, looking down at my own strappy sandals. What Laura doesn't know won't kill her. "What's up?"

"Just checking in to see how things are going on book two," she says. "Selene is wondering if you've got pages to share."

Now I tense all over again. "But I still have three weeks until the first-draft deadline."

I wince as soon as I say it: I sound like a kid protesting bedtime. *Just five more minutes!*

"Marketing wants to get a jump on things early, especially now that *Haunt Me Then* has taken off," Laura explains. "She just wants to give them a taste, since they haven't had an outline or synopsis."

I bite my lip. Laura and Selene both know that I'm a pantser—also known as a writer who flies by the seat of her pants, as the adage goes, instead of creating a detailed outline. Still, they believe in my writing enough to trust me. As part of my book deal for *Haunt Me Then*, my publisher also bought my second novel based on just the loose pitch: Lizzie, a lovable hot mess of an English teacher, butts heads with Liam, the high-strung British architect in charge of building a huge apartment complex next to her elementary school. Of course, enemies-to-lovers ensues.

The problem is that I've had almost a year to draft this book, and the hundred pages I've eked out feel trite and flat, like a soulless, AI-generated replica of every rom-com that's ever existed.

"Right," I say, voice getting even brighter to overcompensate. I dig my nails into my palm. "The thing is, it's still a little unpolished. I want to make sure it's as perfect as possible before I send it their way."

The park looms ahead of me now, bright green and teeming with people and music—stereos blasting, someone playing live guitar. I stop just outside the dog run, cupping my phone closer.

"Of course," Laura says. "But they're not looking for perfection. Anything will do. A few chapters, even."

Something else tips into her voice now—an edge, almost suspicious. I swallow down the paranoia, telling myself that she's not accusing me. She trusts me and my writing. *Even if*, a darker voice whispers, *she shouldn't*.

My mouth suddenly waters for a cool glass of rosé, sweet and burning on my tongue. I take another deep breath.

"Definitely," I say, smiling even though she can't see it. "Let me just clean some things up, and then I can send those chapters over next week."

I try not to picture the look of uncertainty I'm almost positive I can hear through the phone.

"Great," Laura says. "I'll let them know. Thanks, Ivy."

"Of course. Thank you."

"And listen, if you want to workshop anything beforehand, feel free to—"

I don't hear the end of Laura's sentence. It's cut off by a shout behind me, and then a commotion of barks and footsteps. I turn just in time to see an Australian shepherd racing out of the park, its owner running behind.

The man shouts again, eyes wide with fear. "Frank!"

But the dog doesn't stop. He's laser-focused and overjoyed, leash trailing behind him like a comet tail as he barrels straight toward me.

Toward the busy intersection right behind me.

My stomach plummets. Just as the dog is about to leap into the street, I lunge, my phone dropping onto the concrete. The dog crashes into me, and I scramble to grab hold of him. When my fingers brush a collar, I grip tight, and everything slows until there's nothing but fur, puppy breath, and a barrage of hot, sloppy kisses to my face.

"Frank, down."

Through the dog's snuffles and the ricochet of my heart, I hear the owner's footsteps pounding on the sidewalk. His voice is panicked and sharp.

"It's okay," I say, scratching Frank's back. "He's fine."

It's not until I say it that it finally hits me, and I let myself breathe, shaky relief flooding in to replace the adrenaline.

The owner tugs gently at the leash to pull Frank away, and it's there, with my ass on the sidewalk, that I get my first good look at the man.

He's tall, probably over six feet, with thick brown hair, a sharp jaw, and handsome stubble. Everything about him is handsome, actually: the white button-down and slacks tailored perfectly to his lean muscle, professor-style glasses framing his blue eyes, even the sexy leather messenger bag slung over his shoulder. The only giveaway that he was just sprinting through the park is the lock of hair that's fallen from its careful style onto his forehead—that, and the quick rise and fall of his shoulders.

"Thank you," he says. Clipped. Polite. Like a long-lost British prince, right down to the posh accent I've just picked up on. It's actually kind of suspicious how perfect he is—no one this hot should be roaming the streets with the world's cutest dog, unchaperoned—but somehow, he's standing over me, fresh out of a rom-com.

As soon as I have the thought, all the air sucks out of my lungs.

Not just fresh out of any rom-com. The hair, the eyes, the accent, even the ramrod posture. I know this man. Not in real life, but in my head. Standing before me is my latest manuscript brought to life. My hot British architect, the living, breathing embodiment of—

"I'm Liam," he says. "Can I give you a hand?"

2

LIAM?" I REPEAT. IT TAKES everything in me not to add *From my book?* It's impossible, but somehow, this man has walked right out of my laptop and into my orbit. He even has the exact same *name.*

I realize I've been staring at Liam's extended hand for at least five seconds and quickly grab it, his grip warm and strong—still impossibly real. As he pulls me up to standing, logic tugs me back down to earth. Yes, he's startlingly similar to my fictional character, but it's not like "handsome British man named Liam" is an impossible find in a city with eight million people. It's just one hell of a coincidence.

"Thank you," I say. "I'm—"

Frank's leash tangles around my leg, and suddenly I'm falling forward. Liam catches me with one arm around my waist. My hand falls onto his broad chest, and we're almost nose to nose.

Oh god. He smells *good.*

"Sorry!" I step back, untangling my foot from the leash while Frank pants happily.

"No, don't apologize." Liam gives a shy smile as he helps me. "I should be thanking you. I don't know what I'd have done if you hadn't been there to catch him."

"I guess I could say the same thing to you," I joke, indicating the leash.

Liam's eyes lift from Frank to mine, and something strange happens behind them. A flicker and shift, a new lens sliding into place.

"I know you," he says.

The words are like cool breath down the back of my neck, skin prickling to attention. *Me too*, I want to say, but obviously I don't. I'm still half convinced that I was hit by a car back there and this is my bizarre but beautiful version of heaven: my fictional dream man come to life, sprung forth from my brain like Athena from Zeus.

"You do?" I ask instead.

"We met before, haven't we? At the bar on . . . where was it?" Liam's brow furrows, the excitement in his eyes dimming to a low simmer when he realizes I have no idea what he's talking about. "I could have sworn we did."

It hangs in the silence between us, along with my unspoken answer: We couldn't have met at a bar, because I wouldn't have been there—and even if somehow I *was*, I'm pretty sure I wouldn't forget the hottest man I've ever seen.

Frank sniffs at my shoe. Liam is hesitant, a curtain drawing over his expression as he winds the leash around his hand. He's embarrassed, I realize, that I don't recognize him. The thought makes me guilty, because I *do*—just not by any widely understood laws of this universe. I know him in a way that doesn't make sense, which tugs at something low in my gut, an invisible string too powerful to resist.

"Actually, it's funny. When I saw you, I felt like I *did* recognize you." The words tumble out of me before I've considered that they might scare him off, but he's looking at me with those deep blue eyes, and I feel at home in his gaze. "So, I'm an author, and this might be totally weird, but—"

"Wait, that's it." He laughs, and the sound is so nice and musical that I forget what I was saying. "You're Ivy Harcourt."

I stare at him, stunned for a full breath before I remember how to nod.

"I've actually . . ." Liam rubs the back of his neck as his eyes drop to the sidewalk, shy. "I've read your book."

The four sexiest words in the English language, coming from quite possibly the most beautiful man I've ever laid eyes on.

"I'll admit I don't read much romance," Liam adds, "but my sister was raving about it last time we talked, so I picked it up on a rainy day." Another smile, cracking a little wider than the first, and it's like a curtain opening, hinting at the bright lights and wonder on the other side. "I quite liked it."

I was wrong: *Those* are the four sexiest words in our mother tongue, and now I'm at a loss for any of my own. My fault for thinking about tongues.

"Thank you," I say, a little breathless.

Liam holds my gaze, and my heart thuds. I'm not entirely sure that I can keep myself from reaching up and kissing him on that polite mouth, lips quirked slightly like there's a secret behind them. And maybe it really is brain damage, but the bright, wondrous look in his eyes tells me he might be thinking the same thing. Maybe we'd both be forgiven for leaning in and—

Frank barks, tugging on the leash. His tail wags excitedly, like he's forgotten all about his near-death experience.

Liam blinks as if breaking out of a spell and then laughs. "I know, mate. You're getting restless."

I feel it like the shadow of a passing cloud, racing to cover the sun before I've fully soaked in its warmth. He's about to leave, and this beautiful, impossible coincidence will dissipate like a daydream.

"I should be getting Frank home," Liam says. "But is there any chance I can get your number?" His brows lift hopefully. My heart grows wings. "I'd love to take you out for coffee or dinner—to repay you for saving Frank, of course, but also . . ."

A lovely blush deepens his cheeks, and all my fears vanish as I hang on the fishhook of those words.

"I'd like to get to know you, Ivy."

He smiles, a little shyly, and now I'm crashing up through deep blue waters, breathless in the sun-bright air.

"I was worried I'd have to wait until the next time Frank escapes," I tease.

Liam's smile stretches into a brilliant grin. Then he reaches for his messenger bag.

"I think I should have a pen and paper somewhere, or . . ." He stops, a soft, slightly embarrassed laugh bubbling out of him. "Well, er, I do have this."

Even before Liam pulls it out of his bag, I know what it is: a copy of *Haunt Me Then*. I laugh, warmth crackling in my chest like embers stoked in a fireplace.

"You know, I could just put my number in your phone," I say.

Liam's cheeks flush pinker.

"Right." He chuckles, running a hand over his hair. "I'm a little nervous, if I'm honest."

I beam, reaching for my own tote.

"No, I like this better. Besides . . ." I pull out the Sharpie I keep on hand in case I want to sign stock at a store. "I just so happen to have this. Not that I expect to give autographs at a moment's notice." I laugh. "But I like to be prepared."

With a smile that turns my insides molten, Liam flips the book to the first page and hands it to me.

As I write my number, the surreal nature of the moment hits me with full force. Here I am, giving my phone number to a real-life manifestation of my newest fictional love interest. Maybe it should unsettle me that this man appeared out of nowhere with my character's exact name and appearance—with *my book* in his bag—but isn't this exactly the sort of thing that would happen in a rom-com?

As soon as I've had the thought, though, another, darker one swallows it: *It's also the sort of thing that happens at the beginning of a horror movie.*

Fighting a shudder, I give the book back to Liam, and our hands brush with a warm spark that shoots all the way up my arm, landing in my heart with a buzzing certainty: It's too late for me to care. He opens his bag to put the book back, and that's when I notice the reusable water bottle in its pocket, branded with a logo: MEYER AND GREEN ARCHITECTS.

A dry, surprised laugh escapes me. An architect—just like the Liam from my book.

"You all right?" Liam asks, concern dripping into his expression.

I blink, fixing on a smile. "Yeah. I just . . ." I hesitate. Suddenly, explaining this whole coincidence to Liam seems like a bad idea—too intense and off-putting for a first meeting. "Had this weird déjà-vu feeling."

Liam closes his bag with a small chuckle. "I know it well. It really does feel like we've met before, doesn't it?"

When his deep blue eyes lift to mine again, they glint with something I can't quite read—awe mixed with something else. Something dangerous. It tugs at that invisible string again, and I can't help but wonder if this really *is* fate. As soon as I have the thought, a small shudder runs through me. The thing with fate is it can also be deadly: fatal flaws, Achilles' heels, prophecies where all roads lead to death.

But then Liam smiles again, and I forget everything but the warmth in my core.

"I'll see you soon, Ivy. It was lovely to officially meet you."

Excitement flutters in my chest, melting through all my hesitation, and I know there's no turning back: I've stepped over the ledge, a breath away from the familiar fall.

I can only hope that this time, he's there to catch me.

I'm all the way back to my apartment before I remember Laura's text: Got disconnected. Hope everything's ok. Looking forward to your pages next week!—L

All the anxiety I felt on our call has faded, leaving only a big grin on my face as I respond.

So sorry! Had a minor incident with a runaway dog and dropped my phone! Will get you those pages on Monday ☺

Is Monday an optimistic goal? Probably, given that the pages are currently a mess—but I'm still riding on the high of Liam and his text that flew onto my screen mere moments before I remembered Laura's.

I really enjoyed meeting you today (as did Frank!) Hope to see you soon—perhaps next Friday evening, if you're available?

Now I kick off my sandals and sink into my couch, feeling like a heart-eyes cartoon as I write back.

Friday sounds perfect!

The crush-struck part of me wants to sit and stare at my phone until Liam responds, but Laura's deadline lingers like a leak in my ceiling, threatening collapse if I don't handle it soon. I set my phone aside and open my laptop, settling deeper into the cushions.

Since I got my book deal and became a full-time author, my small but cozy studio in Yorkville—one of the more affordable neighborhoods on the Upper East Side, which is to say I'm still paying an arm and a leg—has become my office. At first, I had grand ambitions of being one of those authors who works at trendy cafés or, at the very least, at an immaculately organized desk. But even if I *had* one of those, the truth is that I do my best work when I'm holed up on the couch, usually in sweats and wrapped in blankets like a human burrito. From here, I can face the decorative fireplace that made me fall in love with this apartment, its mantel decorated with my latest struggling succulents, one fern that's hanging on for dear life, and all my favorite books—now including copies of my own.

My heart glows as I think of the day I opened that box from my publisher, my hands shaking with excitement—the first time I held a copy of *Haunt Me Then*. I loved the cover instantly: a cartoon illustration of the two main characters, Cath and Hayden, leaning back-to-back in front of a beautiful Victorian house. It's a modernized reimagining of *Wuthering Heights*, following two childhood friends turned enemies who are forced to spend the summer together in the Westchester historic hotel that Cath's late father used to run, which has now been taken over by Hayden. Of course, they fall in love . . . and in this version, they get their happily-ever-after.

The first draft of *Haunt Me Then* poured out of me in just one month, words flying onto the page like they'd been written already—because in a way, they had. I may have gotten the idea from my favorite book of all time, but there was also so much of *me* in my debut novel: heartbreak, romance, my love of old New York architecture—and, most importantly, hope. I have always loved *Wuthering Heights*, but *Haunt Me Then* was for the version of me who wished, every time I read Brontë's masterpiece, that it had a happier ending—one where they didn't have to die to be together.

Like *Haunt Me Then*, my second novel is technically meant to be a reimagining of a classic, in this case *Pride and Prejudice*, but I can't seem to make it click. Now, after staring at the document for nearly half an hour, I've barely made a dent. All I've done is read over what I've already written, slowly eaten up by a strange new insecurity: The Liam from my book is nowhere near as compelling as the man I met today. Maybe that should inspire me to write, but instead, it leaves me feeling even more blocked.

So I do something I shouldn't.

It is a truth universally acknowledged that authors should never read their Goodreads reviews. Doing so is basically like approaching a wild bear with your arms outstretched and your face covered in honey, but still, I can't help it. It's as irresistible as reading an open diary—one where my own name is scrawled all over the pages. And if I'm honest, the five-star reviews are a hell of a confidence boost when I need one.

When *Haunt Me Then*'s page loads, my breath catches. My stomach sinks. There, at the very top, is a one-star review. Logic screams at me to scroll away, the sort of instinct that stops you from touching a hot stove, but the gnawing curiosity wins over. I read the piercingly brief review, from a user called Heathcliff.

Ivy Harcourt is a fraud.

My hands go cold against the keyboard. A *coincidence*, I think, my heart thrumming. Obviously, the name is a reference to the character from *Wuthering Heights*—plenty of people probably use that name on their profiles. This person's profile picture is a black-and-white portrait of Laurence Olivier as Heathcliff in the 1939 movie adaptation, and when I click on the profile, I can see their information. Twenty-six years old.

Based in Tarrytown, New York. The page was created this month, and *Haunt Me Then* is the only book they've reviewed.

Stomach churning, I drag my cursor over the Report This Review button. *Coincidence*, I tell myself again. *It's nothing. Just—*

My phone rings, jolting me out of my head. When I see the name on the screen, I let out a slow breath, closing my laptop. Then, once I'm certain the panic isn't visible on my face, I answer the video call with a smile.

"Hey, Aunt Mia."

At first, all I can see is her face mushed up close to the screen, squinting through her glasses.

"Can you hear me?" she asks. "I've had this new phone for a whole week and I still can't figure out the volume. I swear, they move things around just to confuse us."

I smile, genuine this time. My aunt has always been a bit of a modern-day hippie. She teaches art at a fancy high school in Los Angeles—the one where I got discounted tuition, thanks to her job there—and when I first moved in with her back when I was fifteen, she still had a flip phone.

"I can hear you," I say. "Can you hear me?"

"Yes!" And then Mia gasps. "Oh no. You're getting a front-row seat to my forehead, aren't you?" She pulls back to reveal herself at the kitchen table, sighing dramatically. "I'm ancient. I'm a dinosaur. It was nice knowing you before the meteor hits."

I chuckle. "Oh, please. You're hardly a day over Mesozoic."

Mia snorts. "Thank you, my dear niece, for that vote of confidence."

"Anytime." I smile, but my nerves prick as I shift on the couch. "So, what's up?"

My aunt and I are pretty close, but she isn't the type to FaceTime me out of the blue, and the anxious, paranoid part of me fears this can only mean bad news.

"I wanted to get your take on hotels," she says, and I relax. "A friend from work recommended some places in the city, but I know the venue is in Westchester, so I was wondering if I should—"

"Wait, hold on," I interrupt. "I thought you were staying with me for Dani's wedding."

Mia hesitates. "Well, I figured since you probably aren't staying with He Who Shall Not Be Named . . ."

"You can call him Xander." I give her a joking eye roll, but hurt thrums beneath it. Originally, the plan had been for Mia to stay in my studio while I crashed at Xander's for the weekend.

I'm so stoked to meet her, he'd told me one night, around two months ago, as we were cuddled up in his bed, my head on his tattooed chest.

You're sure it's not too much? My tone had been playful, but I meant it. Plenty of my relationships had ended because I'd wanted things to get serious too quickly, and part of me still had a wall up with Xander, even though I felt more comfortable with him than I had in ages. *Not just Aunt Mia,* I added, *but the wedding, and—*

Xander interrupted me with a kiss.

I'm sure, he said, sandy hair falling onto his forehead as he gave me a teasing grin. *I'll even wear a suit for you.*

Now none of it would be happening. He'd already been messaging Cat by then, though at the time, I hadn't the slightest idea.

"But don't even think about paying for a hotel," I tell Aunt Mia now, pushing down the thought. "Prices are probably ridiculous a month out from the wedding. I'll just sleep on the couch, and you can take my bed. We'll take the train to New Rochelle together." When Mia still looks uncertain, I add, "It'll be fun!"

She sighs, relieved. Money has always been tight for my aunt, especially after she had to take in the teenage niece she'd never even met—a fact I'm well aware of, even though she never made me feel anything other than welcome. Mia rarely travels, but Dani's wedding, of course, is an exception. As my best friend for the past decade, she's like family to me and Mia both.

"All right," Mia says. "If you're sure."

I give her a serious look. "I am."

"Then it's settled." She smiles. "Now tell me about your day! Writing's still going well?"

Uneasiness churns in my gut as that review flashes through my head, but I push it down.

"Yeah! Actually, speaking of the book . . ." A real smile plays on my lips as Liam takes over my thoughts. "The weirdest thing happened today."

Mia's eyebrows lift, intrigued, and I tell her the highlights: Frank's great escape, how I looked up at his owner and saw my own character staring back at me.

"I mean, *identical*," I say. "Same name, same hair and eye color, same accent. He's even an architect, like the Liam in the book. And here's the weirdest part: He knew me."

Mia gapes. "How?"

"He thought we'd met at a bar, at first," I say. "Which doesn't make sense, obviously—but then he realized that he actually knew me from *my book*. He literally had a copy in his bag."

Even now, my face heats at the memory of Liam—his closeness, those awed blue eyes—but in Mia's expression, there's a subtle shift, barely noticeable if I didn't know her so well. She's concerned.

"Wow," she says. "That's wild, Ives. But—"

"But?" The word slices out of me too sharply.

Mia hesitates, and cold trickles down my spine before she asks the question I know she's thinking.

"You're sure you hadn't met him before?"

I swallow, a strange metallic taste on the back of my tongue.

"I'm sure," I say. "I would have remembered."

"Of course," Mia says gently. "I just want to be sure it hasn't started again."

Somewhere in my memory, there's a distant crackling—a pop of embers. A splinter of wood.

"It hasn't," I say firmly. "If it did, I'd tell you."

My heart thrums for a different reason now—the sudden desperation for her to believe me.

"Of course." Mia's face softens. "I know."

I let out a breath, letting go of my defensive shell.

"So," I say brightly, eager to move on. "Tell me about your week."

Mia launches into her recap, including a detailed update on the squirrels that have taken up residence in her backyard. I smile and laugh along, but in the back of my brain, there's still that quiet hiss and pop, the low warning of a growing flame. Blackening the edges. Hungry.

ELEVEN YEARS AGO

COLD.

That's the first thing I feel, gasping awake in the darkness. Cold and something else, sinking into my hands and knees.

I rock back onto my heels, lifting my palms. As my eyes adjust to the dark, I can see that my hands are wet, dirt and grass caked into my skin. I brush it onto my pants without thinking, smearing mud onto the fuzzy pink fabric.

Pajamas. A hole yawns wide in the pit of my stomach: I should be in bed.

Something creaks behind me, and I turn, heart racing as the thing takes shape in the shadows. A swing set, the old chains blowing in the wind.

My teeth chatter as I get to my feet, legs shaky. Feet numb. Moonlight glints off the green metal play structure, the plastic slide.

I'm at the playground, just a few blocks from home. A breath of relief. I can be home in two minutes, before anyone worries.

But then understanding burrows beneath the thin layer of my tank top, goose bumps rising on my arms.

This isn't my playground. I'm not even in New York state—I'm thousands of miles away in Los Angeles, because home is gone. I live with

Aunt Mia now, in the room that used to be her office, with a bed frame and mattress that she'd had shipped overnight from an online retailer, the chemical smell still clinging to both.

I went to sleep, and I woke up here, at the public park in Mia's neighborhood.

The understanding digs its teeth in, making me shudder: I walked all the way here. It's at least half a mile.

Another gust of wind billows my pajama pants, and I look down at my feet. Bare. Caked in mud.

An uncontrollable shiver takes hold, reaching down to the roots of my teeth.

I don't remember a thing.

3

"**SO." I SET DOWN MY** menu. "Margarita?"

Across the table, Dani lifts a perfectly styled eyebrow.

"I'm getting a soda," I explain quickly. "But I'm also buying a drink for my beautiful and talented best friend."

Now Dani gives a playful roll of her eyes. "You don't have to do that."

"I want to. We're celebrating your graduation *and* your wedding!"

"Graduation's still over two weeks away," she says, ever the pragmatist. "And the wedding's not for a month. But . . ." Dani lifts her water glass in a toast with a little sparkle in her eyes. "I'll allow it."

I tap my own water to hers, grinning. Sitting outside at our favorite Mexican restaurant, my earlier worries have all but vanished in the evening breeze. Pop music drifts through the restaurant's windows, thrown open to welcome the first hints of summer, and the streets are alive with the energy of a Friday night in the West Village. On a night like this, it's easy to forget everything but the good.

"So," Dani says, once our waiter has brought over our drink orders and a basket of chips and salsa. "How are you adjusting to life as a newly minted bestseller?"

Even now, pride beams through me at the reminder.

"Still putting on my pants one leg at a time," I joke. "Except, of course, when they're skirts."

I swish my maxi skirt, and Dani laughs, a delightful snort that most people would never expect from someone so generally poised. "Wise words from the author herself."

As she sips her margarita, the gorgeous diamond glints on Dani's ring finger. She's had it all laid out for as long as I've known her—literally. On the day we met, the first of our sophomore year at my new school in Los Angeles, Dani told me her exact plan: go to Columbia for undergrad and med school, meet a fellow doctor, get engaged at the end of her third year, married between graduation and her OB-GYN residency, have two kids by thirty-five, and then spend her career kicking ass, taking names, and fighting to make the medical industry safer and more equitable, especially for other Black women.

Meanwhile, I barely know what I'm making for dinner tomorrow, much less what my life will look like ten years from now. But that's why we work so well: Dani keeps my feet on the ground when I start to drift, and I remind her to look up at the clouds every once in a while.

"Actually," I say with a thrum of excitement, "you'll never believe what happened to me today."

Dani sets down her drink with an intrigued expression. "Oh?"

Now I tell the full story, including the details I left out for Aunt Mia: my humiliating encounter at the bookstore, the adorable dog, and his even more adorable owner, like my story brought to life.

"And . . ." I pause, building to the last thing I didn't tell my aunt. "He asked me out. We're going on a date next Friday."

For a moment, Dani's face is unreadable, ever so slightly agape. Then she takes a small breath and straightens her spine—the exact series of motions she always makes when she's just been presented with a problem to solve. She grabs her phone.

"What's his last name?"

It's not the question I was expecting, but I hesitate, embarrassed, as I realize that I don't know the answer. Dani cocks her head with a reprimanding look that says, *Ivy*.

"Ivy," she says.

"We didn't get that far!" I throw up my hands in surrender.

Dani starts typing on her phone and then, a few moments later, she spins the screen around to show me.

"Is this him?"

My best friend really is some kind of internet-stalking wizard, because there he is, smiling from my screen. It's his LinkedIn profile photo, perfectly identical to the man I met today: button-down, glasses, gorgeous smile, and deep blue eyes.

Liam Carraway. My stomach flutters. It's a good last name—one I want to say out loud, feel on my lips. At the same time, a part of me relaxes: The character in my book is Liam Darcy, after *Pride and Prejudice*. If their full names had been identical, that would have been a step past charming coincidence, veering straight into creepy. Somehow, this makes it all a lot more plausible.

"That's him," I say with a little smile.

"The profile looks legit." Dani takes the phone back and scrolls. "Architect at the Meyer and Green firm. Went to MIT."

Now my stomach knots into a tight, surprised ball.

"Wait, MIT?" I look at Dani's screen, and sure enough, it's there. "The Liam in my book went to MIT."

Dani's eyes widen. "No way."

Before I can say anything else, she's typing again with renewed intensity. Then she frowns. The knot tightens.

"What?" I ask, too quickly.

"I can't find any other results for him," she says. "No social media or anything."

"That can be good though, right?" I fiddle with my straw wrapper, pushing away the little thrum of anxiety. "Maybe he's just . . . not superficial. Or he doesn't want his personal life online."

With a rumble of uneasiness, I picture what Liam will find if he looks me up: all my socials plastered with selfies and videos of me and my book, shiny graphics made by my publisher. I'm proud of my work, and I love sharing it with people, but I worry that to someone like Liam, my vast digital footprint could come off as vain.

And then there's that review still hovering on my Goodreads page: *Ivy Harcourt is a fraud.* My stomach churns.

"Maybe." Dani gives her screen another glance and then sets the phone down, fixing me with a serious look. "Ivy . . ."

"I know." The words spill out of me, defensive. "Maybe I'm rushing into things again, but I don't know how to explain it. It just feels . . . different. *Right.* And I'm sure the book stuff is all just a weird coincidence. I mean, it's not like I invented hot British architects who went to MIT."

A small smile curves on Dani's lips.

"I guess not," she says. "And I'm really happy for you, Ives. I am. I just want to make sure this guy is going to treat you right."

In her worried expression, Xander's ghost lurks, and I can't fight the little tug of embarrassment. Two weeks ago, Dani was consoling me as I wept into a pint of Van Leeuwen, and now here I am, diving headfirst into someone new.

"I know," I say, "and I appreciate it. I really feel like Liam is a good guy, though. But I'll be careful."

Now Dani's concerned-best-friend expression stretches into a full mischievous grin. "He *is* cute. You'll tell me how it goes on Friday?"

All my anxiety melts away, leaving only warmth. Despite all the failed relationships Dani has helped me through, she still trusts my judgment. She wants the best for me—and even if every romantic prospect in New York City leaves me hanging, I know I'll always have my best friend.

"Promise," I tell her, reaching for a chip.

Just then, my phone lights up on the table. My heart skips a beat: Liam.

How about a walk of the High Line
and then dinner? 6 p.m.?

I break into a grin and show Dani the screen.

"That's him," I say. "Planning our first official date."

Dani gives an approving nod. "Point one for Hot Brit. I like a man with a plan."

I laugh and reread the text, a pop and buzz like a shaken soda can in my heart. Just as I'm about to type a response, another notification flies onto my screen, this one from Instagram. When I see it, all my joy drains away.

Heathcliff2015 wants to send you a message.

Ignore it. The thought slices quickly through me, but I'm numb to the self-protective instinct: I open it before I can stop myself, heart thumping as the DM loads.

It's a video of a bonfire. I don't totally understand what I'm looking at until I realize what's sitting in the middle of the pile: a copy of *Haunt Me Then*, the pages blackening and curling as it burns.

My mouth goes dry. The sounds of the city wash away, leaving only the blood rushing in my ears, roaring and growing until it becomes something else: the distant echo of a scream.

"You okay?" Dani asks.

I snap back into myself with a small shudder, like I'm coming out of a nightmare.

"Yeah, sorry. Totally spaced for a second." I set my phone face down on the table and nod at the menu. "What are you thinking?"

My voice comes out normal, bright, but it feels like someone else's, some other Ivy controlling my avatar. Dani gives me a wary look, but she doesn't push it. As she talks through the taco options, my eyes drift to the other tables, the street around us—a stream of anonymous faces passing through the fading light.

When the waiter comes, Dani orders first. Icy condensation collects on her margarita glass, bright and beckoning.

I force down a sip of my Diet Coke, the carbonation burning my throat. When it's my turn to order, I pick the first thing on the menu. It doesn't matter.

I've lost my appetite.

I manage to get through the rest of dinner as my usual self. Then, as soon as we've said goodbye and gone our separate ways, I whip out my phone, opening Instagram and searching for @heathcliff2015.

Their page is basically empty. The profile picture is that same photo of Laurence Olivier, and the page has no posts. No followers. They're only following one account: mine.

Uneasiness grips me from within, frozen fingers curling around my ribs. It's probably just a troll, I tell myself. As an author with a public profile, I've gotten plenty of weird DMs. Still . . .

A car honks up ahead, jolting me back into myself. The street around me swirls with young people walking hand in hand or in tight packs, spilling from restaurants to bars and back out again, the night thick with possibility.

With a deep breath, I go back to the Heathcliff profile and block it. *There*, I think. *Done.* Then I open my texts and respond to Liam.

Sounds great!

And it is, I tell myself as I keep walking. Everything will be perfect, as long as the past stays where it's buried.

4

IT'S NOT UNTIL THE TRAIN speeds into Hudson Yards the following Friday that my heart begins truly pounding. I hardly get nervous for first dates anymore, but suddenly, I'm a walking collage of all the clichés: sweaty palms, short of breath, my whole body buzzing with the kind of jitters I haven't felt since high school. But there's no going back, even if I wanted to. With a deep breath and a quick glance in my phone's front-facing camera, I step out into the square.

Sunlight dances off the polished-glass buildings, reflecting water and sky like magic mirrors. Tourists gape and snap photos of the Vessel—the giant honeycomb-shaped structure that domes up to the clouds like something from the future. Even the corporate New Yorkers just getting off of work are moving with that slowed-down ease of spring, when the extra stretch of daylight feels like a precious gift, a sweetness to be savored.

"Ivy?"

His voice is like a touch on the small of my back, warm and gentle, and my breath catches. I've spent all week deep in my manuscript pages, filling in Book Liam's outlines with the colors I've gathered from the real one, and still, I'm struck all over again by the reality of him. It's like part of me worried he was never real at all—just some hazy, beautiful projection that would flicker out the moment I caught the right angle.

But here he is, standing with his hands in his pockets and that beautiful smile beaming brighter than any of the buildings around us, stealing all their light.

Real. Definitely still real.

"Liam, hey!" I breeze over to him, and he pulls me into a hug, his hands large and strong on my upper back. "Good to see you."

"You too." Liam pulls back, still close enough for me to see the sun glint off his dark stubble, to smell the freshness of his aftershave.

His gaze dips to take in my dress—tight around my chest, with a long, flowing skirt—but there's no lewdness in the way he looks at me.

"You look beautiful," he says.

Heat creeps up my neck and onto my face. I try to laugh, but it comes out as a soft, surprised breath.

"Thank you," I say. "So do you."

Now two pink spots burn his cheeks, and I grin, pleased to have made it happen. He *does* look beautiful, exactly like the day I met him: a blue button-down instead of white this time, but the slacks, loafers, and glasses are the same—like he walked right out of the meet-cute from my book.

A sudden, irrational thought snaps to the front of my mind: *Of course Liam is dressed like this. It's the only outfit I've written for him.*

Spidery uneasiness crawls down my spine, and I take a step back.

"Did you come straight from work?" I ask, trying to keep the tightness from my voice.

Liam adjusts his messenger bag, and I think I catch a flash of uncertainty in his eyes—but then he smiles.

"The office isn't too far from here," he says. "A lovely walk, actually."

"Meyer and Green, right?"

His expression melts into surprise, and I realize one second too late what I've done.

"I might have looked you up," I admit, pressing an embarrassed hand to my face, which is warm all over again.

To my relief, though, Liam doesn't seem weirded out. He gives a genuine, almost musical laugh.

"I'd say that's only prudent, making sure I don't have any skeletons in the closet."

My stomach flips. He's joking, obviously, but it pricks at something a little too real.

"You'd be surprised," I tease, pushing down the uneasiness. "I once went on a date with a woman who turned out to be a genuine flat-earther."

"No!" Liam gapes. "The horror."

"She had a YouTube channel about it and everything."

"Devastating." Liam shakes his head before giving me a hesitant look. "I suppose there is one thing I should tell you, though."

My heart thumps, and I realize I'm holding my breath.

"It's nothing bad," Liam adds quickly. "I just . . . also have a YouTube channel where I prove, beyond a shadow of a doubt, that Paul McCartney died in 1966 and was replaced by a clone." A smile tugs at the corner of his lips, eyes glimmering playfully. "And I also do a few Beatles covers, of course."

I laugh, flooded with relief and delight at this new discovery: Liam is funny.

"Okay, you got me for a second."

He grins, nodding toward the High Line. "Shall we?"

We make our way to the High Line entrance, joining the slow current of people walking the trail. It runs through an old elevated railway line that, formerly abandoned, has now transformed into a public park with bright greenery and flowers, a strange fairy-tale garden threaded through the steel and glass. For a moment, we're both quiet, taking in the sunny, fresh-air feeling that can be so rare in Manhattan.

"So," I say, "we have a problem."

Liam's expression turns as worried as mine must have been only minutes ago, and I smirk just like he did, letting him in on the joke.

"I'm only just getting to know you, but you've read my book. You've spent three hundred whole pages in my brain, and you presumably also read my bio on the inside flap."

"Studied English at UCLA," he recites with the posture of a diligent schoolboy. "Now lives in New York City with her struggling houseplants."

Now it's my turn to be surprised, my mouth hinging open.

"Good memory," he teases.

"Or obsessed serial killer." I'm joking, but that Heathcliff account flashes, unbidden, through my head.

"I'll never tell." Liam wiggles his eyebrows like a total dork, and I bite back a grin, pushing the anxious thought aside. "I see your point, though," he says. "I know plenty about you, but all you know is that I'm the man who can't keep hold of his dog. And a Paul McCartney conspiracist, of course." He gives me another teasing smile, and I chuckle. "What do you want to know?"

His expression is open and willing, that question like candy presented in beautiful wrapping. For a moment, I let myself taste it. It occurs to me, with a heady rush of irony, that I'm basically living every author's dream: meeting my "character" face-to-face, with an open invitation to learn what makes him tick.

"Why architecture?" I ask.

Liam's face lights up, so bright I want to cup it in my hands like a firefly.

"That's easy," he says. "I've always been fascinated by buildings—and, frankly, a bit bowled over by the fact that humans can make something so big and enduring. It's the simplest sort of magic, turning something from a plan into reality, something you can see and touch." He smiles, giving me a little bump with his shoulder. Heat floods to the spot. "Sort of like what you do."

I can't stop the smile that melts over my face. "I like that."

I like you, I think with a bolt of deep, overwhelming tenderness.

Somewhere within me, a warning bell rings faintly. *Careful, Ivy. Not so fast.* Suddenly, I'm all too aware of the heat of him beside me, our hands close enough to brush.

"What about you?" he asks. "Why writing?"

"It's my favorite thing, too," I say. "The only thing I've ever been good at, really, or even wanted to do." I glance up at him, and another wave of warmth rolls through me, bringing a not-unpleasant heat to my cheeks. "It is a little like magic, isn't it?"

Liam smiles down at me, and I think he feels it, too—that full-body flutter, a flickering flame.

"Well," he says softly, a low smolder in his eyes that could burn me from within, "you're quite good at it."

I'm suddenly so tempted to kiss him right here in the middle of the crowded walkway that I have to bite my cheek and focus on the path ahead of us, the trees with their little white blossoms blowing in the breeze.

"Thank you," I say, face hot. "But if you're trying to flatter me into stopping my interrogation, it's not going to work." I give him a playfully devious look, which he meets with his own. "How'd you end up in the States?"

"MIT, originally."

I nod as if I haven't already noted this other strange similarity to my book character.

"I grew up in London," he adds, "but I always wanted to come here for university."

New uneasiness whispers at the back of my neck. *London.* Book Liam is also from London. Sure, that's basically the first place any American thinks of when they're writing a British character, but paired with the same name, job, *and* alma mater . . .

"And then I got the job in New York after graduation," Liam continues, "so I've been here ever since."

"Is your family still in London?" I ask, willing myself not to linger too deeply on this new coincidence.

He nods. "My parents are, but my sister Phoebe lives in Bristol, working at the university. I love it here, though. I certainly haven't got plans to leave anytime soon." He smiles. "What about your family? I don't think your bio mentioned where you grew up, now that we're on the subject."

I realize too late where I've steered us, and a cold feeling curls in my chest. That question always scrapes at something hollowed-out inside of me, a dark and lonely cavern.

"I grew up in New York," I say, my eyes fixed on the path ahead. "A town called Tarrytown about an hour outside the city. But my parents passed away when I was fifteen, actually. I spent most of high school with my aunt in LA."

I feel it happening, even before I look at him: the little hitch in his breath, the weight settling on his chest. I've gotten so used to saying these facts that sometimes it feels as rote as telling a server that I'm allergic to strawberries. If I'm honest, I almost wish that people would give my tragic past the same reaction—*okay, got it, we'll steer clear*—but they never do. Already, I can see Liam spinning for something to say, some unattainable way to make it better.

"I'm so sorry, Ivy," he says gently. "I can only imagine."

Something in me loosens. I'm used to people saying they *can't* imagine, which has always felt like a lie. *Yes you can*, I always want to say. *You just don't want to.* From the kind, open look on Liam's face, I get the feeling he's different.

"Thank you," I tell him.

It hangs between us for a moment, this quiet understanding.

"How long have you had Frank?" I ask, steering us back, somewhat clumsily, to better first-date territory. "I've always wanted a dog, but I have this feeling that I shouldn't do it until I'm . . . I don't know, older. Settled—and, you know, able to keep a plant alive."

Liam laughs warmly. "I used to feel the same way, actually. I always assumed I wouldn't have a dog until I was in my thirties and probably married, with all the wisdom that comes with old age." He shakes his head, like he's amused with his own naivety. "As if thirty is somehow ancient. But then about a year and a half ago, just after my twenty-eighth birthday, I was lonely and fresh off a breakup, and Frank showed up on a rescue website. Which I may or may not have been checking at least once a day—out of curiosity, naturally."

Liam gives a teasing little smile that squeezes my heart as I do the math: Liam is twenty-nine, though I might have guessed a little older, thanks to the crisp clothes and general air of put-togetherness. *God,* I realize with an almost-shiver, *he probably has good health insurance*—a quality I find unbelievably hot, ever since I turned twenty-six last July and the government kicked me off Aunt Mia's plan, leaving me to shell out almost a third of my rent each month for the cheapest marketplace option.

Quietly, I also clock the mention of a breakup, and a morbid curiosity piques with it.

"And when I saw his name was Frank Lloyd Wright," Liam adds, "what else was I supposed to do?"

My jaw drops, a gleeful laugh bubbling out.

"Oh my god. It was fate."

"Yes," he says, a touch of gravel in his voice. "I think so."

Now the look in his eyes steals my breath. It's flirtatious but also deeper, like he's thinking the same thing: *fate.* We've stopped beside a tree that bursts with pink petals, a crown fanning over Liam's head, and my heart thrums, the moment melting between us like the first ice-cream cone of summer. *He wants to kiss me,* I think, and I want it, too—so much that I almost reach out and touch him, bury my hand in his thick hair, but that same warning bell flares a little louder. We've been on this date for less than an hour, and it feels almost dangerous to want someone this much so quickly.

And then, with another bubbling, unexpected laugh, I realize something: Frank is one of the few details that Book Liam doesn't share with the real one.

"What?" Liam asks, that dreamy look still lingering in his eyes.

"Nothing," I say. "Just . . ."

A thrilling buzz starts up under my skin, like I'm about to spill a secret, and it slips out before I can stop it.

"The male love interest in the book I'm working on is actually an architect."

An amused smirk plays at Liam's lips. "Is he?"

I give him a playful look in return, even as my cheeks heat. "It *is* a total rom-com job."

Now Liam grins, bright as the sun catching in the windows and glassy buildings around us. It's a smile I want to look at forever, and that warning bell rings again, even louder: *Danger.*

"Well, then," he says, "I can't wait to read it."

"I'm sorry, but I refuse to accept it. It's not real!"

"It's *very* real," Liam insists.

I throw him my best exaggerated look of disbelief. "How do we know that cricket isn't a conspiracy invented by the English just to confuse America? Or the biggest Mandela effect of all time? We remember baseball bats; you remember your weird flat cricket sticks."

"Oh, those are also called bats."

"Then what in god's name is a wicket?"

His lips curve in a devilish smirk. "The Crown's evil plan is working."

I laugh, my whole body warm despite the cool night air—almost like I'm drunk, actually, limbs loose and chest buzzing, even though neither of us drank at dinner. When I ordered a lemonade at the adorable Italian restaurant, Liam didn't bat an eye—just ordered one of his own. No questions, no strange little digs about loosening up. Just acceptance.

"So," I say as we wander down Eighth Ave. "What other dastardly schemes does the Crown have in store for this evening?"

My tone is breezy, still a little teasing, but my heart gives a thump. It's already nine thirty—we stayed at our table long after finishing dinner, ordering extra lemonades and moving food around our plates until the host gave us enough pointed looks that Liam asked for the check.

"I could treat us to dessert, if you're up for it," I offer. Personally, I might explode if I eat another bite, but a quieter, hungrier part of myself just doesn't want this date to end.

Liam hesitates, and my heart sinks.

"That sounds lovely, if I didn't have to get home to let Frank out," he says. "But . . ."

Hope stirs again, floating softly upward.

"You could come with me?" Liam's brows lift almost anxiously. "I live on the Upper West Side, not far from the Eighty-First Street stop. I know it's a bit out of the way, but we could watch a movie, maybe—if you're comfortable, of course."

Now it's like wings beating fast in my chest, feathers flying in their wake.

Of the countless mistakes I've made in my dating life, going back to someone's apartment too early is near the top of the list. Aside from the constant low-grade threat of being kidnapped and murdered, there's also the other, more likely emotional peril: being intimate with someone only to realize that's all they ever wanted, and now that they've gotten it, they'll be gone faster than you can say *good morning*. It's a danger I often ignore; I sleep so much better when I'm not alone, and usually, the promise of company in the darkness is enough to look past the obvious risk.

Now that familiar voice is in my head again, rumbling louder and louder with every moment I'm near him: I don't want to go home.

"That sounds lovely," I say.

Liam grins.

Twenty minutes later, we're climbing out of the Eighty-First Street station, Central Park and the Natural History Museum stretching out on either side of us. Streetlamps light the way as we walk, eventually turning down a street lined with beautiful brownstones—the sort I've always dreamed of living in, peering longingly into the windows whenever the lucky few leave their curtains open—until, finally, Liam comes to a stop.

"Here we are," he says.

It takes me half a second to realize that we're standing in front of one of the very homes I've just been admiring. This one is picture-perfect, a New York postcard: the clay-colored brownstone sits snugly between two others, a stone staircase with an iron railing leading up to a doorway framed by a beautiful cornice. On either side, pots spill with bright yellow flowers in a burst of green leaves.

I follow Liam up the stairs and through the door, which opens to an entry hallway with an old wooden staircase leading up and away—to other units, I assume. *So, Liam doesn't live in this whole place by himself,* I think with a strange bit of relief. I don't know how I'd feel about dating someone rich enough to own an entire town house in Manhattan.

Liam veers to a door on our left, slides his key into the lock, and pushes it wide.

As soon as I step into the entryway, I freeze.

Okay, so maybe I was wrong about Liam's wealth. Because he does not live in an apartment. This is a *home*: a living room stretches out before us like something out of a magazine, with a sleek wraparound couch, big airy windows, and a fireplace—an actual wood-burning one, with a stack of logs beside it. To the left of the entrance, a staircase leads down to another floor. A whole second *floor.* In *Manhattan.*

Before I've had time to fully conceptualize Liam's apparent riches, Frank comes bounding up the stairs, tail wagging furiously.

"Hello there!" Liam bends down and wraps his arms around the dog, who puts both paws to his chest and licks his face. "Do you remember Ivy?"

On cue, Frank prances my way, shaking his butt in excitement. I laugh, giving him a good pet.

"Glad to see the escape artist is behaving," I tease.

"Oh, rarely. I'm sure he's eaten something downstairs." Liam chuckles, rising to his feet. "Come on, Frank. Outside."

Liam leads the dog through the house, and I trail behind, taking it all in. A kitchen with droolworthy counter space and sleek appliances leads into a dining room with an actual table, big enough to seat eight. I've barely registered the fact that Liam probably didn't have to build any of this furniture with an Ikea manual and a prayer when he opens the door to the backyard.

"Wow," I breathe, unable to hide my wonder.

A deck leads down to a stone patio and a small garden blooming with color, all of it nestled inside a wooden fence climbing with ivy. Frank leaps down the deck steps, blissfully unaware that he's probably got the best deal of any dog in New York City.

"It's a lot, I know." Liam runs a hand through his hair, like he's suddenly nervous. "It was my nan's. She bought the place back in the seventies, when this neighborhood was still reasonably affordable, and since I'm the only other expat relative, she left it to me when she passed about three years ago."

Tenderness cuts through my surprise when I see the look in Liam's eyes.

"I'm sorry," I say, heart squeezing with a familiar ache. "Were you close?"

"We were." Fondness flickers in his smile. "She was a really wonderful lady."

"What was her name?"

"Margaret."

A breeze rustles through the backyard, ruffling the linen of Liam's shirt as his eyes meet mine.

"She would have liked you," he adds gently.

Warmth spills between my ribs like liquid sunlight, melting everything but a sudden fear that pierces my chest.

"What are you looking for?" I ask before I can stop myself. It's completely the wrong time—certainly not a question to ask after he's just mentioned his grandmother's passing—but I'm overcome with the desperate need to know. "It's just that I've been burned so many times by people who pretend to want something more than they actually do, and I—"

The words die in my throat when he comes closer, tucking a stray piece of hair behind my ear. His hand is warm on my face, his pulse beating against my own as his wrist brushes my neck.

"I think . . ." His eyes search mine, his voice scraping. "I think what I'm looking for is you."

Liam dips my chin upward, so my lips nearly graze his. My breath catches at the heat of his touch, the nearness of him, so close I can taste the lemonade lingering on his lips. And then he kisses me—tender at first, but something burns beneath it, a hunger quickly consuming us both. His fingers bury deeper in my hair as mine find his, raking through the thick locks and then roaming farther down his neck, his broad shoulders.

He grazes the small of my back, and a small breath whooshes out of me.

"Liam . . ."

I don't even know how I'm going to finish that sentence, and I never get to. Frank bounds up to the deck and between us, leaping excitedly for the door.

We both laugh, Liam's hands still on my back. I'm close enough to breathe his air.

"Feels familiar, doesn't it?" he jokes, shooting Frank a pointed look.

I know he means being interrupted by the dog, but that word digs deeper, rooting someplace warm and dark. *Familiar.*

"It does," I say. "Like you wouldn't believe."

We don't watch a movie. I'm not exactly sure how it happens—we don't discuss it—but when the full-home tour ends in Liam's garden-level bedroom, we both know what's going to happen.

His bed is nestled beside the windows, soft white sheets tucked with army corners, and I laugh as he leads me to it. Then my face warms with surprise.

There, resting on the nightstand, is *Haunt Me Then*.

Liam grins and pulls me into his lap.

"Are you trying to seduce me with my own book?" I tease.

He brings his lips close to my ear, stubble grazing my cheek. "Is it working?"

I don't have to answer. As his kisses trail down my neck, gasps whisper out of me at each electric touch. His mouth meets my collarbone, my hands winding in his hair, and suddenly, fear takes hold, cold shuddering down my spine.

We're moving too fast. It's what Dani would say—what any reasonable person would tell me about sleeping with a guy on the first date, especially one who appeared in my life with the kind of coincidence that only happens in books.

My eyes drift to my own cover on the nightstand, and the word starts to rush to my lips. *Wait.* Before I can even say it, Liam stops, like he can feel it.

"Everything okay?" he asks, still so gorgeously polite, as concern swims in the deep pool of his eyes.

I cup his face in my hands, running a thumb along the perfect line of his jaw. *Yes*, I think. *No. Both.*

Instead, what I say is "How are you real?"

It's a quiet plea, almost a prayer—that I won't get hurt. That he won't crumble under my touch like a sandcastle in the tide.

Liam smiles, curving his face into my palm. He kisses my wrist.

"I'm right here," he whispers back.

It's not an answer, but for now, it's all I need.

Later, when I'm nestled beside him, both of us starting to drift off, something occurs to me with a quiet jolt: Liam lives on the Upper West Side, just minutes from Central Park, but on the day we met, he'd brought Frank all the way down to Washington Square Park—significantly out of his way, especially for someone with a dog.

"You all right?" Liam murmurs, pressing a kiss to my shoulder.

My heart thumps.

"Yeah," I say. "Sleepy."

There are plenty of explanations, I tell myself, as I will my muscles to relax and snuggle in closer. Maybe Liam just wanted a change of scenery. Or maybe Frank's vet or groomer is in that area—just another coincidence.

Still, as Liam falls asleep beside me, the thought lodges itself in my head, keeping me awake: How many coincidences is one too many?

5

I WAKE IN A POOL OF sunlight, swaddled in softness.

Liam. His name ghosts on my lips, shorthand for last night and all it held: heat and pleasure, his hands roaming my body like he wanted to prove this was real as badly as I did.

I stretch out my arms, sighing at the pleasant tug in my shoulders. When I brush the space beside me, it's empty.

My heart lurches with the realization: I'm in Liam's bed, but he isn't here.

I jolt up to sitting, glancing around the room—also empty. Maybe he's showering? But when I strain to hear running water, nothing.

"Shit," I mutter, reaching for my phone: 10:30 AM.

Oh god. On any other day, sleeping this late wouldn't jar me—even before I was a full-time writer, my sleep schedule was never built for the nine-to-five lifestyle—but Liam is already up. I've overstayed my welcome.

I pull off the T-shirt I slept in—his, oversized and smelling like him, clean linen and woodsy shampoo—and scramble for my dress on the floor. My phone buzzes with a text from Dani, which, as I emerge from my sleep-addled state, I realize is the fourth she's sent me since last night. I read them all back-to-back.

11:00 PM How did it go?

11:45 PM That well, huh? ;)

12:30 AM I fully support whatever decisions you're making tonight but please send proof of life so I know you didn't get kidnapped

10:32 AM ???

I type out a frantic response.

I'm alive! May or may not be leaving his bed as we speak . . . I'll tell you later 👀

Catching my reflection in Liam's mirror, I wince at how frizzy my waves have become overnight. As I'm doing my best to comb them with my fingers, a memory rushes back to me with a sharp ache: Robert, the lawyer I met two years ago at a cocktail bar in the Village. We talked all night in a martini haze until the bar closed down, and then the next morning, I woke up to him nudging my shoulder, already dressed. *Iris,* he said, frowning. *Hey, Iris, can you get up? I've got a personal-training session in an hour.*

If nothing else, at least Liam knows my name. And if he really wanted me to leave, then he would have kicked me out already, right?

Or maybe he's just being polite.

I settle for a toothpaste-on-my-finger brushing and then creep upstairs, anxiety growing. As I go, a scent wafts in—maple syrup. Music drifts with it, a jazzy instrumental and then a deep baritone hum.

The air seems to still around me, hope crackling to life before I've had the good sense to question it.

Slowly, I walk into the kitchen.

"Morning." Liam turns from the sizzling stove to face me. He's in sweatpants and a T-shirt, a dishcloth thrown over his shoulder—a sight even more beautiful than the breakfast. "Do you like pancakes? I hope so, because it's the only breakfast I can make without disastrous results. The one time I tried a full fry-up, I nearly burned the house to the ground."

A smile melts over my lips, warm as butter.

"Pancakes are one of the best arguments for living."

Liam laughs, and it fizzes my stomach.

"Well, then," he says. "Pull up a seat."

I do, settling in at his kitchen counter as he spoons a few pancakes onto an empty plate for me.

"I've got syrup, butter, all the essentials. Some berries, too, if you like." Liam lifts his eyes to meet mine. "It's only strawberries you're allergic to, right? Not blueberries or blackberries?"

The concern on his face is like a hand reaching through my ribs, squeezing.

"Just strawberries," I say, smiling. "This is perfect, Liam. Thank you." I shake my head in disbelief as he sets the expertly plated dish in front of me. "I seriously don't think I've ever been this spoiled."

He grins, grabbing his own plate. "I'm happy to do it."

I'm reaching for the syrup when something hits me, freezing my hand around the bottle.

"Did I tell you I was allergic to strawberries?"

Liam looks at me from across the counter, brow furrowing. "Didn't you mention it at dinner?"

I spin back through my memories of last night, but I can't remember saying anything about it.

"You said it's fairly severe, right?" he asks.

"Right." I take the syrup, shaking off the uneasy feeling. I must have mentioned it. "I swear I have the memory of a goldfish sometimes."

I laugh, but it comes out weak. Unconvincing. But then Liam joins me at the counter, his knee bumping mine, and all my worries recede. He smiles at me, those blue eyes shining, and there's nothing but the hope still beating through me—a quiet, unspoken promise that last night wasn't a dream.

That for once, someone wants me to stay.

"Two *stories*?" Dani repeats, her voice rising through the phone.

I called her as soon as I left Liam's, and now I'm wandering through Central Park, making my way back to the Upper East Side. A bus would be much quicker, but it's too beautiful a day not to soak up the sun.

"Two," I confirm, barely containing my grin. "With a backyard."

"Wow." Dani lets out a sigh. "The dream."

"And he was sweet," I gush, "and funny, and a gentleman. He made me pancakes. Like, he genuinely might be the perfect man."

Dani laughs. "Breakfast *is* your love language."

Another huge smile stretches on my face. At the memory of the berries, though, uneasiness tugs it down. I still can't remember telling Liam about my strawberry allergy last night, but I must have. It just bothers me that I've forgotten.

Before I can say anything else, two dogs start barking loudly up ahead, both going wild with excitement as their owners pass each other. Like a quiet curl of mist, that other needling thought creeps in—the one that kept me up last night as Liam slept beside me.

"Actually," I say before I can stop myself. "There was one weird thing."

"Oh?"

I chew my lip. Once I voice this to Dani, there's no going back. But then again, if she doesn't think it's worth worrying about, I'll feel a lot better.

"It's probably nothing," I start, keeping my tone light and casual. "Just, Liam lives on the Upper West Side, but we met in Washington Square Park, and last night, as we were falling asleep, I started wondering if that was weird. Like, that's kind of a long way for him to go with a dog, isn't it? Especially since . . ." My heart thrums. "You know, there's all these other coincidences."

"Hmm." Dani's voice is noncommittal, but I can practically see her thinking face through the phone. "Did you ask him about it?"

"No," I say quickly—maybe too brightly. "It was one of those passing thoughts, you know? I'm probably just psyching myself out."

I let out a weak laugh, but Dani's silence makes me squirm.

"Maybe," she says finally. "I mean, it doesn't seem totally out of the question that he'd take the dog downtown. But if you've got a gut feeling that something is off, maybe it's worth investigating."

The anxious feeling deepens, and I bite my lip. "Maybe."

In the quick silence that follows, I feel something shift, softening.

"It sounds like he's a good guy, though, Ives," Dani says. "I wouldn't stress unless it's really bothering you."

Relief unspools inside me. I don't necessarily *need* my best friend's approval, but she's been my gut check since we were teenagers—bringing me back to earth when I spent eleventh grade obsessed with Justin Schulman, who genuinely wouldn't have cared if I got hit by a bus, or talking me down that time I thought about piercing my own ears—and I trust her judgment more than pretty much anyone's. I let out a breath, the tension flooding from my shoulders.

"No, you're right."

I can hear the smile in Dani's voice as she says, "I always am." Then, shifting back into playful curiosity, she asks, "Did you tell him about Book Liam?"

Fresh uneasiness swirls through me. "Sort of."

"Sort of?"

"I told him I'm writing an architect, but I didn't specify that I might accidentally be writing *him*." I cringe. "I was worried it would weird him out."

"No, that's probably the right call. You can always tweak the character's name and details, too, if you don't want it to be identical."

It's a good point, but still, the idea of Liam reading any version of this book makes me nervous. Even with a new name, the similarities are too glaring to miss.

"You know," Dani adds, "maybe this will be good for your research."

Her tone is musing, academic, and I let out a surprised laugh. "You think so?"

"Your first draft is due in two weeks, right?"

"Don't remind me," I grumble. "I sent Laura the first hundred pages, but I've barely made any progress since then."

"So, use this as inspiration," Dani offers. "You've always said you write best from personal experience." After a pause, she adds, with her classic dry humor, "Maybe there's even an argument for your dates to be tax-deductible."

I know Dani's kidding—at least a little—but even after we've hung up, the thought sticks with me. Because the thing is, being with Liam *is* excellent research—a theory that's proven more and more with every passing day.

On Monday, we go on our second date, a tour of the art galleries in Chelsea. I learn that Liam loves the abstract, geometric pieces, while my favorites are the lush, detailed portraits.

On Tuesday, I write a scene where Lizzie and Book Liam work a charity art auction together, and, hating each other's favorite piece, they compete to see who can get more bids.

On Wednesday morning, Liam texts me a video of Frank chasing a squirrel in the yard as I'm heading into Dani's Columbia graduation.

That afternoon, after a celebratory lunch with Dani and her family, I give Book Liam a dog named Louis Sullivan (after Frank Lloyd Wright's mentor.)

On Thursday, we meet for dinner in the West Village, and Liam kisses me in Washington Mews, a tucked-away cobbled street just north of Washington Square Park.

When I get home, I rewrite the first-kiss scene so that it takes place in the exact same spot, Lizzie standing on the raised sidewalk and Liam on the cobbles so they're closer in height, as tangled together as the ivy growing up the beautifully quaint buildings around them.

On Friday night, Liam and I have plans to order in and watch a movie at my apartment—the first time he'll see my place—and for the first time all week, I barely get any writing done at all. I'm too busy tidying every inch of my small square footage, suddenly too aware of how cluttered it is compared to Liam's pristine town house. Half an hour before he's supposed to arrive, I change outfits three times, trying to hit the perfect balance between "casual night in" and "cute date look."

I'm just slipping back into the first pair of leggings I had on when my buzzer sounds. I jump, and then immediately catch myself, staring down my reflection with a hand smushed to each of my flushed cheeks.

"Ivy Harcourt," I command myself, "calm *down*."

I've never been this anxious about inviting anyone over before—but maybe, I think with a little flutter, I've just never liked someone this much.

Or, says a darker voice in my head, *this is that gut feeling Dani was talking about—the little alarm that something is off.*

But there's no time to unpack either possibility: Liam is here, and I have no choice but to shove my discarded clothes into my laundry basket, take a deep breath, and press the button to buzz him in.

When I open the door, Liam stands in the hallway in an outfit I've never seen before: jeans, a T-shirt, and a corduroy jacket. Still dressy, compared to my athleisure, and I can't help but grin.

"Hey." I reach up on my toes and kiss him. "I don't think I've ever seen you in jeans before."

He gives a bashful smile. "Casual Friday."

I step aside, letting him in. For the first time, I notice the package tucked under his arm.

"This was in your lobby when I got here," Liam explains, passing it to me.

It's small, about the size of a shoebox, and completely unmarked, except for my name written in black marker on the cardboard.

"Weird," I mutter to myself as Liam slips off his shoes and sets them on the rack with such typical neatness—perfectly parallel—that I can't help but smile, leading him deeper into my studio. "It's small, but I love it."

Liam gives me a grin that makes me shimmer inside. "It's perfect." He steps up to my fireplace-turned-bookshelf, giving the potted fern a gentle brush. "Now I'd hardly say this one's struggling. It's got some pep in its step!"

I cringe. "That may or may not be a fresh replacement after the old fern died last week."

Liam laughs brightly.

"The circle of life," he teases, gaze drifting to the row of *Haunt Me Then* copies. "I've heard this one is pretty brilliant." He smiles, running a thumb over the spines before turning back to me. "And the author is *quite* fetching."

Warmth pools low in my stomach.

"Well," I tease back as his hands find my waist, "if that's what the people are saying . . ."

Liam kisses me, slow and deep.

"Hello," he says, mouth inches from mine.

"Hi," I say back, voice thick with longing.

Then Liam steps away, maddeningly polite once more—but with a small flicker of a smile, like he knows exactly what he's done to me. Another surprise I've discovered about Liam: Sometimes, he can be devious.

"Could you point me toward the restroom?" he asks.

I do, and then, as Liam shuts the door, I return to the package he brought up from the lobby. I wasn't expecting any mail, and my curiosity piques as I slice through the tape. With a snap, the seal breaks, and I see what's inside.

Confusion tugs my face into a frown. It's a copy of *Haunt Me Then*, identical to the ones on my shelf. I open it, looking for some sort of explanation, and that's when I see the red pen scrawled on the title page, just beneath my name: *Revised Edition*.

A seed of worry calcifies in my gut, some instinctive warning to look away, but I open the book and flip to the next page, the dedication: *For everyone who's still searching for their happily-ever-after.*

Except beneath that, someone has written in the same red pen: *Even the ones who have to steal it?*

Dread rises thick in my chest as I flip again. The next page—the opening chapter of the book—is almost completely blacked out in marker, leaving only a few words visible. Together, they make a brand-new sentence:

you
May
want to
forget

It's an opening, an unfinished thought, and on the next page, I find its conclusion.

but I'm still Here

A scream builds in my throat, so strong I have to bite my tongue to stop it, my mouth filling with the bright copper tang of blood. And then it's there, close enough to taste it: The burning. The smoke.

The bathroom door swings open, and I shove the book back into the package, setting it on the table just as Liam reappears. I feel like a wild animal caught in a trap, my cheeks flushed, my heart thrumming, but I paint on a warm smile.

"What are you thinking for dinner?" I ask.

Concern flickers in Liam's expression for just a moment, but my act must be convincing enough, because he brushes another kiss onto my forehead.

"Whatever you like." Liam glances at the opened package, and I have to resist the urge to snatch it away. "What was it?"

"Another copy of my book," I tell him—technically true. "I'm not sure why they sent it, but I guess it doesn't hurt to have extras."

With another smile that hurts my cheeks, I walk back to the couch, leaving the package behind and praying he won't look more closely. Thankfully, Liam follows, settling into the cushions beside me. I pull out my phone to scroll through dinner menus—normal, easy—but all the while, my brain is humming with panic. That review calling me a fraud and the DM from "Heathcliff" seemed like nothing at first, but now . . .

Understanding slices through me, as sharp and cold as a scalpel. That package had no shipping label, no return address. The only way it could have arrived in my lobby is in the hands of the person who made it.

This book isn't just an accusation. It's also a threat, as impossible to ignore as that angry red pen: *I know where you live.*

And then another understanding whispers from the shadows: *Liam is the one who brought it to me.*

6

I DON'T SLEEP. EVEN WITH LIAM curled in my bed beside me, I can only think of that box and the defaced book inside, the terror keeping me wide awake as Liam gently snores.

I wait a minute, and then another. Once I'm sure that he's fully asleep, I carefully extract myself from his arms and creep over to the package, still on my table, and do what I've wanted to do all night—what I would have done instantly if Liam weren't here, watching: I shove it in the trash.

When I close the garbage can, Liam stirs, and I freeze. I wait a few beats—marking time with the loud thumps of my heart—but he doesn't wake up. Then, as quietly as possible, I creep over to my door and look through the peephole to the hallway outside. One of the lights flickers overhead, illuminating the cracked, dingy tile. Not a soul outside. I let out a shuddering breath.

In the hours since I opened the package, that dark and terrible possibility has haunted me, even as Liam kissed me slowly in my bed—as I let him undress me, his touch roaming over my bare skin.

Liam was the one who carried the package upstairs. He said he found it in the lobby when he got here, but I've only ever seen it in his hands.

Instinctively, I turn back to him, but his shoulders still rise and fall harmlessly with sleep. My chest aches with tenderness. Despite my wild suspicions, one fact remains: Even now, in the absence of his disarming blue eyes, I trust him. The package must have been in the lobby when he got here. Bringing it up was just a kind, innocent gesture.

It's also another coincidence to add to the ever-growing list.

I step away from the door. Then, after double-checking the dead bolt, I crawl carefully back into bed. Liam stirs again, hugging an arm around my waist.

"You're up," he murmurs into my shoulder.

I tense, but when I turn to look at him, his eyes have already fluttered shut again.

Gently, I run a hand through Liam's hair, trying to soothe us both. He snuggles closer, and my heart squeezes. As he sleeps, I fix my eyes on my door, laser-focused through the darkness—waiting for the shadow of an approaching stranger to creep like outstretched fingers from under the crack.

I wake in a flush of sweat, my mouth dry as cotton.

"Morning." Liam chuckles sleepily behind me, unwrapping his arm from my waist. "Did I startle you?"

I turn to face him, my wild heart slowing. He's as beautiful as ever: his usually perfect hair ever so slightly askew, a strip of sunlight from my window catching the golden undertones of his dark stubble.

I let out a breathy laugh. "Sorry. I don't think I slept very well."

"Not my fault, I hope?"

Last night trickles back to me: suspicions tangling up in my head as I stared at the door until well past three in the morning. I don't remember falling asleep.

"Not at all," I lie, smoothing out a stray lock of his hair. "Weird dreams."

"Mm." He pulls me closer, planting a kiss on my shoulder. "What about?"

But then he's kissing up to my collarbone, and my answer is an involuntary sigh. "Don't remember."

Even if I did, I'm pretty sure I'd forget all over again.

He smiles into my neck.

"You know," he says, breath warm, "you talk in your sleep."

I pull back, body going cold.

"Do I?" I ask. "What did I say?"

Liam's smile wavers, and my heart thrums in fear of the answer.

"Nothing, really," he says. "Just a few nonsense words. Something about a fire? It would have been much more of a problem if we were in a crowded theater."

He gives a teasing smile, but the cold intensifies until it swings back to heat, a searing burn.

"Huh," I force myself to say as I reach for my phone—any excuse to turn away, to not let him see the look on my face. "Weird."

"It really didn't bother me," Liam assures me, sounding like he regrets even bringing it up. Guilt curls in my chest, and I turn back to him, pressing a kiss to the worried lines on his forehead.

"It's okay." I smile. "You snore a little, but I like it."

Liam wipes a hand over his embarrassed grin. "You promise?"

In spite of everything, my heart swells. In the light of the morning, last night seems like nothing more than paranoia—just my anxious brain self-sabotaging, afraid to let me trust someone again.

"I swear. Now how do you feel about bagels?"

We stop at my favorite neighborhood spot and then take them to the little park nearby, where we eat side by side on a bench, his knee pressing softly into mine. It's a perfect morning.

It *should be* perfect, if it weren't for the constant hum of worry in my head. Every time I loosen my grip on my thoughts, they wander back to that package, stashed like a secret in my trash.

I'm still here.

"Ivy?"

"Hmm?" I snap back into myself, realizing I've just missed whatever Liam said. "Sorry, lost in a bagel haze."

A smile flashes on his lips.

"Understandable. I was just asking what you're up to for the rest of today. I ought to get home to let Frank out, but I'm not busy otherwise, if you wanted to join me." When I hesitate for a moment, he adds quickly, "Feel free to say no, of course."

The worried look in his eyes widens a crack in my heart. It's a feeling I know too well—realizing you might be coming on a little too strong.

"I'd love to," I say honestly. "But I probably need to work today. My draft is due next Friday, so I can't really take any days off."

His face falls for the briefest moment, but he covers it with another smile. "Of course. That's exciting."

"It is." I smile back. "Stressful, but exciting. Maybe we can do something tomorrow instead?"

My voice lifts hopefully at the end, suddenly anxious to reassure him.

He grins. "That sounds perfect."

We finish eating, and Liam walks me back to my building, where he kisses me goodbye. I watch him go, his tall frame receding down the sunlit street. Then I slip into the shadowed lobby, already pulling my phone out of my pocket.

The call rings for so long that I'm worried he won't pick up until, finally, a voice comes through the phone. "This is Herman."

"Hi!" My voice is chipper and an octave too high. "This is Ivy from apartment 4D. So sorry to call on a Saturday."

"Go ahead," my superintendent says in his usual gruff tone.

I chew my lip, looking up at the security camera mounted above the mailboxes.

"I was wondering if it would be possible to access last night's security footage for the lobby," I say. "I got a weird package, and it was unmarked, so I'm trying to figure out who left it."

Herman hesitates. "What kind of package?"

His voice is suspicious, and automatically, I rush to downplay it—for his sake or mine, I'm not sure.

"Nothing bad. It was just a book, but . . ." I take a breath, willing my heart to slow. "I'd really like to figure out who left it."

Herman is quiet for another moment. Then he sighs.

"Those cameras don't work."

My heart skips a beat.

"What?" I ask, holding the phone closer. "What do you mean?"

"The landlord installed them to scare off package thieves, but they crapped out a long time ago, and he hasn't replaced them. You'd have to take it up with him." There's a weary frustration to Herman's voice that tells me this isn't the first time he's had to deal with stuff like this from the landlord.

"That's okay," I say—bright again, that automatic instinct to minimize. "Thank you anyway."

"No problem," Herman says.

I can feel him about to hang up when I remember something else.

"What about the cameras in the hallway outside my unit?"

But I can hear the answer in his apologetic sigh, even before he says, "Same thing. If you're worried about it, you could install one on your door."

My throat squeezes with the sudden childish urge to cry.

"Okay," I say. "Thanks again. Enjoy your Saturday."

"You too."

Herman hangs up.

I look up again at the camera, its useless eye staring down at me, mocking. A sudden involuntary laugh bubbles out of me, followed by a crawling panic within.

Someone waltzed into my building and left that package undetected, and next time, there's nothing to stop them from going farther—even beyond my front door.

Instead of writing, I go straight to the store and buy a video doorbell. A few YouTube tutorials, a soda, and several expletives later, I manage to get it installed and working. Then I tie up my garbage bag and haul it down to the bins in the basement, where I stuff it and the package out of sight, before I go back to my unit and collapse on the couch with relief.

I'm reaching for my laptop, finally ready to start writing, when my phone dings with a text from Liam: Had a wonderful time last night! Looking forward to seeing you tomorrow—best of luck with the writing :)

A smile stretches on my lips, heart thumping with a stark and sudden happiness.

No matter how many strange coincidences there are, how many doubts have tried to take root in my head, there's the truth I keep clinging to: Being with Liam feels *right*, more than anything has ever felt before—except, maybe, for writing.

And he has no idea who I really am.

The thought comes unbidden, a quiet voice creeping in like smoke. It's not true, I know that. Liam knows me in almost all the ways that really count, even if there are things I've been keeping from him—things that have crept toward the tip of my tongue so many times already that it would be so easy to just let them out, watch them fall to the floor, and see where they splatter.

But telling Liam the truth would mean risking everything—not just us, but *me*. The entire life I've built.

So, for now, that's exactly what I need to focus on: writing this book. Making sure my dream career doesn't slip through my fingers until it's just a distant memory.

Besides, it's still very possible that I'm overreacting about the package, and this is all just someone playing a bad joke. If it isn't, though—if they try something again—I have my dead bolt and my doorbell camera. I'll be ready.

I'm opening my manuscript document when it occurs to me, the snag in that plan: Those things won't save me from someone I've invited inside.

7

ALL WEEK, I WRITE FEVERISHLY. It's a level of focus I haven't felt since *Haunt Me Then*—only different, because this time, the story is fueled not by excitement but sheer determination.

I write from cafés, the library, and mostly my couch: hunched over, fingers flying across the keyboard. I break only for food, the basic maintenance of human life, and, every so often, to text Liam. I haven't seen him since Sunday, when we spent the day wandering the park, seeing a movie, and then cooking dinner at his place. Missing him actually helps: Alone in my apartment, I write him back into existence until I can feel his arms around me, his laughter in warm puffs against my neck.

I write well into each night—technically until the next morning. At the start of the week, there are still nearly a hundred pages to draft, and I couldn't sleep even if I wanted to. As soon as I close my laptop, all I can focus on is my front door. Since Friday, there haven't been any other threats, but even with the new doorbell, I can't stop watching for the shadows to approach, the knob to turn. The first few times I order dinner, the apartment buzzer makes me jump, my heart going hummingbird-fast.

And so, I write—and write and write, until early Friday morning, when it hits me like a plunge into cold water, making my heart race and my skin tingle: I just typed *The End*.

I let out a shaky breath that turns into a laugh, my laptop still warm on my thighs. I did it. The impossible. Two weeks ago, this manuscript was stuck at thirty thousand words and even more dead ends, and now here it is: a completed eighty-thousand-word novel. It's not perfect, not yet, but that's what editors are for. For now, there's only the quiet joy singing out from my core as I bathe in the blue glow of my screen, sudden tears swimming in my gritty, tired eyes.

I did it. The very thing I was terrified I could never do again: I fell in love with my story.

I save the document two times just to be safe, and then, heart thrumming, I draft an email to Laura and Selene.

> Here's the first draft—I hope you like it! I'm feeling really excited about this one :)

I attach the manuscript, schedule the email to send at 9 AM, and then collapse back onto my couch, grinning with exhausted joy as my heavy lids drift shut.

A buzz. Loud, insistent.

And then again: *buzz.*

My eyes fly open, heart pounding. Someone is trying to get into my apartment. I scramble for my phone, frantic to check my doorbell camera, until I pull it from between the couch cushions and realize that it's not my buzzer making that noise: It's an incoming call.

Laura.

I rub the sleep from my eyes and take a long sip of water to fight the dry, thick feeling of my tongue. Before I answer, I note the time on my screen: just after 10 AM. I've been out for hours.

"Hello?"

"Ivy," my agent says. "How are you?"

I tense. There's something stilted in her voice, something I don't understand.

"Good," I say.

It's not true, not when my hands are shaking from being startled awake and the quickly growing nerves, but what else am I supposed to say?

"Feeling really good about this full draft," I add. "I don't know if you saw my email, but—"

"That's actually what I wanted to talk about."

Now I know I'm not imagining the strain in her tone. I sit up straighter, free hand balled into a fist.

"Oh," I say. "Yeah, what's up?"

"The email we got from you this morning was . . . a little concerning."

For a moment, I'm too confused to react.

"Concerning?" I repeat.

Now my brain catches up with me, full spiral: They hate the draft. It's only taken them a few hours to decide, and now—

"Well, yes," Laura says, sounding surprised. "You said that you were pulling out of your contract."

"Wait, *what*?" The question slices out of me in a breathless rush. I race to open my email, and then I see it. Instead of the email I scheduled to send to Laura and Selene at nine, there's a completely different message in my Sent folder.

BOOK 2

Laura and Selene,

I know you're expecting my new draft today, but as hard as I've tried, I can't make it work. I am not the author I've claimed to be, and I can no longer pretend. I'm very sorry, but *Haunt Me Then* will be my last published novel.

That second-to-last line catches me like barbed wire: *I am not the author I've claimed to be* . . . It sounds a whole lot like that Goodreads review: "Ivy Harcourt is a fraud." Heart racing, I reread the final line, *my last published novel*. Buried within those words is a subtle threat, one that's only visible if I tilt my head just right: I might not live to publish another.

Through the roar of blood in my ears, I realize Laura is talking, her voice tinny because I forgot to put her on speaker.

"Laura?" My heart thuds as I press the phone to my ear. "I didn't write this."

For a second, she doesn't respond.

"Oh," she says finally, and I can almost hear her shoulders relaxing. "Well, that's a relief."

"I swear, I don't know how this happened," I tell her. "I had the email with my new draft scheduled to send to you and Selene, but instead . . . someone must have hacked into my email. I'll resend you and Selene the draft right now. I'm so sorry for the confusion."

I cup the phone with my shoulder, opening a new email draft. For a second, I'm terrified that somehow, the manuscript will be gone, but it's still there in my documents folder. I let out a breath, attaching it to the email.

"Good," Laura says. "Thank you for clearing that up, Ivy."

"Of course."

"But . . ."

Laura hesitates, and I freeze with my hands on the keyboard. That *but* feels like a precipice, a hand pressed to my back and nudging me toward the edge.

"I just want to make sure that there's nothing to worry about here," Laura says gently.

There it is—that stomach-plunging drop. Laura's voice is cool and collected, but I hear the warning question in her words: *Is there something you need to tell me?*

"You have nothing to worry about," I tell her as confidently as I can manage. "I intend to publish many more books, and I assure you that this will not happen again."

Laura lets out another small breath, and I can feel the shift: This time, she believes me.

"Great," she says. "I'm sorry if this worried you, and I can't wait to see your draft."

I let out my own relieved sigh, closing my eyes for just a moment.

"I'll send it over right now. Thanks, Laura."

"Thank *you*." She pauses. "And maybe change your email password just in case, okay?"

I send the email as soon as we hang up, triple-checking that everything looks correct and that the document hasn't been tampered with. Then I change my email password to an unguessable string of random numbers and letters. Still, the panic doesn't subside.

No matter what I told Laura, I can't be sure that this won't happen again. Someone—whoever runs these "Heathcliff" accounts, I'm guessing—is hell-bent on haunting me, and they don't just know where I live. They've crept into my *career*, as if to prove how quickly it can all go up in flames.

I'm gnawing on my nails before I've even realized it, an ugly habit I broke years ago—or thought I did. Now my lavender manicure is chipped, the paint flaking from my thumb. I pull it away from my face, scrolling back to the fraudulent email like a wound I can't stop scratching at.

I am not the author I've claimed to be.

My last published novel . . .

It's an expertly subtle threat, leaving just enough room to question what it really means at all. Whoever wrote this understands one cardinal rule of storytelling: Sometimes, the unspoken is even more powerful than the explicit. There, in that negative space, is where your reader's imagination runs wild—and right now, mine is racing away from the memories that reach to drag it back by the ankles.

Cold room. Machines beeping. Pain in my chest, my head.

"Ivy?"

It catches up to me, claws sinking in. Even when I press my hands to my ears, it insists.

I blink blearily, still half asleep.

"Ivy," she says again. "Can you hear me?"

A kind-looking woman I don't recognize stands at the side of the bed.

"Where am I?" I ask her through a dry, scratchy throat. And then, when I look around the empty room, and dread descends, "What happened?"

She takes my hand, smiling sadly as she introduces herself as the hospital's social worker. My heart begins to pound. I know already. I know even before she says, "I have to tell you something that will be very difficult to hear."

I shove the heels of my hands to my eyes, pressing until the stars swim. It's not happening. *Not happening.* That night is gone, buried deep, but my blood thrums like it did then, a slow scream building up inside.

I grab my phone with shaking hands. My first impulse is to call Aunt Mia, but I can't—not about this. As much as that night ties us together, it's also a weight between us, a land mine to dodge.

I could call Liam. I promised to call once I finished my draft anyway, and more than anything, I want to hear his voice, to wrap it around me like a warm blanket. But Liam doesn't know about this, that night, and he'd hear it in my voice. He'd know that something was wrong.

That leaves the other person at the top of my recent-calls list—the one who I know will always pick up. I dial, and as the tone rings, the panic builds inside me, threatening to spill out in a sob or a scream. But when I hear her voice, it's neither.

"Hey, Ives," Dani says.

"Hey!" The brightness in my voice is automatic, compulsive. I don't even know why—if I told Dani what was going on, she would listen. She would try to help.

She would want to talk about it, and maybe, I realize, that's the problem.

"What's up?" Dani asks.

I realize I've been picking at my nails again, a little graveyard of purple chips on my couch, and I brush them aside.

"Just turned in my draft, finally."

"Hell yeah, you did! How are you feeling about it?"

"Really good." I smile, but it strains. "Are you around tonight? I figured we could grab dinner or something, now that I'm officially off deadline."

"I wish I could, but I'm in New Rochelle until Tuesday."

"Right." I pull a hand through my unwashed hair. Dani already told me this, but I'd totally forgotten that they're doing final wedding prep at the venue, which is near her fiancé's childhood home—ironically, not all that far from my own. "God, I can't believe the wedding is next weekend."

"I know." I can hear the excited smile in her voice. Even now, Dani is unflappable: She thrives on a to-do list. Then she gives a quick sigh. "Speaking of which, I'm getting a call from our rep at the venue. But we'll do dinner when I'm back next week?"

"Totally," I say, smiling again. "See you then."

We hang up, and the silence in my apartment seems to grow thicker. In my hand, my phone screen glows, the email app beckoning. I should call Liam, but when I go to dial his number, I hesitate with my thumb over the button, the thought creeping in at a slow drip: If someone hacked into my email, the simplest way would be through my phone or laptop, where I'm already logged in.

For whom would that be easier than the man who's been sleeping beside me?

As soon as I let myself wonder, it's like a cascade of realizations, jagged puzzle pieces locking together: Liam brought up the package. He showed up at the park that day in a coincidence so perfect, it seems made up—almost like he knew I'd be there, my book tucked into his bag. Suddenly, even Liam knowing about my strawberry allergy seems insidious—I still can't remember telling him, but he knew.

And all this—the threats, the messages—only started on the day I met him.

I shoot up from the couch, fueled by a sudden need to move, to separate myself from these suspicions. They cling to me anyway, as thick and suffocating as smoke.

All along, I've been fighting the fear that Liam is too perfect, and for the first time, I'm afraid it's not self-sabotage—it's self-*protection*, and I have been so unbelievably reckless.

I press a hand to my tightened chest, my ricocheting heart. I need to get out of here. Not just this apartment, which seems more unsafe than ever, but out of my own head. I need to stop thinking.

I need to forget.

The solution comes like a hand extended into the darkness. Dangerous. Destructive.

Simple.

Before I can talk myself out of it, I reach for my phone and pull up a number I haven't dialed in a long time.

THERE SHE IS! OUR NEXT great American novelist."

I hear her raspy voice before I see her. When I turn, Sloane is strolling up the sidewalk with a smile, canines slightly pointed. She's fifteen minutes late, which shouldn't surprise me: Sloane has always taken start times as a mere suggestion.

"Hey!" I pull her into a hug—quick and friendly, which she doesn't reciprocate, her arms hanging limply at her sides. My stomach flips over itself with another roll of nerves: This was a bad idea.

"So good to see you," I add as I pull back.

For a moment, Sloane watches me, something sharp glinting in her eyes.

"You know, I was actually really surprised to hear from you. It's been a while."

A *year and a half, to be exact,* even though I don't say it. Something in her expression tells me she's well aware. We haven't talked since we were both servers at a restaurant downtown—me as a struggling writer, Sloane as a struggling actress—until I became not-so-struggling and left. Now, barely a minute into this, I'm already remembering why.

Sloane Morris is a storm: wild and forceful, but every so often, she convinces you it's fun to dance in the rain—just before the lighting picks up and you get struck.

"I know," I say lightly. "I can't believe it."

Sloane pulls a vape from her purse and takes a pull, watching me as the mist curls from her dark-painted lips. It's flavored like some sort of fruit, sickly sweet as she breathes out.

"You could at least come visit."

Her tone is teasing, but there's an edge of truth beneath it that stabs me with guilt. After my book deal, I guess I left a lot of things behind.

"I know," I say. "I'm sorry. I've been—"

I stop myself, realizing that what I was about to say—*I've been sober*—would contradict the entire point of tonight.

"Busy," I say instead. "On deadline."

Sloane shrugs. "Well, even big-time authors need a night out, right?" She laughs, looping her bony arm through mine, and just like that, the strangeness dissipates, and we're back to our old selves. "Come on."

We walk through the grimy Lower East Side streets until we find the first spot Sloane wants to hit, a club in a nondescript brick building with a glowing neon sign and a line out the door. Girls in tiny skirts and sky-high heels, boys with oversized pants and cigarettes, the latter of which I didn't even realize were back in vogue. Actually, the more I look around this crowd, the younger they look. I tug at my high-waisted bell-bottoms, which felt cool when I bought them but now seem hopelessly out of touch with the return of the low-rise jean. The ever-widening chasm between early and late twenties gapes further.

"Are we, like, a little too old to be here?" I whisper as we step into the back of the line.

Sloane, always averse to both subtlety and shame, taps the shoulder of the guy in front of us, who looks fresh out of college.

“Hey,” she says. “How old do you think we are?”

I cringe, but Sloane is undeterred.

“Uh . . .” The guy tousles his shaggy hair, clearly nervous. “Twenty-three?”

I can’t tell if he’s being honest or not, but Sloane smiles her classic fox-like smile.

“Wrong,” she says. “That means you get to buy us a drink inside.”

Secondhand embarrassment takes over for two full seconds before an enthusiastic grin stretches on the young guy’s face.

“How ’bout shots?”

Almost fifteen minutes of waiting later, the bouncer finally whisks us inside with Shots Guy and his cluster of friends. A dark, narrow staircase leads toward a pulsing bass line that vibrates under my palm as I grip the railing to steady myself, sweat prickling under my clothes. I stop, some deep, innate voice begging me not to go any farther. *You know too well*, it says, *what could be waiting in the shadows.*

At the bottom of the stairs, another neon sign with the club’s name flashes pink above the doorway, beckoning. Sloane turns to glance up at me, that pink light glowing on her confused, questioning face, and I force my feet to move again, pushing down the fear. We step through the door like a portal to another world.

A wave of sound crashes into me. Music and voices, buzzing so loud I can’t even hear the thudding of my heart. The air is breath and sweat, multicolored lights flashing in the haze. It’s the kind of place that used to thrill me—that special freedom of being young in New York City, like the world is a glass to be tossed back in one go.

My palms itch, anxious heat crawling under my skin. I could still back out—make up some excuse to get out of here, even call Liam.

“Hey.”

I flinch at the voice in my ear, the sudden presence beside me raising the little hairs on my neck. One of the guys we walked in with, sporting bleached hair and a single hoop earring.

"Want a drink?" he shouts over the music.

I hesitate, hand ghosting over my phone in my back pocket. It's not cheating to let a guy buy me a drink, especially when I have no intention of going farther than that. Liam and I aren't even official. More importantly, I still haven't ruled out the possibility that he's been secretly harassing me for the past three weeks.

I glance over to Sloane, already at the bar with Shots Guy from outside. She tosses her sleek black hair over her shoulder and raises an eyebrow at me, a challenge.

My throat scratches, dry. Thirsty. It's been so long, and it's not like I'm an alcoholic—I only stopped drinking because it messed with my head, made me forget things. And here, in this hot, foggy basement full of recent college grads too drunk to even remember me tomorrow, isn't that exactly the point?

The guy is still waiting for my answer, and I lean closer to tell him.

"Sure."

The room dances with me. Music in my chest, pulsing through my rib cage. Songs bleed together, the drinks, too, until my body is warm and buzzing and I wonder why I ever stopped this, when everything is gold-tinged and wonderful. It's all stretching out before me, floating high and free and waiting for me to capture it like filmy butterfly wings on a corkboard, fireflies in a jar, because I'm the only one who can write it all down.

We're at another bar now. I don't remember exactly when we left the first, or where those guys went—only stepping out into the cool night, arm in arm with Sloane, while we laughed and laughed at something else

I can't remember. Funny how things slip away when you don't hold on so tight.

I'm still dancing, head back and hair sticking to my face in wild, sweaty wisps, when I realize Sloane is saying something.

"—bathroom. I'll be back."

She sounds annoyed, but I don't know why. Then she's going away, and I don't want to follow—it's too good out here, and this song is one of my favorites even though I can't remember the name—but I do have to go, now that she mentions it, so I catch up and trail her through the crowd.

"This is so *fun*," I shout as we walk, only I didn't have to shout, I realize, because now we're in the bathroom, the music muted through the walls.

The stall lurches as I open the door, but I catch myself.

"Careful," Sloane says, glancing at me in the mirror.

"I'm good."

When I'm done, though, the buttons on my jeans elude me, slipping through my fingers each time I try to close them.

"Sloane?" I call through the stall. "My buttons are broken."

"What?"

"Come help?"

I hear her sigh, her heels thudding on the ground. Then she slides into the stall, beautiful and sparkly and also magic, because the buttons work for her.

"Sorcery," I muse as she snaps the last one.

Sloane huffs through her nose. It sounds like a laugh, but not really. "Someone's having a lot of fun."

"Yeah, I needed it." I laugh, too, for real. "Like, you don't even know."

Sloane leans against the stall door, not laughing at all now. Instead, her arms are crossed, her eyes narrowed like she's trying to figure something out.

"So, we're not going to talk about it."

I blink, a crackle like static through the soft clouds in my head.

"What?"

Sloane's face is totally blank except for her plum-red lips, which part in a look of total shock. "That little phone call outside?"

A phone call . . . did I call Liam? Now that she says it, maybe I did, but I don't know why that would make her so angry.

When I'm still too confused to answer, Sloane lets out a cold, dry laugh. "Wow."

Something is wrong. Something is super wrong, but I don't know what she's talking about, and I know this feeling. It's why I came out tonight, exactly what I was searching for: forgetting.

"Sloane . . ."

I wobble in my heeled boots and catch myself on the stall door. Sloane steps back like she's disgusted.

"I'm getting another drink," she says. "Congratulations, Ivy."

Sloane storms out of the bathroom.

Shit. As I scramble to follow her, my fuzzy brain sifts through possible explanations. I said something outside that upset her, clearly, but as hard as I try, I can't grasp it. It's all slipped through the booze-slicked cracks.

Outside, the room pulses, bodies writhing with a heat that snakes under my clothes, my skin. I can't find Sloane in the crowd, and my blood thrums with anxiety. Then I catch sight of her shouldering her way toward the packed bar.

"Sloane!" I call, but the music swallows it up. I push forward.

"Hey." Someone taps on my shoulder, and I spin around. A scruffy guy, probably our age or a little older, thrusts a drink my way. "This is for you."

It's some kind of cocktail, pink and frothy, the glass cool against my palm.

"It's from that girl over there." He gestures with his chin. "She said it was for you."

"Sloane?" I ask, but she's still farther down, trying to get the bartender's attention.

"No idea. Some blond chick." The guy points. "Over there."

I follow his finger, but the dance floor is a soft blur of people and lights, movements lagging. It's been a while since a woman bought me a drink at a bar, and I can't help but be curious.

"I don't . . ."

Someone tugs my hand: Sloane, pulling me away from the guy.

"Don't drink that," she says, grabbing the glass from my hand. "I may be pissed, but I'm not letting you get drugged."

There's a tender squeeze in my heart. Guilt and gratitude.

"I'm sorry. He said . . ."

And then I see her: a woman leaving through the door, blond hair swishing over her shoulders.

Familiarity pulses through me, tugging at a panicked string in my chest. I walk toward the door. Sloane curses under her breath, but her heels start to click behind me.

"Where are you going?"

Outside, the streets are crowded with people walking from bar to bar, their shouts and laughter ringing off-key. I glance left and right, my heart pounding, heat still crawling under my clothes even though it's much cooler outside than it was in the warmth of all those bodies.

And then I see her again, turning the corner.

"This way."

"Seriously, Ivy, what's going on?"

I don't answer. We rush down the sidewalk, dodging clusters of people as we go. The ground shifts under me a few times, and I stumble, my body still weighed down with the sludge of alcohol even as my brain fights to take over. Jolts of music rise and fall as we pass the different bars lining the street until, finally, we turn the corner.

"There," I tell Sloane, pointing at the nearest bar. "Let's go there."

There's no line at this place, but Sloane takes forever to dig her ID out of her purse, and by the time we're inside, my heart is thrumming, knocking at the door of panic.

The room is dark and moody, obscure enough that it's hard to pick out individual people. Jazzy music plays over the din of conversation and clinking glasses, people scattered at tables and the bar. The room stretches back far enough that I can't see everything from the door.

"This place is dead," Sloane mumbles. "What are we doing?"

"I thought I saw someone."

"Who?"

"Just give me a minute."

My pulse thrums as I walk deeper into the room, but the farther I go, the colder I feel.

"Ivy—"

Before Sloane can finish, something flashes nearby. A gust of heat burns my cheeks.

Fire. It roars to life in front of us, swallowing the faces around it in sickly orange. Their jaws hinge open to scream, but the sound is eaten up by the suck and crackle of the flame. The image shudders, dances, and then I understand.

They're melting. Their skin is melting from their faces.

I stumble back as my heart leaps into my throat, a scream reaching up to follow.

Fire. There's a fire. There's—

"It's just a drink." Sloane's voice sounds far away, warped. "Ivy, it's a drink."

I blink, and the people at the table are no longer melting. They're laughing, clapping as a server sets the blazing glass on the table, acrid smoke wafting into the air. It reaches into my lungs, spreading until it chokes me from within.

When I try to breathe, I can only taste the burning. It curls and blackens the room like paper, devouring all but the screams.

ELEVEN YEARS AGO

"Ivy."

A hand on my shoulder, tugging me back into myself. I blink, and my surroundings click into place: a dark bedroom, lit only by a soft lamp and the moonlight crawling under the curtains. Dani's bedroom, I remember, as I look at her immaculately organized desk. Pencils, binders, and books, nothing out of place except the jasmine-scented candle teetering close to the edge.

Even before I turn and see Dani's concerned, sleepy expression, my stomach caves with understanding: *It's happening again.* I should have known. I should have just stayed home.

When I see the lighter in my hand, the chasm widens to a deep, bottomless void.

"What are you doing?" she whispers, folding her arms over her pajama set.

Shame spills from the empty place inside me, twisting up with a cold and terrible fear.

"I'm so sorry." I put the lighter down and back away, hands raised like a criminal. My heart pounds. "I . . ." I swallow, mouth dry. "I think I was sleepwalking?"

Dani tilts her head, brows furrowing, and already, I know it's over: my new friend, my new start. By Monday, everyone at school will know what a freak I am.

But then a hint of a disbelieving smile flickers on Dani's lips.

"You light candles in your sleep?"

My gut clenches. "Did I really light it?"

"You tried. I woke up to the sound of you flicking it, but you couldn't get it to work." She sighs, looking at the lighter on the desk. "Guess it's kind of a fire hazard to have this lying around."

I cover my face, humiliated—even more so as tears start to burn at the back of my nose. "I am *so* sorry. I can't believe I did that."

But I can. Again, that cruel little voice reminds me that I shouldn't have come here, even as desperate as I was to accept Dani's invite to sleep over, clinging eagerly to this chance at my first real friend.

Still, when Dani looks at me now, it's not judgmental: It's a mix of worry and something more casual—almost like interest.

"Have you sleepwalked before?" she asks softly.

I chew on the inside of my cheek, fighting back tears as I look at that candle, still waiting on the desk.

"Yeah," I admit. "It's been happening a little ever since . . ."

The truth winds its way around my tongue, pulling tight.

"Since I moved here," I finish flatly.

Dani nods, understanding. Then she says matter-of-factly, "Well, it's much better than wetting the bed."

In spite of myself, I let out a laugh, and Dani grins.

"What? I'm not joking." She grabs the lighter. "But I *will* go put this away, just in case. Need anything?"

My heart could burst from the gratitude—for her care, for the simple fact that she isn't judging me.

"No," I say. "Thanks, though."

She can't possibly know how much I mean it.

When Dani leaves, I step into her bathroom, locking the door behind me and flicking on the light.

My breath catches when I see my reflection in the mirror.

I don't recognize the girl who stares back at me: her flushed cheeks, her honey-blond waves. Aunt Mia didn't discourage me when she found me in her bathroom with the dye and a mess of towels a few weeks before school started. From what I've gathered, Mia had bright blue hair for most of high school, and she probably figured there were far more destructive forms of reinvention for a grieving teen. We were also still in that strange limbo before the adoption was finalized, where even if she *did* want to forbid me, she wasn't sure if she could; she barely even knew me yet.

I barely know myself. I grip the sink and stare at my reflection, breathing in and out. *Whenever you start to panic*, my therapist told me in one of our earlier sessions, *think about things that are true, facts that ground you*.

My name is Ivy Harcourt, I think now.

I have been in Los Angeles for three months.

My parents are dead, but I am okay.

I like it here. I have friends.

I splash water on my face, towel it off, and then smile at the stranger in front of me until she feels familiar.

I am safe now, and the past can't hurt me.

9

I WAKE WITH A GASP, LUNGS full of smoke. I cough and sputter, clutching at the first things in my grasp: a fuzzy blanket and a scratchy pillow. As my heart slows its wild racing, understanding drifts in like the faded edges of a nightmare.

This is not my apartment.

I jolt up to sitting and look around. I'm on a small white couch. A ray of sun creeps in from the window, catching dust in its beam. In front of me is a coffee table, a TV, and, on the wall above it, a neon sign with pink script that reads HELLO GORGEOUS. The rosy glow ghosts over the room, familiar.

Relief spills through the panic. I'm at Sloane's. She must have moved since we both worked at the restaurant, because I don't recognize this space, but the couch and the HELLO GORGEOUS sign were in her old place in the West Village.

For the first time, I notice the bottle of blue Gatorade on the coffee table, a sticky note pressed to the plastic with messy handwriting:

Had to go to work. Thought you might need this lol

—S

"Oh god," I mutter out loud, suddenly aware of the pounding in my skull.

We went out last night. I *drank* last night. Quickly, I line up the images I can remember: the stairwell, the neon sign that led to the basement bar, a bleach-haired guy offering me drinks, and then . . .

Dread grips me from within. I don't remember what happened next. It's like a curtain drawn over the rest of the night, thick and all-consuming.

I uncap the Gatorade and take a long gulp that soothes the dryness in my throat but does nothing to calm the ache in my head or the anxiety winding deep into my gut.

The last time I blacked out was about a year and a half ago—fittingly, the last time I saw Sloane. That night, we hit up the bars like we always used to do, and the next morning, I woke with my head hammering and a black hole where my memories should be, everything after the third drink gone as quickly as I'd thrown it back.

And now it's happened again. My stomach lurches, and I press my forehead to my knees, breathing until the nausea subsides—but even then, the dread doesn't go away.

For most women in their twenties, blacking out wouldn't be such a huge deal—embarrassing, yes, especially when you're firmly on the other side of twenty-five, but not necessarily something to panic about.

Not for me. For me, a blackout is never just a mistake. It's a threat: a weight strapped to my ankle, pulling me deep into the dark waters of the past.

After I moved in with Aunt Mia in LA, it happened almost weekly. Sometimes, I'd sleepwalk, like that first time, when I went all the way from Mia's to the playground at the park, or the time I tried to light Dani's candle in the middle of the night. Other times, it was smaller: changing clothes, making calls, having conversations I couldn't remember. Somehow, those moments were even more unsettling—because as far as I knew, I'd been wide awake until, with a snap, I wasn't.

The doctors said it was trauma-induced—dissociative episodes, they called them, caused by my grief, as if that itself were the illness. Like most things, the blackouts got better with therapy and age. By the time I left for college, they were all but gone. The only time they'd resurface was when I drank a little too much—but then, I figured, wasn't that just being a college student?

Eventually, though, enough was enough. That morning last year, when I woke with the familiar rising dread and barely a speck of what had happened the night before, I decided it was the last time. I was done drinking—done losing myself to the beckoning dark.

Until last night. Shame stirs low in my gut. *What was I thinking?*

The answer is there, waiting like two glowing eyes in the darkness.

That package. My hacked email.

Liam.

Urgency screams through me: I need to find my phone. Frantic, I dig around the couch cushions before finally finding it on the floor, halfway under the dusty couch bottom. When I press the power button, all I get is a glaring red dead-battery notification.

Shit. I shove my phone in my pocket—still wearing the jeans from last night—and walk deeper into Sloane's apartment, my head swimming. In the kitchen, I squint at the oven clock until the green blurry shapes turn into numbers: 1:57 PM.

Fresh nausea churns in my stomach, and I grip the counter, closing my eyes and breathing through it. When I'm sure I won't puke, I find my way to Sloane's bedroom. It's even messier than mine, a feat I thought impossible, but I find a charger plugged into the wall under a mound of discarded clothes.

As I wait for my phone to boot up again, I pace to the window. I don't see any street signs, but I'm pretty sure I'm in the East Village. People stroll by on the street below: On the other side, there's a stretch of apartments, a Japanese restaurant, and a deli.

Another memory from last night: *Harsh buzzing lights, Sloane at the counter buying a huge bag of chips and two Gatorades.*

"She's fine," Sloane tells the cashier, who's shooting me a suspicious look. "Rough night."

Her voice is sharp. Disdainful.

Sloane is mad at me.

My phone lights up on the floor. I rush to grab it as notifications fill up the screen.

Immediately, I latch on to the two from Liam. First, a text sent at ten thirty last night: Still chugging along with the writing? And then, at nine this morning, a missed call.

My stomach churns. Seeing his name is all it takes for my body to slip, automatically, into the fear that gripped it last night, when my spiral reached its logical conclusion: The threats I've been getting didn't begin until the day I met him.

An incoming call buzzes, and I flinch, my heart hammering. *It's him.*

My finger hovers over the Decline Call button, but then guilt gnaws at me. Ghosting Liam won't solve this—plus, no matter what wild suspicions have been spinning in my head, the fact remains that I totally blew him off last night. He's probably worried about me.

I take a steadying breath and pick up. "Hello?"

"Hello, you."

A wisp of a breath escapes my lips. He sounds so normal, so safe, that for a moment, all the fear goes away.

"Hey," I say, even though I've already greeted him. "Sorry I missed your call. I, um . . . I sort of just woke up."

It's not an admission of guilt, not yet, and I hang on the precipice, waiting for him to ask me why I ignored him all night.

Liam chuckles, warm. "It sounds like you had a bit of fun last night."

I press my fingers to my temple, wincing. "*Fun* is pretty subjective."

And then, with a quick jab of panic, I realize something: There was a knowing lilt to Liam's voice just now, but I don't remember telling him that I was going out last night. Either I did and forgot, or he can tell from the sound of my voice that I'm hungover. I swallow, embarrassed.

"Did I . . . did I tell you I was going out last night?"

"You called me," Liam explains, a little uncertainly—probably concerned that I don't remember. "I missed it, but you left a voicemail."

Hot shame breaks over my skin, and then a cold sweat. *A voicemail.* Vaguely, this rings a bell, but the memory is slippery.

"Right," I manage, burying a hand in my tangled hair. "Yeah. So, I had a few drinks last night with my friend Sloane. I'm regretting it now, obviously. I mean, there's a reason I don't drink anymore—I'm basically a huge lightweight." I laugh, and it rings false, even to my own ears.

For a moment, Liam doesn't say anything, and my heart beats faster.

"You're all right, though?" he asks finally, worry dipping into his voice.

I take a breath, pushing down the uneasiness.

"I am," I say. "I just hope I didn't say anything embarrassing last night."

I force another laugh, but in the silence that follows, fear prickles my skin. I clutch the phone tighter.

"No, not at all," Liam says warmly. "It was sweet, actually. You sounded a little out of it, but you just told me that you missed me, and you wished I was there. And something about a wiener dog in a hat?"

A laugh bubbles out of me, breaking through the lingering anxiety. I remember, now—I called Liam between the first and second bar.

"We passed a woman walking a dog in a fedora," I explain.

"The woman or the dog?"

"The dog, of course. I think I might've been scheming to replace Louis Sullivan."

"The architect?"

"The dog in the book." As soon as I've said it, my face goes hot. "I . . . may or may not have fictionalized Frank Lloyd Wright for my architect character."

"Well, then," Liam says with a smile I can hear through the phone. "Frank and I are touched."

A grin warms my face. It feels cozy, talking to Liam on the phone, like staying up late to read a book under the covers with a flashlight. The paranoid part of my brain wonders if he's only luring me into a false sense of comfort, but with every moment we spend talking, it's drowned out by a growing brightness in my core.

"Wait," Liam says, "I didn't even ask—you turned in your draft?"

The warmth balloons into pride. "I did."

"That's wonderful, Ivy. Congratulations!"

I press a hand to my smile. "Thank you."

"I can't wait to read it."

At that, my stomach flips over itself. I've been so wrapped up in actually finishing the draft that I hadn't stopped to imagine how Liam will respond to it. He was charmed by the dog thing, sure, but will Liam feel the same when he realizes my romantic lead is basically his clone?

The paranoid voice in my head resurfaces: *Unless he already knows.* If Liam hacked into my email, he's almost certainly seen the manuscript. Or maybe he's known from the beginning, and concocted some sort of plan to— What? Get close to me by pretending to be my own character? The idea is ridiculous, like something out of a popcorn thriller.

"I'm just glad it's finished," I say, pushing the worry aside. I don't *have* to show Liam the draft, at least not until I change Book Liam's name—maybe a few details, too, to make it less obvious.

"Well, if you're not busy, we could go out for a celebratory lunch? Or breakfast, if you're just up." I hear a smile flickering in his voice.

"Sounds perfect." I smile, too. "Where should I meet you?"

As we make our plans, the afternoon sun slants through the window, golden with the promise of summer, and my suspicions fade until they're nothing but a dull, almost imperceptible hum.

Liam waits in front of our bagel place with a paper bag and a smile that should be projected on the silver screen, all perfect teeth and dimples. I actually almost stop in my tracks for a moment, knowing that this face is for me—that I get to walk up to him on a sunny Saturday afternoon, my beacon on this bustling Upper East Side street.

"I ordered your usual," he says. "Hope that's all right."

"That's perfect." I pull him in for a hug, breathing in his clean linen smell as warmth puddles in my chest. It seems ridiculous, suddenly, that I ever suspected him of being anything but genuine. "You're perfect."

Liam gives a teasing grin. "If you say so."

I laugh as he hands me the bag and pull out my toasted cinnamon-raisin bagel, slathered in butter that leaks through the paper.

"It is rather un-American that you hate cream cheese, isn't it?" Liam remarks as I unwrap it.

"Oh, my order is an affront to all of New York City." I smile. "But that doesn't make it any less delicious."

We wander with our bagels to the park by my apartment—*our* park, I'm starting to consider it, just like *our* bagel place. I offered to meet Liam on the Upper West Side, but he insisted on meeting in my neighborhood—which thankfully gave me time to change out of last night's clothes.

"So," Liam starts as we settle onto a bench, "where did you get off to last night?"

There's something hesitant in his expression, the way he doesn't quite meet my eyes as he says it. Anxiety burrows into my gut, along with a thrum of embarrassment.

"A few places on the Lower East Side," I say, busying myself with my bagel. "I'm pretty sure we were the oldest people everywhere we went. Which, by the way, did you know the kids are smoking cigarettes again?"

"So I've seen." Liam nods sagely. "It's a dreadful habit, but unfortunately *much* cooler-looking than vaping."

I snort. "It *is*, isn't it? It really sucks."

We settle into a moment of comfortable silence—my knee pressed to his, his elbow against mine, even though the bench is big enough for us to spread out if we wanted. The urge is sudden and deep, as powerful as the impulse to kiss him: I want to tell him the truth.

"So, about last night," I start carefully.

I don't think I'm imagining the small tensing in Liam's body, and it makes my heart skip a beat. I take a breath and force myself to continue.

"I know we haven't totally talked about it, but I'm sure you've noticed that I haven't been drinking," I say. "I was never an alcoholic, or anything. That's not why I stopped. It was more of a lifestyle choice, I guess. I didn't like what it did to my memory."

A glimmer of the whole truth, a little test before I place it all in his hands. Liam watches me with a soft, open expression, ready for whatever I'm going to say.

"So, last night was . . . definitely out of character." I let out a breath, releasing the pent-up shame. "I don't want you to worry, though. I've just been stressed about my deadline, and also . . ."

I hesitate again. If I tell him about the threats I've been getting, then it would give him a chance to put my doubts to rest. But it would also open a door to the darkest parts of me, that locked chamber where they've been safely kept for eleven years.

I take another breath—but before I can decide what I'm going to say next, my phone buzzes with an incoming call.

The words dry up on my tongue, nothing but a startled click coming out of my throat when I see the name on the screen, and the contact photo I still haven't deleted: a selfie I took of us at the park, Xander glancing up from the chapbook he was reading with an amused look of surprise.

I decline the call quickly, but Liam notices.

"What's wrong?" he asks, glancing down toward my screen.

On impulse, I turn it over so he can't see. "Nothing."

My voice is calm, even as my head spins. Why the hell is Xander calling? I haven't heard from him since we broke up over a month ago.

"Anyway," I say, trying to veer the conversation back on course. "I—"

My phone buzzes again, somehow feeling louder. More insistent.

"Are you sure you don't need to take that?" Liam asks, brow furrowing in concern—and something else, too. *Suspicion.* As soon as I notice, it's unmistakable, that flicker in his eyes. He knows I'm hiding something.

The guilt is so immediate and great that I let out a sigh, all my willpower going with it.

"It's my ex," I say. "Xander."

"Ah." Liam sits back, his face frustratingly unreadable.

I chew the inside of my cheek. We haven't talked about past relationships, except for when Liam mentioned that he adopted Frank after a breakup. But this doesn't have to be weird unless I make it.

"We broke up a few weeks before you and I met," I say. "He cheated on me. In hindsight, I'm really glad he did. Otherwise, I don't know if I ever would have woken up to the kind of guy he really was. He was supposed to—" I hesitate again before meeting Liam's eyes, determined to push through. "He was supposed to be my plus-one at Dani's wedding in New Rochelle next weekend."

I hold my breath as Liam takes this in, his eyes soft and free from jealousy or judgment. That's good, I think—unless, *should* he be jealous? I still think about Liam's mysterious ex sometimes, this woman whose absence made him so lonely that he had to adopt a dog.

My phone buzzes again, and I let out a groan. Still Xander. I decline the call, tapping the button harder than I need to.

"I'm sorry," I say. "We don't talk at all. I have no idea what he wants, but hopefully he gets the message."

As if on cue, a text from Xander lights up my screen.

we need to talk.

I feel Liam's eyes on my screen, but it isn't intrusive. Instead, I'm glad he's watching as I block Xander's number.

"There," I say. "Done."

Liam's eyes lift to mine, something swimming in them that I can't quite read.

"You don't have to apologize, you know."

My heart thuds, the intensity of his stare making me suddenly nervous. "What?"

"Just now you said you were sorry. But you shouldn't be. We all have a past. Myself included." His voice is soft and kind to match the little crinkles around his eyes, but my chest tightens.

If he knew the truth, he wouldn't be looking at me that way.

Still, something about the insinuation tugs at me. *Myself included.* It hangs in the space between us, close enough for me to reach out and touch. *Tell me about her.* If I asked, I know he would.

But then Liam puts an arm around me and pulls me close, banishing every thought but those of him, of here and now. I let my head fall onto his shoulder.

"You mentioned the wedding," Liam starts carefully. "I don't want to be too forward, but if you still need a date . . ." He leans closer, his lips nearly brushing my ear. "I'd be more than happy to fill in."

A shudder runs through me at his low, seductive voice, which feels almost inappropriate for a public park. But this isn't just physical. When I meet Liam's eyes, they're open and waiting—*hopeful.* He wants this as much as I do. He wants me, and all the mess and chaos that entails.

"Really?" I ask.

Liam nods with a grin like sun breaking over the water. "Really."

"Then yes," I say. "I'd love that."

I cup his chin and kiss him, his lips tasting like coffee. I want more, but Liam pulls back suddenly.

"Ivy."

"Yeah?"

I'm held in his gaze, suspended above the ground.

"Would you do me the immense honor of being my girlfriend?" Liam asks.

My heart rocks in my chest. This moment—I want to remember it. Liam's cheek under my palm, warm and rough with stubble. His deep blue eyes on mine, and his lips slightly parted, waiting for my answer.

"Yes," I say, kissing him again. We melt into each other, smiling and giddy, his hand resting at the back of my neck as mine winds into his hair. When we pull apart, we don't separate, our foreheads pressed together like we can't bear not touching.

Still, the truth hangs over me like a thick fog, clinging smoke.

I could tell him. I *want* to. Just not now, when this moment is so perfect.

Not when I'm finally happy.

10

THE REST OF THE WEEKEND is perfect. Besides the occasional venture out for food or a walk with Frank, Liam and I spend all of Saturday cocooned in his town house, barely ever leaving his bed. We watch movies, read, and cuddle with the dog. Sometimes, we lie there talking for hours—or, just as often, not talking at all.

On Sunday, we decide to rejoin the world with a trip to the Met before wandering back to my apartment, where we have every intention of ordering dinner, only to end up tumbling back into my bed until well past nine. After, we grab dollar slices at the pizza joint down the street and eat them on the walk back home, giggling like little kids who got away with stealing candy.

It's not until we're back at my apartment door that Liam's smile falls.

"That's new," he says, pointing at my doorbell camera. "I didn't notice before."

Uneasiness churns through me at the reminder of my earlier paranoia, but I play it off with a shrug.

"I found out the security cameras in my building don't actually work," I explain, unlocking the door. "Figured it was better to be safe than sorry."

Liam's frown deepens with concern. "Do you feel unsafe here?"

For a moment, the truth rushes toward my lips: *Yes.* But instead, I reach up and give Liam a quick kiss.

"It's fine," I promise. "Especially when you're here."

At that, Liam's face softens again, a smile curving where I just kissed him.

"Well, if you ever do feel unsafe," he says, worry dipping back into his eyes, "you can call me."

Warmth gushes from my chest all the way to my toes. "Thank you."

"Of course," Liam says softly.

I'm considering dragging him back to my bedroom once again when suddenly, Liam sniffs, brow furrowing.

"Do you smell that?" he asks.

As soon as he mentions it, I do—sugary-sweet and chemical, with something smoky beneath it, almost like . . .

"Shit." I rush deeper into the apartment. The smell thickens in the air, and through the surge of adrenaline, I see it. On the coffee table, my vanilla sugar candle is a roar of flame. I freeze, suddenly transported back to a dark room.

Heat. Melting faces.

My heart crawls into my throat, lodging with a silent scream: *Fire.*

Liam rushes to the kitchen and grabs a metal pan lid, which he shoves on top of the candle. It sputters out in a cloud of dark smoke, wax bubbling and sizzling on the table as we stare in breathless silence.

"Thank you," I finally manage, my whole body shaking. I fold my arms tight around my ribs, my still-hammering heart. "I have no idea how that happened."

"Did you leave it burning when we left?" Liam's expression is concerned, but there's the slightest edge to his tone—almost like an accusation.

"No," I say automatically. "I never leave a candle burning."

But even as I say it, I'm not so sure. I try to remember whether the candle was lit when we left the apartment, but I can't. I usually light it when Liam's coming over, and I always remember to put it out, but tonight . . . I can't actually recall doing either. It's one of those actions like brushing my teeth or turning off the oven—so routine that, as soon as I think too hard about it, I can't be sure if I actually did it or if I'm just remembering some other time. Cold reaches out from my core.

Liam's jaw clenches, but then he lets out a sigh, releasing it.

"It's okay," he says gently. "Let's just clean it up."

After we've scrubbed down the table and tossed the ruined candle into the trash, Liam goes to the bathroom, and an idea worms into my head. Quickly, I pull out my phone and navigate to the app that connects to my doorbell camera.

When it opens, I'm prompted to log in. I frown. Usually I'm logged in automatically, but maybe it kicked me out somehow. I type in my login info, only for an error message to pop up: Incorrect password.

I try again, only to get the same message. Dread pools in my stomach, my hands clenching around my phone as I try and fail for the third time. As the truth becomes undeniable: I am locked out.

After the candle debacle, Liam goes home for the night. He cites an early workday tomorrow, but part of me worries it's more than that—still, I don't fight him. I have things I need to do alone.

As soon as Liam is gone, I curl back on my couch and reset my doorbell-app password, gnawing on my thumbnail as it reloads. When I check the footage, though, there's nothing unusual from tonight. *Because no one broke into my apartment and tried to light it on fire,* I remind myself, sighing with relief as I realize how ridiculous that thought was. I don't like that I forgot about the lit candle, but it's not exactly out of character—and neither is forgetting my password.

It's not until later, when a sweet good-night text from Liam buzzes onto my screen, that the other possibility occurs to me.

Liam has been with me all weekend. It would have been easy as breathing for him to swipe my phone, open my doorbell app, and change my password—just as easy as it would have been for him to light the candle when I wasn't looking.

The idea churns in my head until it's a hurricane raging, my heart racing in the darkness.

With every passing breath, I am more certain of two things: I am falling in love with Liam, and I don't know if I can trust him.

11

WHEN I REACH FOR MY phone in the morning, groggy and bleary-eyed from barely a few hours of sleep, the first thing I see is the calendar notification: Event tonight!

"Shit," I mutter.

I'd forgotten about the book signing, and for a moment, I consider just faking sick and canceling—but then I see Liam's text, sent two hours ago at eight AM.

Can't wait to see you tonight!

My heart gives a tender thump, and in spite of myself, I smile. Then I scrub my hands over my face and let out a sigh. I can do this. Already, last night's panicked suspicion of Liam seems ridiculous. I forgot my password and the candle—two simple mistakes made even likelier by the very real, very handsome distraction in my apartment.

By the time evening falls and I'm slipping into my favorite author outfit—a flowy pink dress that makes me feel like a cross between a Jane Austen character and a cottagecore influencer—I'm actually excited for tonight.

I take the subway down to the romance bookstore in Brooklyn, and as I walk through the shop doors, it's like being wrapped in a cozy blanket. The room is draped in pink ribbons and dusty-rose furniture, and even the air smells romantic, a mix of flowers and ink. I breathe it in, letting it relax me. Nothing can go *that* wrong, I tell myself, when you're surrounded by books.

Still, as I sit in front of the quickly growing audience, I'm alert, scanning the crowd for . . . I'm not sure what, exactly. A familiar face, a jogged memory—anyone who looks like they might want to ruin my life.

"Ivy?"

I almost jump at the sound of Aria's voice—the bookseller who will be my conversation partner for the night.

"Sorry." I fix on a smile, looking away from the crowd. "What's up?"

"We're at ten after, if you're ready to start."

I sneak another glance at the crowd. Liam isn't here yet, but he will be—he's probably just running late from work. In the meantime, there's a room full of excited romance readers to contend with.

I swallow and put on my brightest smile. "Ready."

Aria launches into the event, welcoming the audience with friendly charm. When she introduces me, there's a round of applause that rings in my ears, my cheeks hurting from the grin.

"So, Ivy." Aria turns to me like we're about to share secrets. "We're obviously all obsessed with *Haunt Me Then*, which is such a wonderful reimagining of *Wuthering Heights*. Can you tell us what it was about that book that inspired you?"

A familiar question, one I've answered for every single event and podcast interview. I breathe out, loosening my clenched hands under the table.

"Well, it's probably not hard to guess that *Wuthering Heights* is my favorite book of all time," I start, as I always do. "What I think is really interesting, though, is how the book often gets categorized as a romance. It's a love story, of course, but it's so many other things—a tragic exploration of the cycles of abuse, even a ghost story."

The audience nods along, energized, but suddenly, the "revised edition" of my book creeps into my head, those words scrawled in red.

"But, um . . ." I blink, a small, stuttering beat before I remember what's next. "As much as I love all the contradictions of *Wuthering Heights*, there's always been a little part of me that wishes Cathy and Heathcliff could have had a happier ending—you know, one where they didn't have to die to be reunited."

There are a few chuckles, but my nerves don't ease. Instead, my heart thrums, my foot bobbing in a way I can't control.

"So, that's where the idea for *Haunt Me Then* came from."

At that exact moment, the front door dings open, and Liam slips inside, cheeks flushed like he ran from the subway. He smiles shyly, waving, and for just a moment, I forget to be anxious: There's only us, alone in this room full of books.

"I wanted to write them a happier story," I finish.

Aria moves on with her questions, and the conversation breezes along. Now that Liam is sitting in the back row, watching with such pride in his eyes, I'm not nervous at all—I become my most charming, funny self, thrilled to know he's seeing me in my element. Feeling, for the first time all day, like I'm truly safe.

By the time we get to audience questions, I've almost forgotten my fears entirely.

"First of all, I just wanted to say how much I *love* this book," begins the first reader, a college-age girl with a bright smile. "I'm actually from Westchester, and I loved how real all the descriptions felt."

Alarm pricks the back of my neck, but I keep smiling.

"So, I'm curious why you chose to set the book there," she finishes, "and if you've spent any time in the area."

My grip tightens on the mic. It's a question I've been asked before, one I have a standard answer for, but for the first time, it feels truly dangerous.

"Great question," I say a little too brightly. I pull it back, launching into my usual response. "I've always been really inspired by the towns just outside of New York City, especially the ones along the Hudson. There's so much beautiful nature and architecture there that can sometimes feel a little unsung when Manhattan gets all the attention." Sweat prickles under my arms, and I subtly adjust my sleeve. "I was actually lucky enough to spend some time in . . ."

Before I can say anything else, the front door opens again, the bell jingling. When I see who's standing there, I stop cold. A familiar face, one that needles every inch of my skin with recognition, but not one I expected.

Xander.

The first thing I notice is that he's growing out a mustache. It doesn't suit him, the sandy hairs too scraggly to grow into anything real.

The second thing I notice is that he's a mess. Not just the mustache, but all of him. His clothes and hair are disheveled, and even from the other end of the room, I can see the dark, almost bruise-colored circles under his eyes. When his stare locks on mine, my breath stalls.

He looks wild. Desperate.

And then I notice something else: a ring of purple bruising around his neck.

Coldness wraps around my own throat as tightly as fingers.

I've been silent for too long. People are noticing. A few heads turn toward the door, Liam's included. When he sees Xander, Liam's only reaction is a small furrowing of his brow.

"Sorry," I say, desperate to regain control before it spirals out of reach. "I was saying that, yeah, I've been lucky enough to spend some time in the towns that inspired *Haunt Me Then*."

I barely even see the crowd anymore. Instead, I glance at Xander. He's at the register now, where a bookseller quietly explains that this is an author event, and Xander can purchase my book if he wants it signed.

The Q&A chugs along without any other disturbances, but my confidence has withered. Now I'm on autopilot, running through answers like memorized lines, my voice sounding strange and discordant in my ears. Eventually, Xander sits in the very last row with my book on his lap, only two chairs down from Liam.

When the questions are finally over, I barely hear the applause. Instead, I watch Liam as he glares at Xander with a harsh intensity that sends goose bumps down my skin. By now, Liam has almost certainly realized who he is.

"Okay, folks," Aria announces. "Those of you who've purchased copies of *Haunt Me Then* can line up over here if you'd like Ivy to sign them."

The readers get to their feet, an excited hum of conversation filling the room as the signing line forms. Aria turns to me with a grin.

"Great job," she says. "They loved it!"

"Thank you." I smile back, my eyes darting to the end of the line, where Xander hovers with his shoulders hunched. "I had so much fun."

The line churns forward, and I try to keep my hand from shaking as I sign books. My smile feels plastered on, so tight it hurts my cheeks.

Why the hell is Xander here?

"Abby?" I repeat when the reader in front of me says her name.

"Anna," she corrects me, smiling politely.

My stomach twists. "So sorry! A-n-n-a?"

It feels endless, even though there can't be more than twenty people in this line. When I glance up, Liam is waiting by the shelf of my books, watching Xander with that same dark glare.

Finally, I hand the last reader her signed book, and she thanks me with a grin. Before she's even turned away, Xander silently approaches the table.

Aria's gone to get the rest of the stock for me to sign, so we're alone, except for Liam glaring from a distance. Like he can feel it, Xander glances over his shoulder, scrubbing an anxious hand through his hair. Then he thrusts his book at me.

"I guess you should sign this."

I take the book, trying not to betray my uneasiness to the readers still milling around.

"What are you doing here?" I murmur.

He doesn't immediately answer, just scratches at his neck, and I can't help looking closer at the bruising there—long, narrow smudges, shaped almost like . . .

Worry engulfs my irritation. *Like fingers.*

"Xander . . ."

When his eyes finally lift to mine, they're bloodshot. Determined. "I need to talk to you."

I'm achingly aware of Liam in the distance, probably wondering why I'm not just asking Xander to leave. I probably should. Still, as much as I want to hate Xander, I can't help the concern those bruises stir in my chest.

"Are you okay?" I ask him gently. "Do you need help?"

I'm not expecting the laugh that rips out of him, bitter and biting.

"Do I need help," he repeats, like I've just made some kind of ridiculous joke. His eyes water, and I can't tell if it's from laughter or tears. For the first time, I wonder if he's drunk.

"Is everything all right here?"

We both turn to see Liam towering over the table, at least four inches taller than Xander and well aware of it. His tone is still clipped and polite, so quintessentially British, but there's a danger thrumming beneath it.

Xander's eyes dart from Liam to me. "This your boyfriend?"

There's a joking tilt to the word, minimizing it, and I recognize the sound. It's the same way Xander used to talk about my books. Even when he was outwardly praising me, it was still patronizing— *It's so cool how you can write something that has such broad appeal*, he said once, with the clear implication that "broad appeal" was the exact opposite of what he wanted for his hefty, convoluted poems. All at once, I understand something fundamental about Xander that I can't believe I never noticed before: He's cruel when he's threatened.

"Yes," I say coldly. "He is."

With barely more than a scribble, I sign Xander's book and hand it back to him, throwing in a tight smile.

"Thanks for coming."

With the swiftness of a snake, Xander slaps both hands on the table and leans in close enough to see the flecks of gold in his red-rimmed eyes.

"I know," Xander spits, violent and desperate all at once. "I know what really happened to—"

In a flash, Liam snatches Xander back by the scruff of his T-shirt, so quickly and smoothly that I barely register it happening. Even Xander is too shocked to make a sound, frozen in Liam's lethal grip. My heart races, that unfinished accusation reaching toward me like a hungry ghost.

"She said no, mate," Liam rumbles. The danger in his words is palpable, but somehow, he seems completely composed—the only giveaway is the angry vein bulging in his neck. "Now take your book and go."

With a shove, he releases Xander, who stumbles a few steps before righting himself. Xander throws one last look over his shoulder at me, and terror descends.

But Xander just lifts his hands in defeat, taking a few steps toward the door.

"Fine," he says. "I'm leaving."

The fear is just starting to leach out of me when Xander cuts one last hard look at Liam.

"But you need to ask her about the fire."

The words are a lit match to everything. It crackles and curls, all of it falling away except the shock gripping me from the inside.

I barely even notice as Xander rushes out of the bookstore and the bell jingles, muted, behind him. I feel like the room is full of water—like I'm drowning.

I never told Xander about the fire.

"Ivy . . ."

I look up at Liam, and all that violent rage has melted from his face, leaving only worry. Before he can say anything else, Aria returns with a stack of books.

"Here's the rest of it!" she announces cheerily, either unaware of what just happened at the table or choosing to ignore it. "Would you mind signing?"

I paint on an automatic smile, but the fear still shudders through my body, my brain replaying that image: Liam yanking Xander back like he weighed nothing, simmering with anger. Protective. *Dangerous.* I knew Liam was strong, but for the first time, it strikes me that he's capable of violence.

Maybe I should be frightened, but instead, my hands quiver with fury as I reach for the pen. With those two words—*the fire*—Xander has opened a door that should have been locked tight, and now it could destroy everything.

12

THE WALK FROM THE SUBWAY to Liam's town house is painfully quiet, my heels on the concrete like muffled pops of a gun. Liam's steps barely make a sound. The whole time, my head is spinning, turning the same question over and over: Xander knows about the fire. *But how?*

I'm almost certain now that Xander is the one who's been leaving me those threats as "Heathcliff," even breaking into my apartment. The one thing that doesn't make sense is *why.*

Liam clears his throat, pulling me out of my thoughts.

"Listen," he starts. "About what happened back there . . ."

My blood curdles with dread. I'm not naive enough to think we could avoid this conversation, but still, my body resists it, every part of me tensing.

But what Liam says is "I'm sorry if I overstepped."

His face is so soft with concern that all my worry fades. If nothing else, at least I can be sure now that it isn't Liam who's been threatening me. The thought is such a relief that I forget everything but the desire to comfort him, taking his hand and threading my fingers through his.

"Not at all," I say. "I'm glad you got him to leave. To be honest . . ." My chest squeezes. "I've never had someone defend me like that before."

The smile that breaks over Liam's face is so sweet that I want to kiss him, certain it would taste like sugar. I almost do, but then he stops walking, his face turning serious.

"I'll always defend you, Ivy. Especially from someone like that." He shakes his head, teeth gritting. "I can't stand a man who won't take no for an answer."

That new and unfamiliar intensity flares in his eyes again, and I get a flash of those frightening bruises on Xander's neck, the dark purple ghosts of someone's fingers.

"But I don't usually get physical." Liam's hands dive into his pockets, his gaze dipping downward. "That's not who I am, and I promise you it won't happen again."

When he lifts his eyes, they burn with such sincerity that I can't help myself. I cup my hand over Liam's cheek and bring his lips down to meet mine. He kisses me back, harder, his fingers drifting to the small of my back, and an electric heat zings down to my stomach.

"Sometimes," I breathe, our lips still inches from each other, "I still can't believe you're real."

Liam smiles, laughing softly, and I can feel the puff of his breath.

"Are you kidding?" He pulls back, looking at me like he needs to memorize every detail. "I could say the same about you." He whirls me around in a ballroom-style turn, landing me in a dip with another lingering kiss. "You're perfect."

Worry zips down my spine, but I force a self-effacing smile. "Hardly."

"You are," he insists, helping me back to my feet. "It was so wonderful to see you in your element tonight. I already knew you were made to be an author, but I loved getting to see you in action."

My face flushes, and I'm momentarily shy enough to avert my gaze.

"Thank you," I say. "I'd love to see you in your element, too, by the way. I kind of fantasize about it daily."

Liam laughs, loud and ringing, as he pulls me to his side.

"I think we can arrange that."

As we walk arm in arm, the city seems to glow around us. Sunset drenches the brick and concrete in orange light, the sky a watercolor of lavender and cotton-candy pink. It's the kind of night I'd usually want to write about—perfect and ephemeral, a beauty that might fade faster than I can capture it all.

But with Liam's tall frame beside me, our steps and breath synchronized, I don't think I could write even if I tried. My brain buzzes with a quickly growing certainty, eating me up as the sunset shifts from delicate pastel to burning fire, the clouds darkening like smoke. When we reach his building, I know I can't take another step without telling him.

"Liam."

"Yes?" He stops, concern dipping into his blue eyes. The worry must be written all over my face, too, and I almost want to take it back—to let us live in this in-between before the honeymoon comes to an end.

But as I look into Liam's eyes, so open and kind, his words come back to me: *I'll always defend you, Ivy.* My heart curls open, tiny petals stretching to the sun.

"There's something I should tell you."

My heart beats like bird wings in my chest, trapped and frantic. Liam reaches out to brush a lock of hair behind my ear, his touch lingering on my cheek.

"What is it?" he asks.

"It's about what Xander mentioned at the bookstore." I swallow. "The fire."

Liam nods, patient—like he knew this was coming but wanted to wait until I felt comfortable—and if I wasn't certain before, I would be now. The fire is a piece of me that I always carry, hidden and jagged, its sharp edges jutting into my skin to remind me, every time I meet someone new, that this is something I'll have to tell them, at least if I want them to know me fully.

Very few people do. In fact, I've only ever told this story to two people: Aunt Mia, who technically already knew, and Dani.

And now I want Liam to have it, too. I reach for his hand, still pressed to my cheek, and bring it down to my sternum, holding tight so I can feel the solid weight of him against my skin.

"When I was fifteen, my house burned down. The one I grew up in, an hour outside of New York. That's how my parents died, and . . ." My heart pounds wildly against Liam's hand, and I'm certain he can feel it, that telltale beat. "And I was the only one who made it out."

"Oh, darling." Liam pulls me to him, and it's not until my face is pressed to his shirt that I realize I've started crying. "It's okay."

Now I can hear his heartbeat, strong and steady, each thump a rhythmic echo of those words: *You're perfect. You're perfect.*

If only he knew.

Still, Liam's hand presses gently to the back of my head, stroking my hair.

"That's awful," he croons. "I'm so sorry, Ivy."

I nod, my throat still too tight to speak.

Delicately, Liam lifts my chin so he can look me in the eyes. At first, I want to flinch away, red-eyed and snot-covered as I am, but then he wipes my tears with his thumb, smiling at me like I'm still the most beautiful thing he's ever seen.

"Thank you," Liam says. "For telling me. And if you want to talk more about it, I'm here."

Pulled by a sudden need to prove it, I press both my hands to his chest. Firm and solid. *Real.* The hunger is instant and all-consuming as I kiss him again, every place we touch like a burning promise that this is real. He's here, and he won't slip away.

It's what I tell myself as I lead him up to his town house, the heat of him still scorching my lips.

As the rest of the truth—the whole rotten heart of it—retreats quietly into the dark.

That night, it storms. The clouds roll in so smoothly that we barely notice until the skies have opened, thunder shaking the city. Rain pounds the windows as we curl up together in bed, Liam drifting toward sleep while my mind drifts back to Xander.

I know.

I know what really happened to—

Liam's arms are around my waist, his breath slowing, but I suddenly can't lie still, my body too hot and buzzing. I wait, wide awake in the darkness, until he begins to snore.

Then, when I'm certain he's sleeping deeply enough, I carefully lift his arm off of me and reach for my phone. I tap the screen awake, curling my body around it to block the light. It's just after midnight. Heart thrumming, I unblock Xander and type out a message.

Can we talk? I can explain everything.

I hesitate for half a breath before jabbing the Send button and setting the phone back on the table.

I curl back onto my side and wait, heart pounding as I stare at the screen, both desperate and terrified for it to light up with a response.

NOW

RAIN COATS THE PAVEMENT IN a slick sheen, making it glow like an oil painting: cherry-red taillights, gritty neon signs in blue and green. I pull up the hood of my raincoat, but the drops still fall, cool and stinging on my face. Tonight, the sweet taste of summer is a distant dream.

The building appears, a single lamp glowing yellow above the doorway. As I approach, my breath quickens, too loud in the darkened street.

I buzz.

No answer. It's late, nearly two, so it's possible he's gone to sleep. I'm certain he hasn't.

I buzz again, growing impatient. The rain gets heavier, and I give in, running my finger down every apartment number in the row. I'm lucky: Someone must be waiting on a delivery, or simply too fed up with the noise to be careful about answering the door, because it unlocks with a loud drone.

I step inside, water sluicing from my umbrella and onto the grimy tile.

Drip, drip, drip, in rhythm with my steps as I climb, calming any lingering panic I feel. It's simple. One foot in front of the other.

I reach the door.

I knock.

I'm prepared to take less polite measures, but then it swings open. He stands in the doorway in a ratty T-shirt, his eyes wide with the pathetic expression I've grown used to. But tonight, there's something else in it, something sweet and unfamiliar that shoots a thrill through my blood.

Fear.

I smile. "It's probably time we talked."

He says nothing, but he steps aside. An invitation, even though I didn't need one.

Tonight is inevitable, and we both know it. The only question now is how hard he's going to make this—how much of a mess will be left to clean up in the morning.

13

I JOLT AWAKE WITH A POUNDING heart. By the time I realize I was having a nightmare, I've already forgotten what it was.

Liam's room is dark, the curtains drawn. The sun hasn't risen yet, but the rain has stopped, and Liam sleeps peacefully, his broad shoulders rising and falling, with his back turned to me. My stomach tenses. We always fall asleep and wake up touching—even if we shift during the night, we find each other again, tugged to safe harbor through the churning sea of sleep—and somehow, this feels like an omen. Like he's pulling away from me.

And then I remember: *Xander.*

As quietly as possible, I snatch my phone from the nightstand. It's just after four thirty AM, and I have two texts from Xander. The first one was sent just before one AM in his classic all-lowercase.

fine. come over.

Then, fifteen minutes later:

if you're not going to talk, then i'm going to the police.

Panic spills through me, white-hot and electric. With one glance to make sure Liam is still sleeping, I scramble out of bed and then snatch my shorts from the floor, pulling them on under Liam's oversized T-shirt. As I pad toward the stairs, Frank stirs in his dog bed. I freeze, but he's only twitching in sleep, legs running in the dream world.

Holding my breath, I creep upstairs with my phone gripped tight. Then, once I'm out of earshot of the bedroom, I call Xander.

Voicemail. Still, I try again, gnawing on my thumbnail as it dials.

Same thing.

"Shit," I breathe, pacing across the living room.

Maybe this is nothing. Still, that wild look in his eyes as he slammed the table, getting up in my face. *I know what really happened to—*

I grab Liam's keys from the entry table, the decision made before I can talk myself out of it. Xander sent me that text over three hours ago—more than enough time for him to call the police, if that's what he's really planning. I still don't know for sure, but I have no other choice.

It takes me a minute to find my sneakers—I'd left them in the living room, I thought, but now they're on the shoe rack, nestled neatly between Liam's loafers and a pair of work boots. Liam must have moved them, and the sweetness of the gesture makes my chest squeeze with guilt. I slip them on and creep quietly through the door.

Outside, the world is still dark, streetlamps and lanterns spilling ghostly light onto the pavement. Somewhere in the city, the sleepless among us are stumbling home from bars or into the nearest twenty-four-hour deli, but here on the Upper West Side, everything is quiet, still a little too early for the earliest risers.

The emptiness doesn't lessen my panic. The cliché is right: This city doesn't sleep. The real question is who else is awake and lurking with me in the shadows.

When I get to the subway station, there are only two other people: a woman sleeping on the bench and a man pacing up and down the platform, mumbling quietly to himself. I force myself to breathe and check my phone again. Still no response from Xander.

Finally, the uptown train arrives. I try calling Xander one more time, but there's no answer. The train rockets onward, and I lose my signal.

When I get off twenty minutes later at 145th Street in Harlem, the dark sky is smudged with gray, creeping toward sunrise, and I'm out of breath from my rush up the stairs, heart pounding. Still, I don't slow down, speed-walking the path I've followed so many times before: past the bus stop and the grocery store, its flickering neon light; turn right at the scaffolding that never seems to leave this corner, and then, three blocks later, Xander's building.

I hesitate as I reach the door, gripped with a sudden sense of déjà vu that prickles the back of my neck. I've done this before, countless times, but something about it feels different—like I'm stepping into a scene that's already played out, maybe only in my own head.

I push down the feeling and buzz Xander's unit. No answer. I glance around the street for any approaching tenants I could follow inside, but all I see is a guy standing in front of the next building over, watching me curiously over the glow of his cigarette.

Heart thumping, I take a breath and buzz every unit in the building. It's a skeevy trick, but usually it works—someone's bound to be expecting a package, or just too lazy to get up and check who's there.

The door unlocks, and adrenaline zips through me. I push into the lobby. Inside, it's empty, bright artificial lights buzzing overhead. As I climb the stairs to Xander's floor, that déjà-vu feeling shudders down my spine again, making my heart race faster. The smell of stale cigarette smoke hangs in the air like always—Xander has a neighbor who smokes in the stairwell—but now it feels thicker, curling into my lungs with every inhale. I hold my breath as I walk up to Xander's door and knock.

As soon as my fist hits the wood, though, I realize it's already open, the dead bolt propped against the frame. That familiar eerie feeling nips at the back of my neck as I step inside, shutting the door behind me.

"Xander?" I call out.

No response. There's strange smell in the air, a musty tang mixed with the cigarette smoke from outside, and my stomach squirms.

"Owen?" I try, quieter, but Xander's roommate doesn't seem to be here, either. He practically lives at his girlfriend's most of the time, though, so that's no surprise. I walk deeper into the apartment, the old floorboards creaking under my feet.

When I reach the living room, I freeze.

The first thing I see are the feet: two black socks sticking out from a pair of gray sweats, a hole in one of the frayed heels. One knee is bent, forming an angle on the floor like a rock climber caught mid-ascent.

With a shuddering breath, I force myself to move closer, and then I see it all.

Xander lies stomach down on the kitchen floor, almost like he could be sleeping—if it weren't for the unnatural twist of his bruised neck or his wide, lifeless eyes. The halo of thick, dark blood around his skull.

14

I DON'T SCREAM. I DON'T RUN. Instead, I'm completely frozen, staring at Xander's limp body on the ground like this is some sort of waking dream, one that might go away the moment I blink.

When it doesn't, I rush toward him, putting my hands on his shoulders.

"Xander." My voice is thick, distorted to my own ears. "Xander!"

I shake him a little harder, and his head tilts limply. That's when I see the dent in the back of his skull, dark red matted in the long sandy hair I used to bury my hands in, loving the way the thick strands felt in my fingers. Bile rises in my throat.

Xander is dead, and for a moment, all I can feel is relief.

Almost instantly, the guilt takes over, and I spring to my feet. I pull out my phone to dial 911, but then, just before I press the button, I stop.

I am Xander's ex-girlfriend. Less than twelve hours ago, he had a public altercation with my new boyfriend. There is written proof that he was threatening to call the police on me, and now . . .

I take an instinctive step back, my head swimming. I can't be the one to find Xander's body. I might as well serve myself up on a silver platter labeled PRIME SUSPECT. But I can't just leave him here like this, blood leaking onto the tile.

Then the other truth collides like a blow to the chest: If Xander's building has security footage, then I'm already caught on camera entering his unit. If they catch me leaving again without calling for help, that's even more suspicious.

My heart beats faster, and suddenly, the smoke smell from outside has found me again, only stronger. Sharper. I try to breathe, but it only reaches down into my throat, choking me.

Deep in my memory, I hear it: the crackle. The hiss.

The blood spilling from the back of her head.

I gasp, digging my nails into my palm to ground myself in what's real. Not the sounds, the memories, but the body in front of me.

There is a dead body, and an innocent person would call the police. But first, I have to get rid of the evidence.

Holding my breath, I creep back toward Xander's body and look for his phone. When I don't see it lying anywhere, I have no choice: I go into the cabinet under his sink, grab a pair of rubber gloves, and then feel through his pockets. When I brush the phone, I let out a relieved sigh and then pull it out. The screen prompts me for face ID, and my stomach roils.

Carefully, I hold it over Xander's lifeless face.

The phone unlocks, and I yank it quickly away, opening our messages. I'm his most recent text conversation. Beneath that is Xander's conversation with Cat. My pulse jumps at her name. Xander's last message to her was sent two nights ago: where are you?

She never responded—but clearly, he was still seeing her. The wounded, angry part of me wants to click on their conversation and read every word, but that's not the priority right now. I swipe on Xander's text conversation with me, my finger hovering over the Delete button. If I delete the texts and then, somehow, the police are able to recover them, this will only look more suspicious.

But then there's Xander's last text to me, still glowing from the screen and making my heart pound: if you're not going to talk, then i'm going to the police.

It's even *more* suspicious if they find that text right now, and it will only get worse the longer I wait to call for help. I delete the text conversation as quickly and surely as I'd kill an ant, and then, after putting the phone back in Xander's pocket, I go to my own phone and do the same.

There is only one thing left to do. I dial the number and then wait, heart pounding, for the operator to answer.

"911," she says. "Where is your emergency?"

I rattle off Xander's address, and then, with my nails still digging into my skin, sharp enough to draw blood, I tell her, "I think there's been a murder."

What happens next is a blur. Police arrive. Paramedics, too, though they know almost instantly there is no saving Xander. One of the officers ushers me into the fifth-floor hallway while the others stay behind, and I give him my name and information. I explain to him what happened, as truthfully as I can.

Xander was my ex-boyfriend, and he showed up at my book signing last night demanding to talk. He was clearly agitated, so I refused to speak to him. Then, this morning, I came over hoping we could sort things out. Get some closure.

The officer listens, nodding and jotting things down. My words come out steadily, a little blank with shock. Meanwhile, fear churns inside me, spreading like blood in water.

I have walked into a trap, and I can't be sure whether it's of my own making.

Once I've finished explaining to the officer what happened, he instructs me to wait. There are detectives coming, he says, and he'll just need me to tell them what I told him.

Dread hardens into a stone in my gut. *Detectives.* As irrational as it may be, I wish, in this moment, that I had run when I had the chance—fled like a child from a nightmare.

Still, I force myself to nod like an innocent person would. *I am innocent,* I remind myself.

"Of course," I say.

And then I wait.

When the detectives in question finally arrive, there are two of them: Detective Kelleher, a tall, square-jawed man with a pale bald head, and Detective Lopez, a petite woman with her dark hair slicked into a perfect bun.

They each shake my hand and then tell me that the building's superintendent has given them permission to conduct interviews in an unoccupied third-floor unit.

"For privacy," Detective Kelleher explains.

I follow them downstairs, grateful to leave the crime scene behind, but when Detective Lopez closes the door to the third-floor unit behind us, my heart leaps. Suddenly, I feel like I've been led into a cage.

In the living area, three folding chairs have been set up, and I wonder if they were dragged up here specifically for this purpose. The detectives gesture for me to take a seat.

"Thank you for talking with us, Ivy," Lopez says. "I'm sure this has been a very difficult morning for you."

Her expression is sympathetic, but in a measured way. As a homicide detective, dealing with shaken witnesses must be business as usual. And that's what I am, I remind myself. A witness, not a suspect.

At least for now.

"Can you talk us through what happened today?" Kelleher asks, his forehead bunching with similar empathy.

I walk through the same story I gave the previous officer.

"And what time did you get here?" Lopez asks.

I realize I'm gripping the edge of my chair and try to relax my fingers.

"Around five this morning," I say.

Her eyebrows quirk—a small jolt of suspicion.

"That's pretty early, isn't it?"

Again, I squirm with that childish impulse to run, but I force myself to remain calm, my face relaxed.

"Yeah," I say. "I'd been trying to reach him since last night, but he wasn't answering, and it made me nervous. I guess I couldn't sleep." Then, with a jolt, I remember what I haven't told them yet. "There were these bruises on Xander's neck when he came to the book signing. He didn't say where he got them, but it looked like someone must have grabbed him or tried to strangle him. I was worried about him."

The truth of it seizes me with an eerie chill. Xander must have gotten those bruises somewhere. He was in danger, and I threw him out.

And now . . .

Kelleher leans forward slightly in his seat. "Do you have any guesses of where those bruises might have come from?"

Liam flashes through my head—his strong arms gripping Xander's collar, veins rippling over muscle. I swallow, instantly hoping it doesn't read as a nervous tic.

"No," I say. "We weren't really in contact since the breakup, at least until last night."

"But you were worried about him," Lopez says plainly, as if to confirm. "You came here to talk to him."

I fight the urge for another nervous swallow. Now I can't ignore the suspicion in her eyes. I nod.

"He was acting really strangely last night," I tell her. "It seemed like something was wrong."

"Do you mind telling us what led to the breakup?" Kelleher asks.

I tense, but I know there's no getting out of this.

"He cheated on me," I say, trying to sound as neutral as possible.

The detectives don't outwardly react, but I know I've just given them a motive.

"I found texts on Xander's phone," I add, "with a girl named Cat. I don't know who she is, but . . ."

I trail off, shrugging, but hope rises as I realize what I've also given them: another potential suspect, the other woman.

I try to hold on to that comfort through the rest of the interview, which is mostly just basic questions and confirming the details I've already told them. At the detectives' request, I give them my contact information in case they need to speak with me about anything else. And then, finally, I am free to go.

Kelleher holds the door open for me, and I walk back out to the third floor, feeling almost like I'm in a dream.

"Thank you again, Ivy," he tells me with a nod.

"Of course," I say. "Thank you."

Lopez is silent, that suspicion still glinting beneath her steely expression.

It takes all my self-restraint not to sprint down the stairs. There's another officer stationed at the building door, likely to help secure the crime scene, and he nods as I pass. Outside, the sun has fully risen, drenching the streets in a bright morning glow. Two cop cars are parked on the curb, a few passersby stopping to stare in curiosity.

For a moment, I stand there, not quite sure what to do with myself. Then, when I take my phone out of my pocket, my breath stalls.

I have three missed calls from Liam.

"Shit," I mutter. He must be panicking, having woken up and found me gone.

Heart thrumming, I call him back, gnawing on my thumbnail as the dial tone drones. He answers after one ring.

"Ivy?"

"Hey," I say weakly.

"Where are you?" he asks, voice taut with concern.

I close my eyes, and that's when I realize I'm crying—hot tears spilling silently down my face.

"I'm in Harlem," I say. "At Xander's."

I take a breath, and in the brief hitch, I'm almost certain I can hear Liam tensing.

"He's dead."

15

THE TAXI HAS BARELY PULLED up to the curb before Liam is hopping out and crushing me to his chest. As soon as he does, I'm sobbing, face buried in his shirt.

"Oh, darling," he says, lips against my hair. "I'm so sorry."

"I should have told you," I manage through the tears. "Last night freaked me out, so I came over, and . . ."

Liam squeezes me tighter. "It's okay. I'm just glad you're all right."

He helps me into the cab and then sits beside me, his hand placed gently on my knee.

"Do you want to go back to yours or mine?" he asks.

I hesitate, even as the answer comes instantly. Right now I want nothing more than the soft familiarity of my own bed, but Liam's kindness stirs my guilt.

"Mine," I say. "If that's okay."

"Of course," Liam says gently, and the guilt deepens. A lesser man would be demanding to know why I went to my ex-boyfriend's apartment at five in the morning—a *normal* man, even.

Then Liam asks, a bit hesitantly, "Do you want me to come?"

I reach for his hand, suddenly eager to put his doubts to rest. "Yes, please."

Liam gives my hand a gentle pulse before telling the driver my address.

The rest of the drive is silent as the city rolls past through the windows, the early morning light streaking through the clouds.

When the cab parks at my building, Liam insists on paying the fare and then holding the door open for me, ever the gentleman. Shame winds through me all over again.

"Thank you," I tell Liam as he closes the cab door behind us. "For being here."

The kindness in his expression nearly shatters my heart.

"Of course," he says, as if it's the simplest thing in the world.

By the time we get upstairs, I feel ready to collapse, but when Liam asks if I want to go back to sleep, I find myself shaking my head. The cigarette smell from Xander's hallway lingers on my clothes, and if I get in bed now, I'm afraid it will never leave the sheets.

"I think I'm going to hop in the shower," I say. "You don't have to stay if you don't want to, though. I know Frank probably needs to go out."

Still, when Liam kisses my forehead and says, "I'm staying right here," warmth floods my chest. I don't want to be alone.

I give him one more tight hug before turning to my bathroom, already dreaming of the hottest water possible, itching to scald the last few hours from my skin.

I've barely taken a step inside before I see it, heart springing into my throat.

Red. It's slashed all over my bathroom mirror in an incomprehensible scrawl, the deep cherry of my favorite lipstick, which sits uncapped on the counter like a warning. I stare, open-mouthed, until suddenly, the red slashes become a word.

A *name.*

A scream builds in my throat, and I step back, nearly slipping on the tile. I catch myself on the sink, the lipstick rolling to the floor with a clatter.

"Ivy?" Liam calls.

He rushes inside before I can respond.

"What's happened?" he asks, but I still can't speak. My voice is clamped by that name in undeniable red, written over and over again, the letters overlapping. I watch as Liam sees it, her name obscuring his bewildered face.

"What is this?" He turns to me, but I still don't meet his eyes. "Ivy, who is Cora?"

PART TWO

GHOSTED

THIRTEEN YEARS AGO

CORA

I HAVE ALWAYS BEEN A GHOST, even before I died. The first house I haunted was my own.

On the day that I came to understand this, I was fifteen years old and sitting in the turret nook—my favorite part of our house, because even though it was small, there was space for a reading chair, and enough sunlight filtered through the leaded windows that when it hit my face, I could feel like I was really outside. The window also gave me a small view of our big yard, and it was there, through the decorative glass panels, that I saw them.

There were two of them—a girl and a boy, each riding a bike—and if I could judge correctly from this distance, they were around my age, maybe a couple of years younger.

This wasn't the first time I'd seen people looking at our house. It was an old Victorian, built in the 1800s and sitting back in a big yard in a shroud of trees, tall pines and leafy maples. Even though it was on a private road, people would drive by our house every so often to admire and snap their pictures. There was no fence to ward them off—only a long, winding drive, and then the house, painted a warm clay color and stacked like a strange tiered cake: wraparound porch at the bottom, a second story, and then, above that, the spacious attic floor, everything piped with deep green accents. Dormers and chimneys jutted out almost at random, with windows of different shapes and sizes like so many mismatched eyes—and at the very peak, my turret stretched like a pointed witch's hat to the sky.

But these were not grown-up tourists with cameras, the ones who never came closer than the edge of our property. The kids biking into our yard might have been my classmates—friends, even, if I had them. I leaned closer to the window, breath catching.

They dismounted from their bikes and walked them slowly up the inclined drive, stopping just before it curved up to our porch, like they had silently decided not to go any farther. For a moment, they whispered to each other with an anxious, huddled excitement. I wished I were close enough to read their lips, to be inside their circle, but I didn't have to wait long.

The boy parked his bike and glanced around the empty drive—to ensure, I think, that they were alone. All the cars were gone, Mom at work and Dad picking up my sister from dance class. But they were not alone, not truly.

The house and I were watching.

As the boy crept forward, toward our door, it struck me that I should be nervous—I was home alone—but when my heart began to thrum in my chest, it felt a lot more like excitement. Like we were in on this together—like we had a secret.

With one more glance back at the girl, who looked nervous, the boy straightened his spine and walked all the way up to the covered porch, where he disappeared from view.

I froze with my book still closed around my finger, my racing heartbeats marking time. I should call Mom or Dad, I knew, and tell them. These kids could be trying to sneak in. They may not understand the danger.

Still, I didn't reach for my phone. Instead, I slid my bookmark into my weathered paperback, slipped it under my arm, and crept out of the turret, hesitating at the top of the stairs.

We had a secret language, the house and me. The others didn't know it, and I never told them—they'd think it was silly, even childish—but it was true. The house wanted to keep me safe. If I listened, it had answers. I only had to ask.

Carefully, I pressed my foot to the first step, holding my breath—but it didn't creak. I let out a sigh. *Yes.* Before the house could change its mind, I raced down the stairs, every one of them silent, keeping my secrets.

I didn't stop until I reached the parlor, where I hid myself beside the doorway to the foyer and caught my breath. Through the open archway, I could see late afternoon sun dappling the foyer rug, dust motes floating in the beam like fairy dust. I took a breath, and then, bracing myself, I peeked my head in—just in time to see the boy approaching the door.

I jumped back immediately, hiding myself again. *Did he see me?* My heart pounded even faster, so hard I wondered for a moment if something was wrong—like, call-for-help wrong, even if that was impossible. In this house, I was safe, just as long as they stayed outside.

Still, I didn't dare move—couldn't bring myself to retreat to the safety of my turret. I was curious in the way danger always inspires, that unstoppable urge to hold my finger over a flame and see if it really burns.

More steps sounded on the porch—the girl. I held my breath. Waited. And then through the locked door came a muffled voice.

"I heard she can only go outside in a bubble." It was the girl, her snark unmissable even through the glass. "Doesn't she have that disease where the air can kill you?"

My cheeks went hot. Every inch of my skin, suddenly, was burning in the way I've read about in books but never experienced until this moment—with the realization that they were talking about me, and that I wasn't supposed to hear.

The girl was wrong. I didn't live in a bubble. What I did have was a severely compromised immune system, thanks to the stem-cell transplant I had when I was two years old. While the transplant saved my life and put my leukemia into remission, it also left me with a series of chronic complications and a lifetime of immunosuppressant medications, which meant I had to be careful: no crowds, no regular school classrooms, and no being around anyone sick. Because of this, my sister and I were both homeschooled. I never strayed farther than the edge of our large, wooded property, except to go to the hospital. The last time, I was five years old, and I'd caught a cold that nearly killed me.

The isolation had never really bothered me, because I knew the alternative. Besides, I had my family. I had our house and a world of books contained within its walls. I was safe, and I was happy with that.

At least, I thought so.

The boy stepped forward and cupped his hands against the glass. I heard—but didn't see—the thump of his feet, his hands on our clean, pretty window. When he spoke again, his voice seemed louder, reaching toward me, curling deep in my chest.

"I heard she's already dead," he said. "And her family just pretends she isn't."

All at once, the heat in my blood turned ice-cold. Because there it was: the consequence of my curiosity. The flame singeing my finger and proving what I knew all along.

The rage that rushed up in me was so sudden and strong that I nearly cried out. For one bright, hot moment, I wanted to rush into the foyer and fly to the door like the very ghost they thought I was. I even curled my fists, my weight tipping forward onto my toes, ready—and then I heard someone else approaching outside.

"What the hell, guys?" It was another girl—a bit older, I thought, from the sound of her voice. "I told you not to come over here. Come on, Mom's going to be pissed if she finds out."

I heard their groans and laughter. Then I heard their feet thumping back down the porch steps.

On impulse, I rushed into the foyer, making it to the door just in time to see them walking to their bikes, their backs turned to the house. The new girl wasn't that much older, from what I could see now—maybe only a year or so older than me. She was tall and slim, with brown hair cut just above her shoulders and a bright blue bike helmet tucked under her arm. She shepherded the boy and the other girl back to their bikes and then, suddenly, glanced back toward the house.

I froze. Her eyes met mine. They widened, her mouth falling open like she was staring at a ghost.

I took a breath, as if to say something, but I didn't have time to decide what—because just then, Dad's car pulled into the driveway. The girl looked back at the other kids and called something I couldn't hear. They all hopped on their bikes and pedaled away just as Dad was rolling down the window.

"Hey," he called. "What are you kids doing?"

They didn't answer. Or if they did, I didn't hear. I ran deeper into the house, safely tucked into the kitchen by the time the back door opened. As I waited, the book positioned like a prop in my hands, my heart thrummed a fast *thumpthumpthump* that I could feel in my neck. I didn't know why I felt like this, like I was caught—I hadn't done anything wrong. I didn't go outside, didn't speak to those strangers.

Maybe it was because if Dad hadn't arrived home at that moment, I would have—if only to show them that I existed. That I wasn't their ghost.

"Cora!" Dad called out, voice pinched with anxiety. "Where are you?"

"In here," I said, trying to keep my own steady.

He came in with an armful of groceries, visibly relaxing when he saw that I was here and safe and not anywhere near those teenagers, their germs that could kill me if I wasn't careful. Before he could say anything else, my little sister came bounding in, sliding in her socked feet across the black-and-white tile floor.

"I *almost* got my double pirouette," she said, slinging her dance bag onto the floor. "I was so close today, but Miss Claudine was staring at me, like, every time, and it totally threw me off."

As she talked—a mile a minute, like always—she stepped into a preparation and then spun around on one foot, arms flying to catch her balance as she fell out of the turn.

"Ugh," she groaned with classic drama, already setting up for another turn.

"Ivy, don't spin like that in here," Dad scolded as he set the bags down, but he was chuckling. "You could fall and hit your head."

"Honestly, I think Miss Claudine would *love* that." Ivy collapsed onto the nearest chair. "*Très tragique*."

I laughed, my heart slowing at the familiarity of my sister's boundless energy. For this year, eighth grade, Ivy had switched her language studies from Spanish to French, determined to learn all the ballet words, but I guessed she'd give up dance for a new obsession by the end of the year. She always did: Last year, it had been marine biology, until she decided that fish were gross and the ocean freaked her out.

"What have you been up to, Cor?" Dad asked cheerfully, but I could hear the worry still humming beneath it, which made me feel guiltier. Those kids had really scared him.

"Nothing much." I shrugged, averting my gaze so he couldn't see the truth there. "Reading."

"*Withering Heights*?" Ivy squinted, reading the cover in my hands.

I suppressed a chuckle. "It's *Wuthering Heights*."

"What's it about?"

"Love," I said. "Family. Also ghosts."

"Can I read it?"

"Maybe when Cora's finished," Dad suggested, winking at me.

I smiled. Even though she was about to turn fourteen and wanted everyone to know it, Ivy still had the little-sister habit of wanting to borrow all my stuff.

I looked back down at the book, but now, when I tried to read, my mind wandered back to those kids at the door—the older girl and her stunned, frightened face—and suddenly, I understood something important.

I was a ghost, like Cathy knocking on the window of Wuthering Heights, only in reverse. I didn't want to come inside: I was a spirit watching from within, hungry for the world outside the glass. The world I could never have.

16

THE QUESTION RINGS IN MY ears, as loud as the bright red letters screaming back at me from the mirror.

Who is Cora?

A ghost. One that's been haunting me for eleven years.

"My sister," I whisper—or maybe it only feels that way, my own voice muted by the roar of my blood. *Her name.* I'm still too afraid to say it out loud, as if it's some kind of incantation—a word you whisper three times in the mirror to make something horrible appear.

I shut my eyes, breathing until the noise quiets. Until I can finally look at Liam's concerned face again.

"She died in the fire."

"Oh." Liam melts in understanding. "Oh, Ivy." And then, quieter, "I had no idea."

Translation: *You never mentioned her.* This feeling—the terrible tightness in my chest, the blinding guilt—is the reason why.

"I don't talk about her much," I say blankly. "I don't mean to hide her, but it's just . . ." I let out a breath, turning away from the garish mess of the mirror, gripping the sink behind me for balance.

The last time I shared this with anyone, it was Dani at our first sleepover, that night when I almost lit the candle in my sleep—that unconscious part of me still drawn, somehow, to the destruction that haunted me.

For most of my time in LA, I didn't tell anyone about the fire. The select few who got close enough knew that I lived with my aunt, and that my parents had died, but most people were never bold enough to ask for the full story—until later that night, when we were both lying awake in the darkness, and Dani said, "You never talk about your life before you came here."

It wasn't probing, or even too curious—it was an observation, simple and scientific. And suddenly, I found myself telling my family's story for the first time since I got there, exactly as I'm doing now.

"She was sick," I say. "She had cancer as a little kid, and when she was almost two—the year I was born—she got a stem-cell transplant to beat it, but it left her severely immunocompromised. She couldn't really go to regular school, so we were both homeschooled. I still had a pretty normal childhood aside from that, but Cora . . ." My breath catches as I say her name. "She never really went farther than our front yard."

"That's awful," Liam breathes. "I'm so sorry."

I shrug, an instinct to minimize.

"Once I got to LA, it felt easier not to tell the full story. Usually, I just said I lost my parents in a fire, and that was enough. Most people were too scared or sad to ask for more, and . . ." My voice hitches. "I guess that's what I did to you, too."

Liam takes my hand. I look up at his kind, empathetic expression, and my chest tightens, eyes stinging all over again.

"I'm really glad you told me," he says. "I want to know everything about you."

Now I can't fight the tears. He pulls me to his chest, his chin resting on the top of my head. For a minute, we just stand there, Liam rocking me slowly as I cry.

And then he draws a careful breath.

"Why would someone do this?" he asks, bewildered.

I tense. He means the mirror, and now my heart is thrumming.

"I don't know," I lie. "But—"

I hesitate. There is still so much I can't tell Liam, but as reckless as it may be, I trust him. I want to widen the crack in the door, let him deeper inside.

"Someone has been stalking me," I tell him.

Instantly, Liam tenses, as if ready to fight whoever's done this to me. "What? Who?"

"I don't know," I say. "But I've been getting these threatening messages online, and then the package you brought up the other week . . ." My face goes hot as I admit what I've hidden from him. "It was a defaced copy of my book. Whoever left it knows where I live."

Liam's face softens for a moment. "That's why you got that doorbell camera." Then his eyes widen. "Do you think it was Xander?"

My stomach plummets. *His lifeless eyes, blood pouring from his skull.*

"I had the thought," I say quietly. "Especially after he came to the bookstore. But now I'm not sure. I never told Xander about Cora or the fire." I steel myself as another admission trips through my lips. "Harcourt isn't my original last name. It's my aunt's—technically her husband's, who died a long time ago—and I took it when she adopted me, so nothing about the fire or my family comes up when you search 'Ivy Harcourt.' But I guess Xander could have found out somehow."

It also occurs to me that Xander could have done this to my mirror before he died. He could have broken into my apartment and scrawled the lipstick sometime after the event last night, when I was at Liam's. I don't know how Xander would have known about Cora, but he clearly knew much more than I'd thought. That violent, bloodshot look in his eyes as he slammed his hands onto the table at the bookstore . . .

It hits me with a chill: If Xander really did this, then I'm safer now that he's gone.

Liam frowns, tucking a piece of my hair behind my ear. Every inch of my skin buzzes at the touch, all of me an exposed nerve.

"I'm so sorry you were going through this on your own," he says quietly.

The guilt surges, and I'm afraid that if he keeps looking at me like that, I'll confess. I wrap my arms around him, pulling him close so I don't have to meet his eyes, but it's not enough—more tears slip out anyway, wetting Liam's chest.

"It's all right," he says softly, noticing. "You're safe now."

An anxious jolt zings down my spine. The way he said it, it's almost like he's read my mind. Like he knows.

I hold him tighter, pushing the thought away. Then, once I'm sure I'm strong enough, I pull back and wipe my eyes.

"Okay." I turn to the mirror, still red with her name. "Let's get this cleaned up."

We go back to Liam's. After helping me scrub the lipstick from my mirror, he insists: If I don't feel safe in my apartment, then of course I should stay with him. Relief spills through my chest as I pack my duffel. Even with her name washed away, my home still feels haunted.

For the rest of the day, Liam takes care of me. He's called out of work by now, which only makes me feel a little guilty. Still, I'm grateful; I don't think I could have handled being alone.

Cuddled together on the sofa with Frank, we watch movies until the sun starts to dip behind the clouds. I show Liam my two favorite rom-coms, *You've Got Mail* and *When Harry Met Sally . . .* He puts on his favorite, *Phantom Thread*, and I argue that it's way too dark to count as a rom-com, and he insists that that's what makes it beautiful. Shocking myself, I agree.

We take Frank on a walk. We make popcorn. We set aside everything dark—Xander, Cora, the past—and then, around eight, when we both realize we're starving, Liam insists I stay here while he picks up dinner.

"You should relax," he says. "Take a shower, if you like. I'll be back before you know it."

I want to protest, but I never did get around to showering earlier, and my hair still feels greasy and smoky, my body exhausted. Before I can talk myself out of it, Liam kisses me on the forehead and steps out into the night.

Alone with Frank in my lap, I check my phone for the first time in hours. There's a missed call from Dani, and then a text.

I just saw the news about
Xander. They said you found
him? Are you okay??

Warmth gushes in my chest, and then, just as quickly, I feel a stab of guilt for missing the message. I dial her number, and Dani picks up on the second ring.

"Ivy?"

"Hey," I say, throat stinging at the worry in her voice. "Sorry, I just saw your text."

"Don't apologize," she insists. "How are you?"

I let out a breath, settling deeper into Liam's couch.

"Okay, considering." Frank nuzzles my arm, and I smile. "Liam's been taking good care of me. I'm staying at his."

Dani goes silent, and my breath hitches. I can't see her face, but I know, somehow, that there's something she's not saying.

"Dani?" I press, when she still hasn't spoken.

"There's something I should tell you." Her voice is steady, but urgency hums beneath it.

"What?" I ask. Dread churns through me, and I already know that whatever she says next will knock me off my axis.

Dani takes a slow, measured breath.

"Jeremy's uncle works for Liam's firm. He mentioned it at dinner the other night, and when I told him that your boyfriend works there, Jeremy's uncle asked for his name." She pauses. "He'd never heard of a Liam Carraway."

Uneasiness buzzes down my spine, the feeling like pins and needles, but I shake it off.

"That doesn't mean anything," I say. "It's a big firm. Maybe they haven't crossed paths."

But Dani doesn't relent. "I looked Liam up again, and there's no proof anywhere that he works for Meyer and Green, except for on his LinkedIn—which wouldn't be that hard to fake."

"What are you saying?"

Panic creeps into my voice, but Dani remains cool and collected.

"You haven't known him for very long," she says simply. "He just appeared in your life one day, basically identical to a character from the book you're writing. I mean, you said it yourself—there have been some weird things about how and where you met."

My hackles rise. "You didn't think it was weird before."

"I know, but now . . ."

"If you're suggesting that Liam is lying to me and, like, pretending he's this character I made up so I'd fall in love with him, then that's ridiculous. How would he even know about my book? No one's seen it besides me, my agent, and my editor."

My tone is edging into anger, but when Dani speaks again, it's calm, just like always—Dani holding it together while I go off the deep end.

"You email yourself drafts as a backup method, right?" she asks. "Maybe he got into your email somehow."

I tense. Dani doesn't even know about my hacked email, and still, the possibility occurred to her.

"Or he could work at your publisher or your agency," Dani says. "There are plenty of explanations. The point is . . ." She hesitates again before delivering the final blow. "I don't trust him, Ivy."

"This is so typical." It comes out of me on instinct, a knee-jerk defense.

Frank hops off of my lap, like the change in tone has surprised him.

"What?" Dani sounds stunned.

"You never trust my judgment," I argue, knowing I'm being unkind and letting it build anyway, letting anger harden the fear. "We both know I didn't exactly have your picture-perfect childhood, but I'm not some broken teenager who never recovered from what happened to me. I'm an adult, and I can make my own decisions."

For a moment, Dani is silent. Frank trots over to the door, his collar jingling as he sniffs at his leash.

"I didn't mean for it to come off that way," she says, wounded. "But Ivy . . ."

"I'm sorry." My voice is blank, momentarily distracted from the guilt. "I have to go."

I hang up, uneasiness building in my chest as I get up and join Frank—because I've just noticed something on the shoe rack, right where the dog is snuffling.

Earlier this morning, when I was looking for my sneakers, they were beside Liam's loafers and a pair of work boots. Both of those shoes are still there, but for the first time, it strikes me that until today, I'd never seen those boots before.

I bend down to look closer. They're brown and worn-looking, the sort of thing you might wear to tromp through mud. Sure enough, when I lift one of the shoes, the bottom is caked with dirt.

Fresh dirt. With a jolt of understanding, I reach out and touch it. It rubs off onto my finger, drying but still wet.

Dread crawls through me like unfurling smoke. I've never seen Liam wear these boots. When he came to pick me up at Xander's this morning, he was in his sneakers—the same ones he slipped on again when he went out to get dinner just now. I can't remember what he wore to the book signing, but I'm almost positive it was his loafers.

And yet, these boots are freshly worn, covered with the kind of dirt that must have been everywhere last night, thanks to the storm.

My breath stalls as the truth descends like the slice of a waiting blade: Liam left the house on the night of Xander's murder, and for some reason, he's hiding it from me.

THIRTEEN YEARS AGO

CORA

THE FLAME DANCED, PAINTING THEIR faces a ghostly orange as we sang.

"Happy birthday to you!"

With a hearty gust, Ivy blew out the candles, and the room went dark again, a small tendril of smoke snaking up toward her grin.

"Fourteen already," Mom mused, nostalgic, as she flicked on the kitchen light.

Dad beamed, clapping Ivy's shoulder as if aging were an improbable feat. It wasn't—not for Ivy, whose survival was a given and not a constant battle to be won.

"Can you believe it, Cor?" Dad asked.

I caught my sister's eyes and smiled. "Seems like she was thirteen just yesterday."

Ivy snort-laughed—as usual, the only one who seemed to find my dry humor funny, or maybe the only one who understood that I was joking at all.

"We should get going." Mom glanced at her watch. "Reservation's at six thirty."

Dinner at Ivy's favorite Italian place with all her friends—who, as I understood, were many, and from all over the place: dance, book club, homeschool meetups. There was much discussion of how she'd possibly whittle the guest list down to only six, which was as many as our parents would offer to feed on their own dime. Kayla, Jessie, Abigail—I saw all their names in my head like pictures of desserts I'd like to try, bright and colorful but tasteless with intangibility.

"Arthur, will you grab the cake?" Mom asked.

Dad obliged, removing the candles and setting them gently back in the box. They'd be lit again at dinner, of course. This whole family ritual had been all for my sake, much like the piece of cake that Dad had already cut for me before we started singing.

As Dad closed the cake box, Ivy got up and pulled me into a tight hug. She still hugged me that way, like she was just a kid who needed her big sister—and she was, really, even though her life experience trumped mine in every way that counted.

"I wish you could come," she said.

And she did, I knew. In the earliest phases of birthday planning, Ivy had asked if she could invite friends here, to the house—always forbidden, but it was a special occasion, she reasoned. They could stay in the backyard.

I wished she'd never asked. Not because I didn't appreciate it, but because it stung too much to watch her face fall at the answer.

You know that wouldn't be safe for Cora, Mom had said, morphing into doctor mode. She was a pediatric oncologist and all too aware of the specific dangers that threatened me every time I took a breath; so often, it was Mom who had to be the bad guy.

I hugged Ivy back, which I was still allowed to do because she hadn't been contaminated yet. And then I remembered. "Wait, I forgot to give you your present."

I walked over to the living room, where I'd wrapped it in some of Dad's old newspapers, tied with bright red string from one of our many miscellaneous drawers. I had thought it looked nice, but now, when I handed the gift to Ivy, self-conscious heat prickled my skin.

"It's nothing fancy," I said quickly. "But I thought you'd like it."

She grinned, tearing into the paper with her usual finesse. When Ivy saw what was inside, she gasped.

"Cora," she said, giving me a cautious look. "This is yours."

I shook my head, smiling at the weathered copy of *Wuthering Heights* that peeked through the wrapping.

"It's yours now," I said. "I know how much you wanted to read it."

Ivy pulled me into a tight hug. Over her shoulder, Dad smiled at me and winked, just like he did a few weeks ago when Ivy had asked if she could read the book. I also knew that at dinner tonight, Mom and Dad were gifting her with a personalized book embosser, with a stamp that read FROM THE LIBRARY OF IVY PARKER. I knew she'd want to add this book to the collection.

"Thank you," Ivy gushed, pulling back to look at the cover. "I can't wait."

I smiled, chest warming at her excitement.

"All right, birthday girl," Mom urged. "We really don't want to be late." She gave me a quick hug before grabbing her keys. "Text us if you need anything."

I promised, and Dad gave me a kiss on the head before carting the cake to the door. When Mom followed him, Ivy stayed behind, leaning in conspiratorially.

"I made sure Dad cut you a good piece," she whispered, as if it were a secret. "A corner one with lots of icing."

I smiled as I pictured them unveiling Ivy's cake at the restaurant, one square already missing—proof to the world that I existed, the mysterious sick sister.

Then Ivy joined our parents in filing out the door.

I lingered in the foyer to watch them go. I always felt compelled to stand guard, a dark voice whispering that if I looked away, they'd die in a car accident, or get murdered, or any other tragedy that could befall them, and it would be my fault.

So tonight, once again, I watched as the rectangle of the outside world shrank behind the door, a sliver of sunlight stretching on the rug until it disappeared, sealing me inside.

Alone.

I was tempted to move immediately, to break up the quiet so it didn't settle into stagnant weight so quickly, but I forced myself to stand there until I heard the car engine start, the tires pulling out of the driveway.

And then I listened for the house to make its decision.

The last time, it was instant: a loud bang from somewhere in our cellar, which lay behind a door at the end of the hall—a clear and resounding *no*. Other times, it hadn't been so easy to understand. A gurgle of water from the drain, an indeterminate beep of the smoke detector. Those times, I'd decided to stay on the safe side. It was a big question, and it required a clear answer.

My hopes were beginning to fade when, finally, I heard it: a quiet, metallic *plink*, almost like the pluck of a guitar string.

I smiled. I'd heard this sound before. It came from somewhere near the kitchen window, though I wasn't sure of the exact source. That's what made it such a good answer—try as I might, there was no clear explanation. It was the house itself bestowing me with this small gift, an undeniable whisper of *yes*.

I gathered what I needed: an N95 mask and surgical gloves from the stash in the hallway closet; my shoes, which I slipped on beside the back door. And then, one final step: I left my phone on the table. My parents, protective as always, had made me and Ivy download a family safety app so we could share our locations. They didn't always check it—it's not like I ever went anywhere—but I couldn't risk them knowing, not about this.

I didn't hesitate until I was at the back door with my hand on the knob, heart suddenly thrumming like a caged hummingbird.

The idea had come to me first as more of a daydream than a possibility. I had been sitting in my turret nook reading when, suddenly, it was there, my page lost to the vision. I went over it so many times, smoothing out the edges until I could comfortably fit it in my palm—until it became less of a wild imagining and more of an inevitability.

The last time I passed our property line, I was five years old and being rushed to the hospital, so racked with fever that I couldn't even remember it. Today, that was all going to change.

I finally had the house's blessing.

With the mask safely fastened over my face, I took a breath and turned the knob. The July air floated in to meet me.

As I stepped outside, I thought of those kids on their bikes. It had been almost a month since they came, and now here I was—walking around the side of the house and then down our empty driveway, the end getting closer with every step. I was alone, and I was alive.

I was not their ghost.

The thought lifted my feet until I was running all the way down our driveway, laughing as gravity pulled me forward, uncontrollable. The sun warmed my skin, the air filled my lungs, and anything could happen.

Anything could go wrong.

Still, I urged myself onward, past our driveway and toward the end of our yard, where the grass dipped into a low ditch. I hopped over it and onto the sun-dappled road that wound through the trees, telling myself that if something bad happened, I wasn't really that far away. All I'd have to do was turn back.

But nothing would happen—not when the house had given me its sign.

As the end of our private road drew closer, my chest nearly fizzled with possibility. I couldn't remember what lay at the end. Other houses, maybe. A river.

I took the final bend, heart lifting—and then froze.

Our private road ended at another, bigger road, stretching gray and endless in both directions. I could follow it, but I didn't know where it led. I didn't remember this road, and I didn't know how I'd get back home.

The buzzing in my chest veered into panic. For a moment, I had the irrational fear that this was all there was, the end of the earth.

And then I heard it: the hushed approach of wheels. Not a car, not that fast, but something smaller—a bike, cresting the road.

A rider.

My pulse raced. I needed to go, needed to run, but I couldn't make myself move—all I could do was stand, stunned, as the bike came closer. As she saw me.

The girl stopped her bike with one sneakered foot and then took off her helmet—blue and shiny, winking in the sun like a beetle's exoskeleton. Dark brown hair tumbled out, cut just above her shoulders.

"Hey," she said. "Are you okay?"

I stared, too stunned to speak. Because I'd just realized who she was.

The girl frowned, confused. "Do you—"

"You were here before," I blurted as my voice found me again, skin burning with a combination of excitement and nerves. "In our yard, with those kids." And then, all at once, that heat turned to anger. "You were talking about me."

The girl's eyes widened and then cast downward with embarrassment.

"Oh," she said, winding the helmet strap around her fingers. "Yeah, my little brother and his friend rode over here when I was supposed to be watching them." Her gaze lifted to mine. "I'm sorry."

Her eyes were wide set and brown, I thought, maybe a little hazel—from this distance, it was hard to be sure of anything except the intense way they looked at me, making me want to turn to stone even as my heart sped up, blood running hotter.

Part of me wanted to turn back around and leave her there with her apology. Part of me wanted to scream. But most of all, another familiar feeling bubbled inside me, as intense as it was on the first day I saw her in the yard: that clenched-fist, racing-heart need to prove that I existed.

"I don't have 'bubble-boy disease,'" I snapped, even though it wasn't her who'd said it before.

She blinked. Her eyes were hazel, I decided, as the sun hit them, lighting up a spark of greenish gold. Definitely hazel.

"I'm just immunocompromised," I continued, face going hot under the weight of her stare. "I'm homeschooled, but I do go outside. I just have to be careful, which is why I wear the mask. But I'm definitely not *dead*."

Her mouth twitched, and my heart pounded, both eager and afraid for her reaction. Then her lips curled into a smile.

"Well, I'm glad," she said.

It was contagious—a smile warmed my own cheeks, cupped beneath the mask.

"I'm Gabby, by the way," the girl said.

A thrill zinged down to my fingertips as I realized that, for the first time in as long as I could remember, I was about to introduce myself to someone new.

"Cora."

The next idea came swiftly, almost inevitably, like a cool breeze ruffling my hair.

Maybe I should have asked the house—should have sensed the brewing danger, the *no* it almost certainly would have given me. But the house was too far away, and it wouldn't have mattered. I was riding too high on my first secret escape, and all my doubts were drowned out by the eager beat of my heart as I asked the question that would change everything.

"Do you want to come over?"

17

WE EAT AT THE DINING table, tucked into one corner. It feels wrong, too formal, even though we've eaten here before. Now it's like those six vacant chairs are watching us, an invisible jury.

"You all right?"

Liam's voice almost makes me jump. He's speaking at a normal volume, but it feels too loud, an alarm ringing in my ears.

"Yeah." I wind my lo mein around my fork, even though my hunger fled the second I found those boots. "Just a little spacey, I guess."

Liam places a hand on my knee, and I flinch. He lifts his hand, surprise and hurt mingling in his expression, and my worry morphs into guilt. I'm being weird—it's obvious—and if I want to trust Liam again, then I just need to tell him what's on my mind. Maybe if he just explains it, then I'll feel silly for even wondering.

I set down my fork.

"Did you go out last night?" I try to keep my voice casual, even as it wavers slightly.

"Out?" Liam frowns. "Like . . ."

"I feel like I remember you getting out of bed." Realizing how out of the blue this is, I pivot, looking down at my plate. "I, um . . . I used to sleepwalk sometimes, after the fire, and I guess I can't tell if I'm remembering wrong, or if something happened last night."

Liam's expression turns empathetic. Open.

Before he can say anything, I add, "But I think I remember you leaving."

Maybe it's just my imagination, but the words seem to charge the space between us. Carefully, Liam sets his own fork down in a perfectly straight line beside his plate. Then he nods like he's just remembered something.

"Now that you mention it, I did go to the bathroom."

"Do you remember when?"

Something flashes in Liam's eyes. Still, his voice comes out relaxed.

"I don't recall."

I nod, but my heart thrums.

"I'm sure you didn't sleepwalk," he says carefully. "I would have noticed. And even if you did, it's okay. There's nothing to worry about."

He touches my knee again, and this time, I don't flinch away. He's the same Liam as always: kind, understanding.

But that doesn't explain the muddy boots.

I take a breath, reminding myself that I can trust him. And I will—just as soon as I get this idea out of my head.

"I know," I say. "I'm probably overreacting, but I'm still just thrown from everything with Xander, and . . ."

Come on, Ivy. Just spit it out.

"I noticed your boots were muddy. So I wondered if you'd gone out in the rain last night."

Liam doesn't flinch.

He doesn't even blink.

Frank's collar jingles, making me jump, but he's just getting up from his spot on the floor, clearly taking this as the perfect opportunity to beg for food. Liam chuckles, tossing him a little sliver of chicken.

"Right," Liam says, all uneasiness gone. "I'd completely forgotten. Frank was being a real menace last night, so I let him outside. Probably around one in the morning, I'd say."

Frank's tongue lolls, his tail wagging as if he corroborates this story.

"He's a spoiled little prince, isn't he?" Liam croons as he scratches him lovingly.

"He is." I smile, but it feels strained.

Because that's the thing: Frank Lloyd Wright *is* spoiled. His luxury dog bed is imported from Sweden. He lives in an Upper West Side town house, for crying out loud. But most importantly, Frank hates getting wet. I know this for a fact—we tried to take him on a walk last week when it was just barely drizzling, and Frank made it a block before plopping onto the concrete and refusing to go on.

So why would Frank want to go outside last night in the rain? And why did Liam need his boots if he was just letting Frank out in the backyard? He could have stood at the door and watched from inside, barefoot.

"Want a dumpling?" Liam offers me the container. "You've barely touched them."

Before I can accept, Liam is already spooning one onto my plate, as gentlemanly as always.

My shoulders loosen. Liam takes care of me. I trust him. His explanation, though strange, is perfectly plausible. It's like I told him: I'm just shaken up about Xander—about earlier, too, the lipstick scrawled all over my mirror.

As I stab my fork into the dumpling, it occurs to me, with a little jab of irony, that Liam is the first partner I've told about Cora. He's the only one I've ever fully trusted with her, and that's terrifying, in its own way: Now there is so much more to lose.

After dinner, Liam insists on cleaning up our plates while I go get ready for bed.

When I come back upstairs, Liam is on the sofa with Frank and a book, a perfect tableau. He lifts his eyes from the pages to mine, a handsome smile curving on his lips.

"Hello, beautiful."

A hunger tips into his voice now, and it reaches low into my belly, a flame crackling to life. I walk toward him.

As I pass the door, though, I can't help glancing at the shoe rack.

Liam's boots are scrubbed clean, like the mud was never there at all.

In the morning, Liam has to go to work. There's no way around it—he already took yesterday off to take care of me—but even if he offered, I wouldn't let him stay. I don't want him to feel like I'm so fragile that I can't be on my own.

"I'll be back around six," he tells me, standing at the door in his perfectly pressed button-down and slacks.

Meanwhile, I'm still draped in his oversized T-shirt, eyes bleary. No matter how much my body wanted to pull me under last night, my brain was too loud to sleep.

"Frank is all set with his food bowl," Liam adds, "but he'd probably love a walk later, if you're up for it."

Hearing his name, Frank jingles over. I smile.

"I think we can handle that, right?" I say, scratching Frank's ears.

He snuffles in agreement.

"All right, then Frank," Liam says. "It seems like you're in excellent hands." Then he pulls me to him for another lingering kiss. "Don't hesitate to call if you need anything, yeah?"

"Thank you," I say, my arms still locked around his shoulders. "For everything."

Liam tips his forehead to mine. "Thank *you*."

It strikes me that this is what I've always wanted: this picture of domestic bliss, watching my partner leave for work as his T-shirt hangs down to my knees, a full day of writing ahead of me.

As the door shuts after Liam, though, the fantasy shatters. I won't be writing today.

It's my first day alone in Liam's apartment, and I have work to do.

I start with his home office. It seems like the most likely place he'd try to hide something, if he had anything to hide—which, I remind myself, I can't be sure that he does. As I open his desk drawer, guilt swarms in my gut, but I'm not doing this to break Liam's trust. I'm doing it so he can regain mine. So I can be certain, once and for all, that all my fears are only in my imagination.

The desk is expertly organized, both inside and out. No clutter, no secrets. He took his laptop with him—work or personal, I'm not sure, but I don't see another one here to investigate.

"Damn," I mutter to myself.

Frank's collar jingles as he approaches, poking his head through the door. I give him a look.

"You know, this would be a lot easier if you could talk."

I search around some more for a computer but find none—and anyway, breaking in might be a step too far. I'll try the other rooms first, see if I find anything there.

The bedroom is next: I check Liam's nightstand drawers, closet, and even the medicine cabinets in his bathroom, but nothing strikes me as unusual. His bookshelf grabs my attention next, the *Haunt Me Then* cover standing out among the spines. I take it off the shelf and flip to the title page, where I scrawled my phone number in Sharpie on the day we met. A small, dark laugh escapes me. Because it's the ultimate irony, isn't it? Starry-eyed romantic meets the perfect man who gives her every indication that he truly cares, and still, she can't let herself believe it.

I put the book back and turn away from the shelf, stomach lurching.

An hour later, I've searched practically the entire town house, and still,

I've found nothing. Maybe that should settle me, but instead, my mind keeps racing. The absence of evidence isn't concrete proof that Liam is telling me the truth. It just means I can't be certain that he's lying to me.

There's only one thing left to do. With a slowly building dread, I pull up the location-sharing app on my phone.

This morning, when Liam went to the bathroom, he left his phone on the bedside table. I'd wrestled with my conscience for a few frenzied moments before that gnawing instinct in my gut took over, and I swiped the phone. Quickly, I shared his location with myself and then erased the proof that I'd done so, closing the app. When Liam came out again, his phone was exactly where he'd left it.

I'm not proud of this. I never thought that this is the type of girlfriend I'd become—paranoid, snooping for his secrets. But I can't trust him completely until I know for sure.

Now I hold my breath as the people section of the app loads.

There's the little blue dot showing my location. Another showing Dani's location at her apartment on Ninety-Seventh Street.

And there, toward the bottom of the map, is Liam's dot in the East Village.

My chest constricts. *The East Village.* Liam said his office was near Hudson Yards, didn't he? Quickly, I close the app and google Liam's firm, and sure enough, there's an address in Chelsea—on the opposite side of Manhattan from the East Village.

Heart racing, I open the location app again and zoom in on Liam's initials, still hovering on Second Avenue. The dread reaches out from my core, stretching all the way down to my fingertips as I clutch the phone tighter.

Liam isn't at work right now. He lied to me, and I need to know why.

A few minutes later, I'm dressed and speeding down the street toward the subway. As I go, it hits me that I could be reading this all wrong. Maybe Liam's on a site visit, or some other perfectly logical reason for leaving the office, and I'm overreacting once again. I try to hold on to that hope, but my feet won't slow down. There's a tight ball of fear in my stomach, almost like a premonition, getting stronger as I board the train downtown. My gut knows better than my heart or my head.

When the train shrieks to a stop at Second Avenue, I rush for the doors so quickly that I almost lose my balance. My heart pounds with every step up the stairs, and I'm not sure which is more responsible: the shame of knowing that I'm basically stalking my boyfriend, or the fear of what I'll find.

I pause when I make it up to the street, consulting my phone again. Liam's location hovers between Ninth and Tenth, so I move in that direction, pumping my legs so quickly that I'm nearly out of breath. When I get to the right block, I force myself to slow down enough to peek through the windows. A grocery store, a hair salon, a smoke shop—and Liam isn't in any of them.

Then, as I'm passing the coffee shop next door, I freeze, something in me knowing even before I've seen him.

Liam, arms folded on a café table with a serious expression on his face. But that's not what makes my stomach drop so quickly it might as well splatter on the concrete.

Liam isn't alone. On the other side of the table, a woman sips from a mug, her sleek black hair spilling over one shoulder as she reaches out to place a gentle hand on his forearm.

Sloane.

18

ALL THEY'D HAVE TO DO is turn their heads to see me framed in the big coffee-shop window, but I can't move. I'm fixated on Sloane, the improbability of her sitting there across from Liam, touching him.

And Liam doesn't flinch away. Instead, he hangs his head like her touch is a relief.

Anger hisses inside of me like steam, rushing up until I'm sure it has to explode into action—throwing the door wide and marching inside, demanding an explanation. My fists curl, my weight tipping toward the door—but before I can move, Sloane's gaze shifts toward the window.

In an instant, all that rage fizzles out, leaving only the fear of a trapped animal. And so, I do what they do best: I flee.

Tears sting my eyes as I speed down Second Avenue, my chest tightening until there's barely room to breathe. I don't know if they saw me or not. I don't know which is worse. I focus on putting one foot in front of the other, breathing in and out, until my thoughts start to slow and sharpen.

Maybe I was misreading the situation. That touch wasn't necessarily romantic—it could have been a friendly gesture. Maybe they know each other from somewhere else.

But that doesn't explain why Liam didn't just tell me. Why he lied about where he was going.

I stop walking, pain landing in my chest like a physical blow. I've spent all day searching for proof that Liam was lying to me, thinking the certainty would soothe my panic, but now that I have it, I wish I'd never gone looking.

I wipe my eyes and reach for my phone. No texts from Sloane or Liam. Either they didn't see me after all, or they're still figuring out how to react.

Doubt creeps in again as I remember Sloane's anger that night at the bar. Why would she have been upset with me if *she's* the one who's having a clandestine meeting with my boyfriend? There's something here I'm missing—there must be.

With a deep breath, I do what I should have done the moment Dani raised her suspicions. I google Liam's architecture firm and call the phone number listed online.

After a few rings, a cheery woman's voice answers.

"Meyer and Green."

"Hi," I say, trying to match her chipper tone, but it comes out sounding nervous. "Is Liam Carraway in today? I'm a client, and he gave me this number to call."

I have no idea if Liam even *has* clients, but the receptionist doesn't contradict it. Instead, her fingers click on a keyboard, and I hold my breath.

"I'm sorry," she says finally. "We don't have anyone by that name employed here."

It's like the buildings press in around me, threatening to collapse in a mountain of brick and glass. Dani was right. I should have listened, but instead, I shut her out.

"Okay," I force out. "Thank you."

"Anytime. Have a good day."

The call disconnects.

I lower my phone and let out a dry laugh, overcome by the irony of it all. Sun slants over the city, honeyed and warm, the scent of early summer drifting in the air: fresh leaves, something spicy and delicious floating out from a nearby restaurant. It's the sort of day I love, alive with promise. Just like the day I met Liam, when it felt like everything was falling into place.

A cavern yawns open inside me. I can't believe I ever let myself believe that fantasy when I knew, deep in my gut, that it was too good to be true. Still, I trusted Liam with Cora, with my grief, and the whole time, he's been lying to me—about his job, about whatever's going on with Sloane.

And I'm certain he lied to me about those muddy boots. Maybe he was with Sloane that night, or maybe . . .

My head rushes, spinning back through the details. Xander sent me that threatening text around one AM, but I didn't see it until four thirty. I found his body just after five AM, which leaves a sizeable window of time that's unaccounted for. If Liam snuck out of bed before I woke up, sometime between midnight and four thirty, slipped on those boots, and crept out into the rain . . .

I'm heading for the subway before I've even fully made the decision. Xander and Liam had their altercation at the bookstore less than twelve hours before I found his body. I can picture it perfectly: Liam striding up to Xander's door with a confident knock. *We need to talk about Ivy.* The door shutting quietly behind them, trapping them both inside.

I rush down the steps to the platform, reaching it just as the train hurtles into the station. The doors close behind me, soft but final.

This is a bad idea. A terrible idea, really, given that I may or may not be the police's number-one suspect for Xander's murder. I could go straight to the cops with my theory, but that might make me look even more suspicious, especially since I wouldn't have any proof—just a hunch and some circumstantial possibilities. I can't outright accuse Liam unless

I'm sure, beyond a shadow of a doubt, that he's guilty of more than just lying to me.

And so, half an hour later, I'm back in an echo of yesterday morning: walking to Xander's building, desperate to get inside.

The street is empty of cop cars now, but I hesitate outside the building door. I won't even be able to get inside Xander's apartment unless his roommate, Owen, is there to let me in—but if he is, Owen could tell the cops that I was here. Or, I realize, he might not even be allowed to stay here at all, since it's technically a crime scene. I'm still debating whether or not this is all a doomed plan when I hear someone approaching behind me.

I turn around, heart racing, but it's only a delivery guy. I relax slightly, but the anxiety doesn't fully subside as the guy presses the buzzer. He could still place me here if the cops come asking.

But it's too late to turn back. The door unlocks, and I push down my paranoia, following the delivery guy inside. He veers over to the mailboxes as I head for the stairs, leaving him behind.

As I climb up to the fifth floor, my heart pounds. It seems impossible that it was only yesterday morning the last time I was here, with no idea what waited for me on the other side of that door. The cigarette smell of Xander's hallway grows nearer, but just before I reach it, I pause, listening. When I don't hear anyone, I step all the way onto the fifth floor.

"He's dead."

I whirl around, nearly yelping at the sudden raspy voice. There, on the stairwell up to the sixth floor, Xander's neighbor Marge sits with a cigarette dangling from her fingertips, fresh smoke curling in a cloud around her gray hair.

"Although I guess you knew that," she adds in her thick New York accent, looking me up and down with a mix of recognition and wariness. "I heard you found him."

I've only ever met Marge a few times in passing, and she always looks at me like she's suspicious. I try not to read too much into it now, even as my heart thrums.

"Hi, Marge." My voice goes high and overly friendly—nervous. I take a breath, remind myself that I'm innocent. "Do you know if Owen's home? I realized I left some things of mine here, and, well . . ." I swallow, shaping myself into the grieving ex. "I was also just kind of hoping for a minute alone to say goodbye."

Marge coughs into her sleeve.

"Owen's gone," she says. "Didn't feel too cozy sleeping at a murder scene, I guess."

"Do you know when he'll be back?"

She shrugs. "Not anytime soon, if I had to guess."

Marge brings the cigarette back to her lips, still assessing me with her sharp gray eyes, and a new idea flashes into my head.

"Sorry if this is too much to ask," I start carefully, "but did you happen to see anyone that night, or hear anything? I just . . ." Genuine pain racks through my chest. "It's been killing me, not knowing who did this."

Marge tips her chin up at me, blowing more smoke.

"Sorry. I already told the cops I don't know."

There's a hitch in her voice, though, and I sense something behind the words. She *told* the cops she didn't know anything, but that doesn't mean it was true.

"Please," I beg, dropping any pretense. "We didn't end on good terms, and it will always haunt me if—" I stop, desperation choking me up. Now no part of me is pretending. "I just need to know."

For a long moment, Marge studies me over the glowing tip of her cigarette. Maybe I'm imagining it, but I swear something in her expression softens.

"Fifty bucks, and I'll help you get inside."

When I gape at the brazen offer, she just shrugs.

I'm in no position to argue, anyway, and Marge tells me she'll take

Venmo, so I send over the cash. She double-checks the notification, stubs out her cigarette on the wall, and then walks over to Xander's unit. I watch as Marge jimmies a credit card around in the door until, a few moments later, the lock clicks. At my stunned expression, Marge lifts an eyebrow.

"That trick works pretty much anywhere as old as this place."

I don't *love* what that says about the security of buildings like mine and Xander's, but it's not the main source of my surprise—even I picked a few locks in my teenage years. If it's that easy to break into Xander's apartment, then it could have been anyone.

"Need anything else?" Marge asks impatiently.

"No," I say. "Thank you."

Marge doesn't linger. She turns down the hall and heads back to her unit, the door shutting behind her.

Alone, I turn back to Xander's open door. Everything in me screams to turn around, to shut the door on whatever awful secrets lie inside. But I already paid Marge the fifty bucks—and if I want to know for sure whether Liam was here on the night Xander died, then I need proof. Something, anything tangible.

I step inside, closing the door gently behind me.

The first thing I notice is the smell: stale, almost chemical. I take a careful step deeper, and the floor creaks beneath my foot. I freeze, heart jumping. Every sound feels amplified—my own breath, my heartbeat—and I wait, suddenly terrified that other noises will materialize in the silence.

I take a slow inhale. Blow it out. Then I move into the kitchen.

The floor is spotless, all the blood scrubbed away. It makes sense—they probably clean up this type of thing as soon as they've documented everything—but still, grief spills through my chest. It's like he was never even here.

And if there's any proof that Liam was here, too, it's probably already gone.

Regret gnaws at me again. This was a bad idea. Still, I need *something*, and I'm already here. I take a breath, the sharp bleach smell stinging my throat as I walk down the hall to Xander's bedroom and push the door open.

My breath catches. This room, unlike the kitchen, is still full of Xander's presence. It smells like him, a little bit of musk and the incense he always burned. I'm sure the police have gone through his things, too, but it's impossible to tell, because his room is as messy as always: clothes scattered on the floor, his dark bed rumpled, a haphazard stack of poetry books and novellas on the nightstand. Carefully, I pick up the one on top: *Love Is a Dog from Hell.*

My eyes go misty as I'm transported back to the night we met in October, at a Halloween party Dani and Jeremy were hosting. Xander was a friend of a friend, invited by one of Jeremy's med-school buddies, and the first thing I noticed, after his obvious lack of costume, was the tattoo on his bicep: DON'T TRY, the infamous quote from Charles Bukowski's gravestone. I recognized it instantly—one of those factoids English majors can't seem to escape—and, adjusting the ruffled collar of my Emily Brontë costume, I marched right up to him and said, *That's a little on the nose, right? Unless that cigarette is actually part of a Charles Bukowski costume, in which case gross, but fair play.*

He'd grinned, hitting me with another Bukowski quote: "*My ambition is handicapped by laziness.*"

Just like that, we were talking for hours—and I knew, in that moment, that we could keep talking forever.

Or so I thought.

A tear slips down my cheek, and I wipe it away, setting the Bukowski book back on the nightstand. As I do, an idea snags me.

Crouching down, I dive under Xander's bed and feel through the mess of storage bins and dust bunnies until I find what I'm looking for: an old wooden box. I brush it off with my sleeve, coughing a little as dust flies up from the surface. It's about the size of a jewelry box, maybe a little bigger, with dark-stained wood and a brass clasp. I pop it open, the empty velvet lining like a black hole. Then I feel around for the little hook and pull the false bottom away, revealing what's really inside.

"Classic," I mutter to myself with a small smile at Xander's weed stash. When he found this box at a flea market, he was instantly obsessed—it was the perfect place to hide his drugs, like he was a teenager and not an adult living in his own apartment. *I don't want Owen to steal my good stuff*, he insisted, even though I'm pretty sure Owen has never stolen anything in his life.

I push the weed aside, revealing the next thing in the box: a small black flash drive. I pick it up, turning it over, but there's nothing identifiable about it. Still, dread fills my gut.

I glance around the room, but I don't see Xander's laptop. Of course not, I realize—they must have taken it for the investigation. My own laptop is still stashed in the tote bag over my shoulder, but I hesitate. If this is evidence, do I really want it on my computer?

I hold up the drive and take another deep breath. As I release it, I know my decision is made: I've already broken into the scene of a crime for which I am clearly a person of interest, if not their only suspect. I can't turn back without making this worth it.

I slide the drive into my laptop's port and open the screen, my whole body thrumming with anxiety as it loads. The drive's icon appears on the screen. Its name is nondescript, and I hold my breath as I click it to see what's inside.

It's a series of documents, all of them saved with generic names. I click on the first one, and my heart nearly stops. As the article PDF loads, I have to blink to clear my vision, like someone's shone a bright light directly into my eyes. In my ears, a quiet ringing drones.

VICTIMS IDENTIFIED IN DEADLY TARRYTOWN HOUSE FIRE

My mouse hovers on the page. I don't want to read it—can't—but I can't look away either, can't make myself close it.

JUNE 29, 2015

A house fire killed two adults and one child in Westchester County early Monday morning. Firefighters responded to a call around 1:00 a.m., and upon arrival, they found the bodies of the three victims inside the home, as well as a surviving 15-year-old girl, who was transported to the hospital.

The victims have been identified as Melanie and Arthur Parker, both aged 53, and their daughter Cora, 17.

Fire officials have yet to determine the cause of the blaze.

My breath stalls, a hot stone lodged in my throat. I know all this. I've lived it, but still, it's like the floor is quaking beneath me.

Because why the hell does Xander have this?

I fumble as I click on the next document, another printed article from a different news outlet.

ARSON SUSPECTED IN TARRYTOWN HOUSE FIRE

All the blood drains from my hands, leaving them cold on the keyboard. At the very top of the page is a full-color image of our burned home's remains, our beautiful Victorian blackened. I can barely even read the words, only the familiar phrases jumping out at me like scattering embers.

Presence of accelerant.

Investigation is ongoing.

No arrests made . . .

I rip out the flash drive and close the laptop, impulsive and desperate to look away. I turn back to the box, a sob building in my throat, and that's when I notice there's still something left inside. It looks like a photo turned upside down, so only the back faces out.

I pull it out of the box and flip it over.

All the breath leaves my lungs as I see the familiar ghost staring back at me.

Cora grins at the camera like she's glowing from within. In the sunlight, her ice-blond hair sparkles, and her blue eyes glimmer like clear, cool water. One hand cups her chin, and on that pale, pale wrist, her veins are bright blue rivers. She looks happy. *Free.*

She has no idea what's coming.

I shove the photo back in the box, head spinning.

Xander knew about Cora. He had a photo that, the last time I checked, was hidden under my bed, one of the few pieces of her that I kept—and now it's here, buried in this box like a tomb. I don't know how long Xander's had it. I can't be certain what he was planning, either, but as I shove the box into my tote, flash drive and all, there's one thing I know for certain: I am in even more danger than I realized.

THIRTEEN YEARS AGO

CORA

IT WASN'T JUST THE HOUSE keeping my secrets. Now there was Gabby.

That first day, we sat in the backyard at a safe distance apart and talked. I told Gabby about my family, how we had always lived in our centuries-old house, and what it was like being homeschooled; she told me that she'd turned sixteen in April, she had just finished her sophomore year, and she lived down the road with her mom and little brother, Alex. I learned that she hated English and liked math, but she did love to read—it was just the essays she didn't like, how there wasn't always one right answer.

Next week, she came again. We'd exchanged phone numbers so that I could tell her when it was safe; I explained that my parents were overprotective and would be angry if they knew I was having a friend over, even just to the backyard. She told me that her mom was the opposite: She was always working, so Gabby was often left to babysit Alex, who was a year younger than Ivy and even more rambunctious.

For months, we continued our backyard meetings whenever we could. I collected little pieces of her, slipping them into an invisible treasure box like cracked geodes or river-smoothed stones: She liked science fiction and fantasy but hated horror; she had a scar on her elbow from falling off her bike as a kid; she only saw her dad at Christmas, because he'd moved to Seattle with his new wife after the divorce, which happened when Gabby was three.

She had questions for me, too—not just about my illness, but my favorite books, how I saw things. I didn't get the sense that it was morbid curiosity, either, even when we talked about my being sick. It felt like Gabby wanted to understand everything. Like she treasured my pieces, too.

Once, in late September, we were lying with our backs on the grass when she asked me, "If you could go anywhere, where would you go?"

I turned to give her a dubious expression.

"In a perfect world," she added. "Where it didn't matter."

I looked up at the clouds as if thinking, even though my answer came immediately.

"England," I said. "The West Yorkshire moors."

"Like *Wuthering Heights*?" Gabby guessed.

I smiled. She hadn't read the book, but she knew it was my favorite, and she could do an eerily good impression of the Kate Bush song.

"Maybe it would be cold and lonely," I said. "But sometimes, I think about all that space stretching on and on, just grass and hills and sky . . ." My breath caught at the thought. "I feel like I'd just run forever."

For a second, Gabby was quiet, and I worried that was a strange thing to say.

Then she said, in a voice like a prayer, "That sounds really nice—running forever."

There was something dark in it, pricking at my concern, but before I could voice it, a grin lit up behind Gabby's mask.

"Also, I'd totally roll down a hill with you."

I laughed. "Deal."

As I looked back up at the clouds, though, a sudden sadness pierced my chest. It was all only a fantasy. I could never sit on a plane to England, breathing in recycled air. In all likelihood, I would die like Emily Brontë did: a recluse, far too young.

"It's funny," I said, the thought flowing out of me before I realized it, "but the Brontë sisters went almost nowhere. Emily only ever left home four times, and every time, she was so homesick that she came back. They lived really isolated from society, making up these imaginary worlds with each other. It's kind of incredible that they were able to write such rich stories."

Gabby gave me a look that sent a shiver of heat down my spine.

"You could do that, you know."

"Like, write?" I asked, not sure why my heart was thumping.

She nodded, lifting her hazel eyes back up to the sky. "Have you ever thought about it?"

The truth was, I had. It was a secret I hadn't told anyone, and for a moment, I considered keeping it that way—hidden as deeply as the journals of abandoned stories stashed under my bed. But when I followed Gabby's gaze up to the clouds, I found myself saying, "Yeah, actually. I have."

She sat up, reaching for her backpack.

"What are you doing?" I asked, sitting up with her.

In answer, she pulled something out of the bag: a camera.

"Taking your author photo," she explained with a mischievous flick of her eyebrow. "I'm supposed to fill up this roll for my photography class."

I started to protest, but Gabby held up a hand.

"Please," she said, adopting a joking, French-adjacent accent. "You are interrupting ze creative flow."

I let out a snorting laugh, and at that moment, the camera clicked.

"Wait, no!" I argued. "That can't be it."

"Oh, I think it is." Her eyes lit up as she went back to her French-photographer persona. "I'm an artist. I know these things."

I rolled my eyes, but my smile hurt my cheeks.

"Let me take a different one," I pleaded. "Without my mask."

Gabby's eyes widened. "Is that okay?"

My heart thrummed. I hadn't even thought about it as it slipped out of me, but suddenly, I was overcome with the certainty that it was. We were far enough apart, and I trusted her. Maybe that shouldn't have made sense—germs don't respond to feelings—but to me, it did.

Carefully, I lifted one string off of my ear, the mask falling away. Gabby let out a quiet breath, and I couldn't quite tell if it was surprise or fear—maybe both.

"Okay." She lifted her camera, a little hesitant, and I wondered if her heart was beating as fast as mine. "Smile."

A breeze stirred around us, tickling my nose, and it was like something in me had loosened, fallen away. When I smiled—when Gabby smiled back at me—I felt light beaming from the spot.

Gabby snapped the picture. She lowered the camera, grinning under the mask she still wore.

"Perfect," she said, even though there was no way to check on the film camera.

Her eyes were still locked on mine.

A couple weeks later, Gabby texted me a picture of the final product, printed out in her school's darkroom. When I saw it, my breath whooshed out of me. Even in the grainy phone image, I looked like someone different. *Radiant*, I found myself thinking.

GABBY, I texted back, all-caps. You're right. This is officially my new author photo.

She texted back a row of emojis, a stack of books and a bunch of different smileys. I chuckled, curling into my turret nook as I wrote back.

Do you want to come over? My mom's still at work and my dad took Ivy to dance class

Gabby's typing bubble appeared, then disappeared again. A sudden uneasiness squirmed in my gut. A minute later, she finally responded.

Idk if I can . . . it looks like it's going to storm

I looked out the window and saw the clouds gathering, heavy and gray. As if on cue, thunder rumbled overhead.

Behind me, the radiator punctuated it with a sudden, harsh clang: the house's answer to the question that had already slithered into my head.

Gabby had been coming to the backyard for weeks, and I'd been fine. Wouldn't the same apply if we were inside, as long as we wore our masks and kept our distance?

I looked out the window again, and a feeling brewed in my chest like the coming storm, dark and electric. For once, I wanted something badly enough to defy the house's warnings.

I texted Gabby before I could change my mind.

We could hang out inside if we're careful

I held my breath until she replied.

Ok, if you're sure

I was. It seemed silly, suddenly, to put so much faith in the house's mystical answers, a childish game. In the end, it was me who was in control of my own actions, my own safety—wasn't it?

Yes, I texted Gabby. Totally.

If only I'd known how wrong I was.

19

MY HEART RACES IN TIME with my rush down the stairs, each step unsteady as I breathe in Marge's lingering cigarette smoke. Even when I'm back outside, it clings to my clothes as surely as the memory of Xander at the bookstore, his cruel, biting look as he turned to Liam.

You need to ask her about the fire.

A horn blares. I step back from the curb as a truck barrels through the intersection, the driver shooting me a dirty look as he passes. The breath that escapes me is reed-thin. If that driver had seen me any later, he would have hit me.

The walk light turns on, but I'm frozen, cold sweat clinging to my body. I didn't find any proof that Liam killed Xander, but I may have found something much worse.

My phone buzzes, startling me out of my head.

Liam.

I decline the call and cross the street, moving at an anxious clip, but it's too late: He's lodged himself back in my brain. Liam in the café, Sloane's hand on his arm. Liam's muddy boots wiped clean.

My phone buzzes again. I walk faster, keeping time with my heart. Maybe I should just answer and get this over with. I don't have proof that he's guilty of anything besides whatever's going on with Sloane—and maybe that's all it is.

When I go to answer the call, though, I've just missed it. It goes to voicemail.

I stop walking, taking a breath to calm my pounding heart. If he calls again, I decide, I'll answer.

My phone buzzes. I flinch.

This time, though, it's a number I don't recognize. An eerie feeling tickles the back of my neck as I pick up.

"Hello?"

"Ivy." The male voice is familiar and chipper. "This is Detective Kelleher."

My stomach plummets. They must have seen me leaving Xander's apartment, or maybe Marge ratted me out—they *know*, and now I'm about to be caught with the flash drive and photo stashed in my bag.

I take a breath, clutching the tote strap. *I am innocent*, I remind myself. So, I do what an innocent person would do.

"Hi," I say, matching his tone. "Is everything okay?"

"Actually, Detective Lopez and I were hoping to ask you some questions. Are you home?"

Panic surges, sparking through my chest. Just then, my phone beeps with another incoming call—Liam again. I decline it, staying on the line with Kelleher, anxious heat shuddering down my back.

"I'm not," I say. "I could talk over the phone, though?"

I hate how nervous I sound. I clench my hand into a fist, nails jabbing into my palm.

"We'd prefer to talk in person, if that's all right," Kelleher says. "We're actually at your apartment now, but we could wait until you get home."

My blood runs ice cold. *Say no*, I think. *Ask for a lawyer.* But that would make me sound guilty, and I don't know any lawyers, and the silence is stretching on too long—and so I say, with the stifled resignation of someone who knows they're walking into a trap and can't stop it, "Okay. I'll be back in half an hour."

When I walk up to my building, the detectives are waiting casually outside, as if I've invited them over for book club.

"Ivy." Kelleher smiles, giving a little wave. "Good to see you again."

Lopez just watches me with that same calculating expression.

"Hi," I say, heart thrumming. "So sorry you had to wait."

I unlock the door and lead them upstairs, breathing quietly through the panic. *I am innocent,* I think with each step. *I am trying to help.*

When we get to my floor, I pull the tote bag closer to my side, the flash drive feeling impossibly heavy as I open the door to my unit and gesture for them to step inside.

"I don't have a lot of places to sit," I say apologetically as they glance around my small living area.

"That's all right." Kelleher smiles that same friendly smile as he takes the couch, Lopez joining him. "We promise we won't take up too much of your time."

Realizing I should sit, too, I lower myself onto my unmade bed—the only other seating in my tiny apartment—and set the tote bag at my feet, afraid my hands might start to shake. I fold them in my lap.

"No problem," I say, giving an appropriately sad smile. "Anything I can do to help."

Kelleher returns the expression, while Lopez's face is careful and professional, ready to get down to business.

"Can you tell us again about the last time you saw Xander?" she asks.

My nerves jump, but I nod.

"It was on Monday, at my book event. He came in wanting to talk to me, and he seemed really out of sorts, I guess. He had those bruises on his neck, which worried me." My throat twitches as I think of Liam springing for Xander, that glare in his yes. "But I told him I couldn't talk, and then he left."

"And that was the last time you saw him?" Lopez asks.

"It was."

"You're sure?"

I hesitate, throat twitching.

"Yes," I say. "I mean, besides that morning, when I . . . when I found him."

What happens next is something that I can't quite put my finger on: a glance between the officers, a spark in the air. No one has spoken yet, but I get the terrible sense that I've messed up. That it's too late to fix it.

"I see," Kelleher says easily, shifting his attention back to me. "Then is there any reason why you would have been at Xander's apartment on the night he was murdered?"

Everything stops. The sounds of traffic outside, my heartbeat, the breath in my lungs. Lopez made me nervous from the beginning, but now it's clear that Kelleher was the one I should have feared. Where her stare has been probing, calculating, his shines with restrained delight—a winning hand plunked down on the table with a self-satisfied *gotcha*.

My voice comes out as a small, terrified whisper. "What?"

Kelleher is unmoving, that predator's glimmer still in his pale eyes.

"We have security footage of a woman entering Xander's building just before two AM on the day he was murdered—three hours before you reported his body. And, Ms. Harcourt, we have reason to believe that woman was you."

THIRTEEN YEARS AGO

CORA

"WHOA." GABBY LOOKED AROUND AS she stepped into the house, jaw dropping beneath her mask.

My face warmed with a mix of pride and strange vulnerability. I was so used to the house that I rarely tried to see it through someone else's eyes: the old foyer leading to the grand staircase and then, down the hall, the parlor and connected living room; beyond that, the kitchen and the door leading to the backyard. Everything was full of dark wood and damask, the walls painted a menagerie of colors: dark greens, blues, and even reds. It was a world on its own, our house. Not just a place, but a being.

"I love it," Gabby added, and I released my held breath. Having spent nearly sixteen years here, I was inextricable from the house; if she didn't like it, some part of me would be certain that she couldn't like me.

"Me too," I said, smiling. "Want to see upstairs?"

The stairs creaked beneath our feet as we climbed, noisy giveaways, but no one was home. On the second floor, I showed Gabby Ivy's room and then my parents', each door shooting off from the large sitting room.

Finally, I showed her my own, leaning nervously in the doorway as she looked at my bed on its pretty white frame, the curtains drawn so light spilled onto my desk. When she stopped in front of my bookshelves, my heart climbed into my throat. I had never shown them to anyone outside of my family, and suddenly, it felt like opening my ribs and inviting her to peek inside.

"Wow," Gabby breathed, picking up a book. "You've practically got a library in here."

I came closer to see which one she had in her hands: *Jane Eyre*, another old copy I'd pilfered from Mom's collection. I smiled. "That's kind of the dream."

Gabby grinned. Then she gasped. "Wait, I almost forgot."

She dug around in her backpack and pulled out a glossy piece of paper, which she handed to me. When I saw it, my breath stalled. It was the photo she'd taken of me, my smile beaming up from the print. I was so afraid to smudge it that my fingers hovered over the paper.

"Don't you need this for class?" I asked, heart squeezing. "Or . . ."

"It's yours." Gabby gave a shy smile. I couldn't see from behind her mask, but I could have sworn her cheeks were red.

"Thank you," I breathed. Something churned inside of me, a desperate urge to hug her. I swallowed it down, asking instead, "Want to see the third floor?"

She gaped. "This house gets even *bigger*?"

I laughed. "You haven't even seen the best part."

We raced up the stairs to the attic, the large space decorated with bookshelves, a TV area, some old toys that my parents had been too sentimental to get rid of, and then, on the other side of the room, a big round table and chairs.

"This is where Ivy and I do school," I said, nodding at the supplies on the table—neat on my side, and a veritable tornado of books and papers on Ivy's.

"Your dad still teaches you?" Gabby asked.

"We can do most of our work independently now," I said. "But yeah."

"Have you thought about college?"

I hesitated, and so did Gabby, as if she hadn't fully considered that question before asking.

"I mean, there are online schools and stuff, right?" she tried.

I folded my arms, keeping my eyes on the table. Suddenly, it looked small.

"Maybe," I said, shrugging. "But I still have a couple years." I turned to the door that lay just past the work area. "Want to see my favorite part of the house?"

Gabby nodded, and I led her to the door, opening it wide.

"Go ahead," I said, gesturing to the staircase inside.

She took a tentative step, and I followed, leaving the door open as we climbed. When we got to the turret, Gabby gasped.

"Oh my god," she said. "This is so cool."

I couldn't help beaming. "Isn't it?"

"It's like a castle, or something." She walked deeper into the small nook, running a hand over my reading chair, the bookshelf across from it.

When her eyes met mine again, I froze, that same open-chest feeling shuddering through me. This time, though, it wasn't just vulnerable—it was pleasant. Cozy.

Maybe that's why I found myself saying, "I used to think it talked to me."

Gabby made a face like she wasn't sure if I was joking. "This room?"

"The whole house," I said, with a fizzy feeling in my blood, like I was telling a secret. I supposed I was. "I'll ask it a question, sometimes, and it answers."

I hadn't immediately noticed my switch from past to present tense, this little admission.

"Like . . . should we go get a snack?" I looked up at the ceiling, playing up my waiting expression.

Somewhere above us, something creaked.

"Shit." Gabby's eyes widened. "That's so creepy."

"I'm not sure what that one means, though," I joked, wiggling my fingers. "*Ask again later.*"

Gabby snorted. "How about . . . should we go to England?"

We waited a few breaths. The house said nothing.

"Indecisive, I guess." I shrugged, still teasing, but something cinched my ribs.

"Hmm." Gabby narrowed her eyes in thought. Then she brightened. "Okay, house. Should Cora introduce me to her family?"

A tiny flare of panic lit up in my chest. Gabby sounded like she was still playing this game, but something in her eyes told me she wasn't entirely kidding.

"Maybe we should . . ."

Before I could finish, there was a sound outside. Not from the house itself—I rushed over to the window just in time to see Dad's car pulling into the driveway.

"Shit," I breathed. "You have to go."

Gabby frowned. "What?"

"My dad is home. Come on, he can't find you here." I waved my hands for her to follow me, and then sped down the attic stairs, Gabby behind me.

"Where should I go?" she asked, anxious. "Through the back?"

"I don't know." We landed on the second floor and then rounded to the grand staircase, taking it all the way down. My heart was a hammer in my chest, knocking so hard I could feel it in my teeth.

"Cora . . ."

Just as we reached the ground floor, footsteps thumped onto the front porch. Panic surged through me, a raging flame beneath my skin. Gabby still hovered on the staircase, her eyes wide with fear and something else.

Something like hurt.

My eyes snapped to the cellar door at the end of the hall, and I grabbed Gabby's hand. She flinched at my touch, but there was no time to think about it.

"In here," I said, pulling her toward the cellar and fumbling with the key, which waited in the lock on the door.

Distantly, I could hear Dad's key rattling at the front entrance. My fingers slipped, and I nearly dropped the cellar key, but I slid it back into the lock just in time, twisting it and pulling the door open.

Gabby looked down at the dark, wooden staircase with terror on her face.

"Please," I begged. "Just until there's a chance to sneak you out."

She took a breath and then nodded. Relief flooded through me as Gabby descended. I closed the door and locked it just as I heard Dad's voice in the foyer.

"Cora?" he called out. "We're back!"

The key was in my pocket by the time he and Ivy appeared in the hall.

"What's wrong?" Dad asked, frowning.

"Nothing," I lied. "Just . . ." Realizing I still had my mask on, I pulled it off. "Sorry, I put this on because I didn't know who was at the door. I didn't think you'd be back so early."

"We missed the memo that class was canceled," Ivy said, breezing through toward the kitchen. "Power outage at the studio."

"Oh," I said. "That sucks."

Dad gave me a look that wasn't quite suspicion—more like there was something in me that he didn't understand.

"Well," he said, "I'm going to get started on dinner. How's spaghetti?"

I nodded, forcing a smile. "Great."

As Dad followed Ivy, thunder cracked, making me jump. Overhead, the lights flickered.

"Darn," I heard Dad mutter to Ivy. "Hope it doesn't get us, too."

I stood in the hall, heart still thrumming. When Ivy appeared again with a bag of chips, I flinched as surely as I did from the thunder.

She made a face. "You're being weird."

I crossed my arms like it could stop her from seeing through me. "Just don't want the power to go out."

"Yeah, that would suck," Ivy agreed as she walked toward the staircase, casual. "Want to watch a movie or something?"

"Maybe later," I said.

"Okay." She stopped as she climbed onto the first step, turning back to me like she just remembered something. "Did you get a bike?"

I froze, panic surging. "No?"

"Oh." Ivy frowned. "Then whose is that outside?"

My heart pounded so loudly I was certain she could hear it. Somehow, I managed a shrug. "No idea."

Ivy watched me for a moment, but then she shrugged back. "Weird."

With that, she ran up the stairs like she'd forgotten the whole thing already, feet thudding on every step.

I waited, my blood still thumping in my ears long after her footsteps had faded. That was close. Way too close.

In the kitchen, Dad started to hum like he always did when he cooked. If I had an opening, it was now—but then, just as I was turning toward the cellar door, I heard another car outside. Mom's.

My heart crumpled, a weak breath escaping my lips.

I couldn't get Gabby out now. As Mom's steps thumped lightly on the porch, I whipped out my phone and sent Gabby a text.

Can you wait a little longer?

Her typing bubble appeared and then disappeared for a long time before her response finally whooshed through.

Ok

Guilty heart thumping, I turned away from the girl I'd hidden in the cellar like a dark and dangerous secret.

20

I CAN'T SPEAK. CAN'T MOVE. CAN'T do anything but stare at Kelleher's smug face as he watches me like a twisted mirror, reflecting all my darkest fears.

"That wasn't me." The defense comes out on impulse, but it's true. It has to be. "I wasn't there that night."

Even as I say it, a growing tide of dread rushes up to drown me. That strange déjà-vu feeling I had just before I found Xander's body . . . almost like I'd already been there. Like I'd already opened that door.

Kelleher leans closer.

"Are you sure about that?"

Panic descends. I don't remember going to Xander's that night, but if there's one thing I know I can't trust anymore, it's my own memory.

Someone knocks at the door before I can answer, so loud it echoes in my bones. All three of us turn to face it, and for a wild moment, I expect the door to explode with a steel-toed kick, a squadron of cops flooding my small studio.

"Ivy?"

At the sound of Liam's voice, fear spills through my veins before it's dulled by unexpected relief. I don't know what would have happened, what I would have said if he hadn't just knocked on my door. When I jump up and open it, he's standing there, a little breathless, like he just ran up the stairs.

"I've been trying to reach you," he says. "I—"

Liam stops short. Maybe it's the torment in my expression, or the tangible presence of someone else in the room. He steps past me, already leaping into protective mode before he sees the detectives standing up from the couch.

"Hello." Liam stops, blinking in surprise before turning back to me. "Is everything all right?"

Kelleher straightens to his full height, which is still several inches shorter than Liam, and extends a hand.

"Detective Kelleher," he says. "And you are?"

"Liam Carraway." He glares down at him. "Ivy's boyfriend. Now what is this about?"

Kelleher and Lopez exchange a look.

"We were just speaking with Ivy about her whereabouts on the night of Xander's murder," Lopez says with her usual icy cool. "We have footage of a woman entering Xander's apartment around two AM that night—a woman we believe was Ivy."

It's slight, but Liam can't hide the widening of his eyes. Just as quickly, he morphs back into protective boyfriend.

"That's impossible," he says without even looking my way. "Ivy was at home with me on the Upper West Side."

Kelleher lifts a suspicious eyebrow. "All night?"

Now Liam glances at me. It's so quick, I can't read it before he looks back at the detectives.

"Yes," he says. "All night."

Gratitude pools inside me, but Kelleher's chin tips upward in a challenge.

"Were you awake around two AM?" he asks. "Can you be sure that Ivy didn't slip out?"

Liam's glare deepens.

"Can we see this 'footage'?" He says the word like it's about as plausible as the Loch Ness Monster.

I feel another pulse of gratitude for Liam, even as my nerves roil beneath it. I fix Kelleher with my best cool stare.

"I'd like to see it," I agree.

A tangle of fear and anticipation twists in my chest as the detectives exchange another look. Kelleher seems to hesitate, but Lopez sighs, pulling out a phone and turning the screen so we can see it.

"This was recorded in Xander's building on Tuesday morning at one fifty-two AM."

Liam and I have to press close together to see, his heat radiating onto my skin. I want to lean against him, let him hold me up, just as much as I'm terrified to touch him.

I focus on the grainy black-and-white video on the screen. I recognize Xander's lobby, the dirty tile and row of old mailboxes. In the corner of the screen, the seconds tick by at an increased speed. At first, nothing happens. But then, about ten seconds into the video, the door of the building swings open and someone walks inside. A woman, I'm guessing from her size, a raincoat hood pulled over her head so that we can't see her face. She walks to the stairwell, disappearing from the frame.

I let out a small breath. *That's it?* You can't even see her face. They can't possibly be sure it's me. But then the video changes to another feed: the hallway on Xander's floor. From behind, we can see the same woman turning and walking to Xander's unit, still hidden by her raincoat. It's large and trendy, hanging down to her knees and stopping just above the top of her rain boots. At Xander's door, she pauses with her back still to the camera, shaking out the half-closed umbrella in her hand.

My blood turns to ice. Now I can see the umbrella more clearly, the familiar daisy pattern distinct even in black and white. I know that umbrella.

And, I think, with a shudder of dread, *I know that raincoat and those boots.*

As the woman knocks on Xander's door, my chest squirms with the uneasiness of watching a horror movie. For a few moments, nothing happens. Then the door opens. From this angle, we can't see their faces, but they seem to be talking.

The woman steps inside.

"We have her leaving again at two fifteen," Lopez explains, fast-forwarding to another clip: the woman stepping through Xander's apartment door and into the hallway. She's walking toward the camera now, with her head dipped so the hood still conceals most of her face.

The rest of it is hidden by a dark surgical mask.

My heart pounds, panic jolting all the way down to my fingertips as I wait for the woman to lift her chin, to show the camera her face. But she never does—just turns and disappears down the staircase, umbrella still in her hand. The clip switches back to the lobby, where the woman walks quickly and quietly outside. That's the end of it.

Liam responds first.

"You can't see this woman's face in any of these videos," he says, indignant. "How can you possibly be certain this is Ivy?"

Another charged glance between the detectives. Kelleher opens his mouth to speak, but Lopez beats him to it.

"We can't be positive about the ID yet, but when we showed this footage to witnesses and asked if anyone recognized the woman walking into Xander's apartment, Ivy's name came up—as well as their recent breakup."

My stomach flips. Was it Xander's roommate, Owen? Marge, or someone else from the building who recognized me?

Liam scoffs. "So this is all speculation, then. You have no witness actually confirming that Ivy was there on the night of Xander's murder."

"Mr. Carraway—"

"Is Ivy under arrest?"

Kelleher blinks, his mouth opening and shutting like a fish.

"Not at the moment," he manages finally. "She invited us inside."

"Respectfully, officers, I think it's time for you to go." Liam breezes back to my door and holds it open for them, the polite British gentleman again. "Thank you for coming by."

"This is Ivy's apartment, isn't it?" Lopez glances my way. "I didn't hear her dismiss us."

She and Kelleher stay planted, and the panicked, frightened part of me wants to give in—to blurt my confession.

But then I meet Liam's eyes, and I stand taller.

"I think I've given you all the help I can," I say icily, turning back to the detectives. "Thanks for coming by."

The outright defiance in my voice sends shivers of excitement through me for a few moments before Kelleher's withering stare burns it all away.

I'd almost forgotten about the flash drive hidden in my tote bag.

I'd almost forgotten the truth.

"Have a good day, Ms. Harcourt," Kelleher says, every word a threat.

With that, he turns and strides out of my apartment, Lopez behind him. Liam shuts the door, and the sound reverberates in the silence.

For a moment, we just stand there—Liam at the door, me hovering in the hall between my bedroom and kitchen, our breaths feeling loud in the quiet.

"Thank you," I say finally, forcing myself to meet his eyes. When I do, guilt digs roots in my chest. Liam's expression is as soft as always, but with something cracked open and vulnerable beneath it. Hurt.

"You didn't answer my calls," he says without moving closer. "I was worried."

"I know." The roots stretch deeper. "I—"

I stop as it rocks back into me, so fresh and stark it nearly sends me backward.

"I saw you earlier," I tell him, throat tightening. "At the coffee shop with Sloane."

I don't know how I'm expecting him to react—with shock, regret, pleading—but none of that is what happens. Instead, Liam drops his gaze to the ground with a tired sigh.

"I thought I might have seen you there," he says quietly.

Anger spins in my chest, coiling tight.

"That's it?" I snap.

"I can explain." He comes closer, hands outstretched like he wants to touch me, but I back up.

"I know you lied about work, too. About—"

I stop short, wracked with a sudden exhaustion that sends me crumpling onto my couch, the smell of Kelleher's cologne still clinging to the cushions. I could hurl all my accusations at Liam, each one a sharpened stone in my hand, but it wouldn't purge the fear eating me from inside. Liam lied, yes, but after that video, I know for a fact that he didn't kill Xander.

Not after seeing that rain gear.

"Ivy . . ."

The delicate care in his voice is enough to shatter me.

"They don't have any real proof," Liam says. "You're safe. I know you didn't do it, and so will they."

Sweet Liam, with his inexhaustible care. His trust. I shake my head, tears blurring my vision.

"They won't," I say.

"Of course they will. They just—"

"Liam, they *won't*." I force myself to face him, hot tears streaming down my cheeks as I say the words that I know will end this forever. "I think I might have killed him."

THIRTEEN YEARS AGO

CORA

"CORA?" MOM CALLED UP FROM the bottom of the turret stairs.

I turned my phone face down in my lap, hiding it even though I hadn't been looking at anything dangerous—just the blank screen, waiting for a text that wouldn't appear.

"Yeah?" I answered, reaching for my book as Mom climbed up to the reading nook.

"Just checking in," she said with a small, worried smile. "You've been up here all night."

Anxiety churned in my gut. It had been a full day since Gabby left—I was finally able to sneak her out last night around midnight, when everyone was asleep—and I hadn't heard from her since. Of course I hadn't. I still couldn't forget that cold, blank look on her face as I led her through the darkened house to the backyard, quietly apologizing while she just shook her head and said, in a tone terser than I'd ever heard from her, *Bye, Cora*.

I'd already hidden the photo she took of me, the only remaining evidence of her presence in the house stashed safely under my mattress.

Since then, I'd spent most of my time in here, aside from dinner tonight. Every time Ivy opened her mouth at the table, I silently panicked that it would be about the strange bike she'd seen in the yard, but it never was.

"I'm okay," I told Mom now. "Just tired."

Her steps creaked on the old floorboards as she came to perch on the edge of my chair. Instinctively, I curled my legs closer to my body. Mom frowned, and my heart leaped into my throat.

"You sure you're feeling okay?" She placed a cool hand to my forehead, already back in doctor mode. "You barely ate."

She seemed so worried that, for a moment, it all rushed up inside of me: *No*, I wanted to shout. *I'm not okay. I won't ever be okay as long as I'm stuck here, pretending that this is a real life.*

The thought was so loud and clear that my stomach churned. I had been sad before, and I'd been lonely, but never once had I felt *this*—a sharp, dangerous feeling that I was slowly beginning to understand as rage.

"I'm fine," I said tightly, pushing it down. "Promise."

"All right. Well, let me know if that changes."

Mom kissed me on the forehead and then turned back toward the stairs. My heart thumped. She started to descend, and in that moment, I was seized by the sudden terror that if I didn't say something now, it would rot and die inside of me, never to be spoken again, and so I blurted it out like a secret.

"Am I ever going to get better?"

Mom turned around, surprised.

"What do you mean, honey?"

The rage stoked again, hot and dangerous. "I mean, am I ever going to be able to live a normal life?"

It wasn't a question anymore, but a demand veering into accusation.

Mom's eyes widened. "Where is this coming from?"

She took a step toward me, and I shot up, moving away from her.

"I've looked it up," I said, back pressed to the wall as if to hold me up. "Most people who've gotten a stem-cell transplant can live a totally normal life, even if they're immunocompromised. They can go to school and be around other people. It just takes extra precautions."

The words tumbled out of me like they'd always been there, and I realized that they had. They'd just been stowed in the back of my brain, pushed into the dark because I knew—or maybe just assumed—that they would never be welcomed. But maybe I was wrong. Maybe, I thought, as my mother looked at me with tears shining in her eyes, there was a chance.

"Oh, Cora," she murmured. "I wish so badly that you could."

All my rage was snuffed with those few soft words.

"You're right that that's the case for some people," she continued gently. "But I've talked it over with your other doctors. I've seen it firsthand."

Tears stung my eyes, spilling hot onto my cheeks. Mom crossed to me, pulling me to her chest.

"Do you remember when Dad took you and Ivy to that playgroup when you were little?" she asked, smoothing my hair.

I nodded, even though I didn't want to hear it. I knew how this story ended.

"He'd been so adamant that we try to socialize you more," she said wistfully. "Eventually, he convinced me that it was worth the risk. You were only at that park for one hour, masked and distanced, with maybe five other kids." Mom pulled back, cupping my face in her hands. I could see that she was crying, too. "You got so sick, it nearly killed you."

A pit opened in my stomach. *I know,* I wanted to tell her, even if I didn't have the words. *I remember.* That trip to the hospital was the last time I ever went farther than our front yard, until the day I met Gabby.

"But that was ten years ago," I argued. "I'm older now. My immune system could get stronger, if we—"

Mom's hands tightened on either side of my face, freezing me in place.

"I'm so sorry, honey," she said, fixing me in her stare. "But it's just not possible."

"Yes, it is." My voice was so fierce that it surprised both of us.

Mom stepped back, letting me go.

"It is," I said again, my heart pounding.

I could feel it about to spill over, so intense I itched with it: *Because I made a friend and she's been coming over for months. I took off my mask around her, and she even came inside, and I'm totally fine, because—*

"Cora?"

It wasn't until Mom said it that I even noticed something was wrong. But she saw it first—that feverish heat bubbling up inside of me like boiling water, making my head all fizzy. The way my heart hadn't slowed down, and now, suddenly, it was like I couldn't breathe.

She always saw it first.

"Cora!"

I tried to answer her, but she was too far away, and the ground was rushing up to meet me.

In the moment before I fell, I understood that this was my answer and my punishment. Somewhere above, a light flickered: the house's silent elegy for the life I'd been foolish enough to want.

21

IT HITS LIAM LIKE A small electric jolt: a twitch in his shoulders, his lips almost curving up into a smile like he thinks I'm making a dark joke for about a millisecond before he understands how serious I am.

"Ivy . . ."

Now the only thing on his face is pure concern—whether for me or for his own safety, I can't be sure.

I get up from the couch and march to the small closet in my front entrance, swinging open the door. I hear Liam follow me while I comb through the detritus until I find them: the trendy raincoat, boots, and blue daisy umbrella from the video. I thrust each one at Liam, fear quaking my hands.

"They're mine," I say. "That was me."

Liam's eyes search mine, the terror catching. "What are you saying?"

"I don't remember going to Xander's, but I had a weird feeling when I went to his apartment, just before I found his body, like I'd been there already." My voice tightens, both desperate and afraid for him to understand. "And now that video . . ."

Understanding flickers over his face.

"You think you were sleepwalking."

I nod, a black pit yawning inside of me.

"But why would you . . . ?" Liam shakes his head, unable to say the words. "It doesn't make sense."

The answer is a lump in my throat, clogging my voice. It doesn't make sense, and yet it's the only explanation that does. Even that email to my publisher, the candle nearly burning my apartment . . . I don't remember doing any of it, but that doesn't mean anything. It never has.

"Ivy . . ."

He reaches for me, and I flinch away.

"Xander was stalking me," I argue, my whole body shaking as the certainty builds. "He knew about the fire, and . . ."

My heart is pounding. I can't explain this to Liam—not without telling him the truth.

"Maybe I was afraid of what he'd do," I finish quietly.

Liam watches me with an intensity that sends a shiver down my spine. I can't tell what he's thinking, and for a moment, I'm terrified.

Then he pulls me to his chest.

"You didn't kill him," he says simply.

"You don't know that," I argue, pushing back to look up at him.

"I do." His eyes flash with conviction. "For one thing, I've seen plenty of women in Manhattan with raincoats and umbrellas that look just like yours."

My jaw clenches, but he does have a point. They're all pretty popular brands—but still, all of them together?

Before I can voice it, Liam adds, like he's read my mind, "And someone has been breaking into your apartment, right? They could have taken these from your closet."

Now my jaw drops. I hadn't thought of it until now, but he's right. Whoever left that lipstick on my mirror could have taken the clothes, too, intending to frame me.

Unless it was me all along.

The thought sends ice straight to my core.

"More importantly," Liam says, taking a small step toward me, "that video was taken at two AM. To get to Xander's, you would have had to leave mine by one thirty—even earlier if you came here first to get the raincoat and everything—but that's not possible."

"Why?" I press, heart speeding with a growing suspicion.

"Because," Liam says carefully, "I was awake just before."

I step back, holding him in my stare. *The muddy boots.*

"That's when you were up to let Frank out," I say, but my meaning is clear: That's the story he told me, and I don't believe him.

He stares back at me, his eyes making quick, restless darts over my face as the air between us hums with an almost palpable charge. We both know Liam lied about why he went outside that night. Now we're holding our breath, waiting on a knife's edge while he decides whether or not to tell me the truth.

He breaks the standstill first, letting out a defeated sigh that gives me my answer.

"I wasn't entirely honest with you about that night."

My stomach clenches, but I give a small nod, bracing myself for what's next.

"I didn't get up to let Frank out," he says. "Sloane came over."

Her name is a pinprick to my skin, shocking it to hyperawareness. Once again, I was so wrapped up in my panic that I almost forgot the sting of that specific betrayal.

"How long has it been going on?" I'm ashamed of the desperate crack to my voice, but I need to hear it from him.

Liam's forehead bunches in genuine confusion. "I thought you knew."

When he sees his expression magnified on my own face, Liam shakes his head urgently.

"There is nothing going on between Sloane and me—at least not anymore. I hadn't spoken to her in over a year." He reaches for my hands, squeezing them gently. "She's my ex-girlfriend."

All my blood rushes to where Liam's palms touch mine, leaving the rest of me cold.

"What?" I breathe.

"We dated for about six months, and we didn't end on the best of terms."

The timeline stitches together, and like a blow to the chest, I understand: Sloane is the mysterious ex, the breakup that spurred him to adopt Frank. Then I notice the look on Liam's face. It's a look I'm well acquainted with—one that tells me there's something I'm missing. My stomach churns.

"What happened?" I ask, almost a whisper.

"It was my fault, I'm afraid." Liam runs one hand through his hair, the other still anchored to mine. When he meets my eyes, his gaze is soft. "I met someone else."

I pull my hand from his. "You cheated on her."

"No." Confusion flickers in Liam's expression before his lips press into a firm line. "I've never cheated on anyone. Would never. But when I started to have feelings, I thought it best to break things off rather than hurt Sloane any further."

His eyes search mine again like he's waiting for me to say something, but I don't have the words.

"I didn't realize you and Sloane were still in touch until the night you met up with her," Liam continues. "I suppose she must have put it together then, too, when you called me. After, she sent me a few messages about—well, her concern."

Liam averts his gaze now, uncomfortable.

"Concern about what?" I ask. "Us?"

Slowly, his eyes slip back to mine. "About you."

I rear back.

"She was worried about your drinking," he explains. "She said you seemed unwell. You'd forgotten things, and she thought you might be . . . seeing things."

My ears start to ring, so faint I'm not sure if I'm imagining it. Familiar images flicker in my memory, a frantic kaleidoscope: *Lights and neon. Roar of fire, melting faces.*

It's not until Liam catches me by the waist that I realize I was tipping slowly to the side, losing my balance.

"Do you need to sit down?" he asks.

I shake my head, even though it swims. I will not fall apart, not now.

Liam's touch falls from me, his face melting into pure regret. "I should have known something was wrong when you called me that night. I figured it wasn't my place to worry about your drinking, and you seemed all right the next day, but—" He lets out a sharp, disheartened breath. "I didn't want to believe Sloane. She was angry with me, rightfully, and I thought she might have been lashing out."

Awareness zings down my spine. *Angry. Lashing out.* Liam's expression is as genuine as ever, but those words hold a grim weight. It's exactly the kind of thing a man says to diminish and discredit a woman when he knows she's right.

I take a step back, defensive.

"Why did she come over that night?"

Liam smooths a hand over his hair, and I wonder if it's a nervous gesture, a tell.

"I'd been ignoring her calls and messages," he says. "I was a coward, if I'm honest. We'd never really had it out after the breakup, and there were a lot of things still unsaid. When she showed up that night, Sloane had been drinking, and she was angry." His eyes lift to mine with a vulnerability that makes me feel undressed. "She thought I was taking advantage of you."

A bolt of awareness shoots down my spine, like when I can feel a stranger's stare on a crowded subway car. There's meaning in Liam's expression that's just outside of my grasp, tickling the back of my neck.

"Why would she think that?" I ask.

Now the look in his eyes is something far more unsettling: bewilderment.

"Do you really not remember?"

Those five words—a plea with which I'm intimately familiar. Now, though, they feel like a curse, one I confirm with the question I have to ask next.

"Remember what?"

It's small but unmissable: Liam steps back, like he's suddenly wary of me.

"The night we met."

22

I TUMBLE THROUGH MY MEMORY, TRIPPING and spinning until I land on one unforgettable image: Liam watching me with awed recognition at the park, a hint of a smile in his eyes. *I know you.*

"It was at that bar in the Village," he says now. "I can't remember the name of it now."

Already, my broken memory wakes to fill in the blanks. Dark, moody lighting saturated by the alcohol, pink cosmopolitan staining my tongue. The handsome stranger at the bar, his button-down rolled up at the sleeves as he shook my hand and those blue eyes met mine, his other hand on the waist of Sloane's short black dress.

"You were there with Sloane," I say, like I'm intoning the words of an old poem I once memorized. "She was introducing me to you."

Her mysterious boyfriend, the one she'd been mentioning at work for the past few months, even though none of us had met him—not until that night, when Sloane decided to show him off. That night when our eyes locked for the first time, both of us thrown off our axis, exactly like he's looking at me now.

"You had this wonderful smile," Liam says, low and tender. "And this energy about you, so genuine and warm. Most people in this city wear cynicism like a badge of honor—hell, I'm English, and so do we—but you just seemed so . . . happy, and so unashamed to care about things you love. I don't think it was two minutes before you were gushing to me about your favorite books." He chuckles before fading again into a serious expression. "I'd never met anyone who seemed to know so clearly who they are."

I have a sudden image of my lips crashing into his, drunk and messy.

"Oh god, did we . . . ?"

"No." Liam's eyes widen. "God, no. I can't say it didn't cross my mind, but we'd both been drinking, and Sloane . . ." He trails off, guilty again. "We only talked. But the more we did, the more I wished I could spend the rest of the night talking to you."

The image recedes, blurring around the edges. It was just a fantasy—a lingering picture of what I'd wanted so feverishly in that moment, hating myself for it even then. It's probably why I kept drinking that night, the jealousy and self-loathing nudging me into the oblivion I craved.

"You said . . ." Liam starts, a smile cracking on his lips.

Like a gasp of cold water, I remember.

"I said I was going to base a character off of you."

It's all so painfully obvious now. I had it all backward: Liam wasn't my character come to life. He was my muse. That night was lost to the fog of alcohol, but the evidence remained in the message I found typed in my Notes app a few days later: sexy British arcjitect named Liam. USE IN NRXT BOOK!!!

I'd forgotten all about that note. It was hardly remarkable, one of countless others I'd scrawled to myself, like so many authors do, in a sleep-deprived or drunken fog of inspiration.

But even if I couldn't remember him, Liam stuck. Some part of him was permanently etched into my consciousness.

A laugh escapes me, wondrous and disbelieving. "You're Book Liam."

His eyebrows lift in teasing surprise. "Book Liam?"

I cover my burning face. "I *did* base a character off of you. I just sort of forgot that you were a real person."

"Well," Liam says with a little relieved huff. "That explains quite a bit."

"You thought I didn't remember you that day at the park," I say. "I mean, you were right. I *didn't*."

"I was embarrassed, to say the least." A shy smile curves at the corner of his mouth. "Here was the woman who'd so bewitched me that I ended my relationship, and she didn't even recognize me."

Shame drops like a stone in my stomach as the full weight of this revelation settles there. I'm the reason Liam broke up with Sloane, and now she thinks I'm callously dating her ex—because I *am*. Suddenly, more memories rush back: Sloane stepping away from me in the bar bathroom, angry. *So, we're not going to talk about it.* Oh god, I called Liam between bars, didn't I? She must have thought I was flaunting it.

"I wanted to reach out to you afterward, but it didn't seem right," Liam says. "You were friends, and then Sloane said you'd quit the restaurant after your book deal. She was hurt, and I wasn't even sure the connection I'd felt between us was real. We'd both been drinking, after all. So, I told myself to forget it, and then spent a year and a half thinking about you, pining like a schoolboy. Reading your book." He chuckles like he's astounded at himself. At us. "I didn't know what else to do. I was so desperate to see you again, and so afraid at the same time, and then suddenly I was taking Frank home from the groomer and there you were—materialized like a vision in the park, saving his life."

I can't help the smile that breaks over my face like a beam of sunlight. So it really was a meet-cute after all—just with a completely different shape than I'd thought, all jagged and bent.

"When I realized you didn't remember me, I panicked a bit."

"You pretended you knew me from my book," I say, understanding.

Liam nods, his smile growing before it falls away completely. "I should have told you the truth, but I was embarrassed. I thought *you* might be embarrassed, so . . ."

"You went along with it."

Regret tugs at Liam's face. "I never meant to lie to you, Ivy. I swear."

Like a handful of sand dropped into the wind, the fantasy drifts away.

"But you did," I tell him. "About your job."

"Ah." Liam pulls back, shame coloring his face. "Yes."

I stare, unrelenting, as he gathers himself again.

"I did work for Meyer and Green," Liam says. "That wasn't a lie. I was laid off on the day of our first date, and when you mentioned my firm that night, I suppose it felt easier to go along with it than to admit the truth."

"You let me believe you were going to work every day." Embarrassment surges, and I cross my arms like a shield against the tide. "Where were you even going?"

He chews on his lip, a gesture I've never seen him make before. It makes him look much younger, like an insecure boy.

"A café, usually. I'd sit and apply for jobs." He sighs, running a hand through his hair. "My nan left me some money in addition to the apartment. Until then, it had all been in savings, so I'd been using it to get by while I searched for work." His eyes brighten. "I have an interview next week. I was going to tell you, I just—I wanted it to be certain. And with everything else going on, with Xander . . ."

Liam watches me, searching. He's desperate for my forgiveness, and as hurt as I am that he lied to me, I can already feel myself tipping over the edge. Still, part of me holds back, aware that I might be falling for another delusion.

When he reaches for my hand, I let him take it.

"I should have told you," he says. "About everything—work, Sloane, how you and I really met. I just didn't know how. When you asked me about my boots and if I'd gotten up the night before, I didn't know where to start. I was afraid that if I told you, you'd be angry that I lied, and then I'd lose you again."

Something in me loosens.

"I kept things from you, too," I admit, surprising him. "Not just about my past, but . . ." I hesitate, stopping before the whole truth tumbles out. "I literally wrote an entire book about you," I pivot, "and didn't tell you because I was worried it would scare you off."

A small smile flickers on his lips. "Well, I consider that a bit of an honor."

My heart swells. Still, I'm wary of accepting this all too quickly—not until I can be certain.

"So then the dirt on your shoes," I start carefully. "That was because . . . ?"

"I walked Sloane back to the subway," Liam says. "And what you saw today was just the rest of that conversation. I owed it to her, I thought—just not when she'd been drinking." Liam squeezes my hand. "That's all."

The clenched fist inside of me releases. *I believe him.* Maybe it's misguided, just wishful thinking, but the relief is so overwhelming that I fall into his arms again, his forehead tipping down to meet mine.

"I can't believe I thought I made you up," I say into his chest.

Liam laughs warmly and kisses the top of my head. "We're quite a pair, aren't we?"

"We are."

I look up at him, and we hover there for a moment, our lips nearly brushing. I'm desperate to close the gap, but a sudden terror curls up from the darkness within me, clawing to come out.

"What time did you go back to sleep?" I ask him. "After Sloane left."

He frowns, thinking.

"She came around twelve forty-five, so . . ." He hesitates. "I think I was asleep again by one fifteen."

It hangs in the narrow space between us, the unspoken truth curling like smoke. There's still time for me to have gotten up and left for Xander's by one thirty.

"Liam . . ."

"You didn't," he says fiercely. "You'd remember."

I want so badly to believe it, but we both know by now that my memory can't be trusted.

"What if I don't?" I whisper.

Liam cups my chin with his hand, silencing my thoughts with his touch. For a breath, I wonder if he's also trying to silence his own.

"I love you," he says.

My heart soars, featherlight and ablaze. It's not an answer, but it's a promise: From here on out, we go into this with eyes wide open. No matter how ugly.

No matter what we've done.

"I love you, too," I say.

And then I kiss him, fierce and hungry as a flame, all my fears devoured in its wake.

ELEVEN YEARS AGO

CORA

FOR NEARLY TWO YEARS, I forgot her. It was easy, at first—I was too sick even to think about it. The days that followed my attack were blurry, a wash of semiconsciousness in bed, rushing to the bathroom to be sick, and pain. That's mainly what I remember: the ache in my entire body, an almost constant throbbing.

Mom was able to treat me at home, and soon, the pain subsided. I slept. I ate what I could.

And I knew, as soon as I was lucid enough to think of anything but how close I'd scraped to death, that I could never see Gabby again.

I didn't tell my parents about her. I couldn't bring myself to admit to their constantly frightened faces that this was my fault. I'd disobeyed them, flown too close to the sun, and then nearly paid the price. We all did.

Ivy took it worst of all. She hovered at the edge of my bedroom, teary-eyed, like if she came any closer it might break me.

"I'm sorry," she whispered once, in those early days, when she thought I was asleep. "I think it's my fault."

I wanted to tell her that it wasn't—this wasn't some illness she'd unwillingly brought home from a friend—but my tongue was too leaden. Sleep had pulled me under once more.

It got worse once I was better. As soon as I was well enough to move around the house again, everything reminded me of Gabby: the books she'd touched, the way her footsteps had sounded. I couldn't even look at the cellar door.

There were so many times that I thought about texting her and trying to explain. But every time I got close, I'd remember that she hadn't texted me, either. She had every right. I'd locked her in the dark like a dirty secret for hours, and then I'd thrown her out into the rain.

In the end, I deleted her number. It was better for both of us. Gabby could live her life, and I'd remain safely in mine. Not living, not quite, but alive—and that had to be enough. Even though it broke my heart, I knew I was saving my family from the same fate. If I died, they'd never recover.

The one thing I couldn't get rid of was the photo Gabby had given me. I couldn't bring myself to do it—instead, I slipped it out from under my mattress and then hid it even deeper, in a shoebox of old stuff I kept under my bed.

As I put the lid back onto the box and slid it under the bed frame, I noticed another box—the one full of my notebooks, all gathering dust. I reached for the newest notebook and brushed off the cover, flipping through the empty, untarnished pages.

I carried it to Ivy's room and knocked on her door.

"Do you want this?" I asked.

She was lying stomach down on her bed, my gifted copy of *Wuthering Heights* in her hands.

"For what?" Ivy asked, setting the book quickly aside like she was embarrassed to be rereading it so soon.

I smiled. "To write something."

I set the notebook on the dresser beside her door.

"Or whatever you want," I said, shrugging. "I don't need it anymore."

And so, time passed. Two Decembers, two birthdays. Dad made me my favorite red-velvet cake and stuck seventeen whole candles in the frosting—extravagant, maybe, but each new birthday was a battle won, another year of my precarious life survived. Christmas passed, and then, in the blink of an eye, it was summer again: late June, a few weeks before Ivy's sixteenth birthday.

I was up in the turret again, reading a copy of *The Bell Jar,* when my phone buzzed with a text from an unsaved number.

Saw this at the bookstore, it said. Thought of you.

There was a photo attached: a beautiful edition of *Wuthering Heights* with gold-sprayed edges and glittering foil, held in a familiar hand—suntanned skin dotted with a little constellation of moles, dark purple nail polish.

My breath caught. *Gabby.* Before I could stop myself, I was writing back.

Tell me you bought it!

When her response dinged, I grinned so wide it hurt my face. It was a selfie of Gabby holding the book, smiling and doing a thumbs-up.

She had changed in the past two years. Her hair was longer, curling a couple inches past her shoulders. She wore different makeup, too—darker, thicker eyeliner that made her hazel eyes pop.

I couldn't help myself. I called her, heart thrumming as it rang.

"Hello?" Her voice poured into my ear again, and goose bumps ran down my back.

"Hey," I said. "Sorry, I didn't know if it was weird to call."

For a second, she was silent, and anxious heat broke out over my skin.

"No," she said finally. "Not weird at all."

We talked for hours that night, catching each other up on everything we missed. Gabby told me she was taking a gap year after graduation to save up and figure out what she wanted to do next; she might even move to the city. She asked me if I'd been writing, and I told her, a quiet shame heating my cheeks, that I hadn't—but Ivy actually had. I'd read some of her stories, and they were good.

I told Gabby what happened that day, when we were almost caught. As I explained how sick I'd gotten, and the decision I'd had to make, her silence felt like a weight through the phone, one I could almost reach out and hold. When I was done, it hung there between us for a few moments more.

"Jesus, Cora," she said gently. "I'm so sorry."

"It's not your fault," I insisted. "And, for what it's worth, I'm really sorry I locked you in the cellar."

I could almost hear Gabby's smile. "It was very *Jane Eyre* of you."

I laughed, warmth spilling through me. "At least Bertha Mason had the attic. Way nicer than the cellar."

And just like that, we were us again—like only hours had passed instead of two years. When Dad finally called up to me that dinner was ready, my chest pinched at the thought of hanging up.

"I have to go," I told Gabby. "But . . ."

I hesitated, my heart thumping. The idea had come to me over an hour ago, but now, suddenly, I was nervous to say it. I glanced at the turret stairs, listening to ensure that no one was coming, and then lowered my voice.

"My family is actually going to be out of town this weekend," I said. "Visiting our grandparents in Florida. I'll be here, obviously, if . . ." I took a breath, willing my heart to slow its wild beating. "Do you want to come over then?"

I counted three rapid pulses in my chest before Gabby said, "Yeah. That would be really nice."

When I opened the door, we both froze.

"Hi," I said.

"Hi."

When Gabby texted me that she was on the way over, I spent ten minutes pacing the house, heart thrumming with nerves. Now I was completely still, struck by the presence of her after so long. Her eyes. Her ever-fidgeting hands, which sprang immediately to her hair, tucking a wavy strand behind her ear.

"Should I come in, or do you want to . . . ?"

"I'll come out there," I said quickly, stepping out onto the back porch. I hadn't asked the house for guidance—I'd grown out of the habit in the last two years—but I knew, deep in my gut, that we shouldn't risk going inside, at least not right away.

I closed the door behind us, gesturing to the porch seats.

"Do you want to sit?"

"Sure." Gabby nodded a few times too many, and I knew that she was nervous, too. Not just that, I realized as she sat down in the farthest chair—she was afraid of hurting me again.

I sat in the chair opposite, the length of the bench stretching between us.

"So," I said, at the same time that she took a breath to say something else. We both stopped, laughing awkwardly.

"You first," I said.

"No, you."

I hesitated, missing our old ease.

"I'm really glad you're here," I said finally.

"Me too."

Another moment stretched between us, quiet and polite, and suddenly, I couldn't take it.

"Why did you text me?" I asked.

Gabby blinked, looking uncomfortable, but not entirely surprised at the question. Her gaze dipped to her hands.

"I don't know," she said quietly. "I saw the book, and maybe I was looking for an excuse, but I just . . ." Her eyes lifted to meet mine. "I missed you."

The words were a vise around my heart, squeezing.

"Oh," I said weakly, afraid that if I said anything more, I wouldn't be able to hold back tears.

Gabby let out a pent-up sigh, like a wall had fallen between us.

"I missed you a lot, actually," she said. "I kept waiting for you to reach out, but . . ."

"You didn't reach out either." I was surprised by the sudden frustration beating through me. "You could have."

"Could I?" Gabby snapped back, anguish in her expression. "You locked me in the basement for five hours to avoid letting your parents know about me, Cora. The ball was sort of in your court."

I tensed, stomach lurching. "I almost died."

"I didn't know that!" Gabby jumped up from her seat, pacing away. Hurt warped her voice, softening it. "How was I supposed to know that?"

"I don't know." Now I couldn't stop the tears. I wiped them away, embarrassed, but more kept flowing. "I don't know."

Gabby stopped, something in her stare that I couldn't quite read. She took a step toward me and then hesitated, like she was afraid to cross the invisible boundary.

"I'm sorry," she said softly. "I feel awful that I didn't know." She shook her head, scrubbing at her own teary eyes. "It doesn't have to be like this going forward, though. We can be better at communicating, and—"

"And what?" I snapped, the word dredged from somewhere dark and broken. Maybe that's where it all came from, the anger, the hurt, and the sadness—that same black hole inside me. "You'll leave eventually, and I'll still be stuck here."

"You don't know that," Gabby said, but I could see somewhere behind her eyes that she didn't believe it.

"Maybe we were right before." I pressed my lips together, breathing through the awful tightness in my throat. "Maybe you should just go."

Gabby watched me for a long moment, almost like she was waiting for me to take it back. I pulled my knees to my chest and dropped my chin to them, a tight, protective ball.

"I'm really sorry, Gabby," I said quietly.

"Yeah," she said, even softer. "Me too."

And then she turned and walked away.

I stayed there, curled in my chair, telling myself that this was the only way. I needed to let Gabby go so that she could live a real life—the kind that I would never have. I had my family, my books. I could be content, I told myself, just like I had been these past two years.

You are not content. The voice rose up like smoke from somewhere hidden inside me—or maybe it was the house itself. *You are numb,* it said, *and you are already dying.*

I looked up to find the yard empty, Gabby gone. Panic surged through me, followed by a pulse of desperate, white-hot clarity: *I am going to die somehow.* And if I let Gabby leave, I might as well be dead.

I raced down the stairs, nearly stumbling into the yard. She'd already made it around the house and back to the driveway, where she was getting onto her bike. Seeing me, Gabby froze. Her mask was already off, dangling from her wrist, so I could see the hesitation written all over her face—but not just that.

I saw hope, too.

It happened quickly, a growing chorus of sounds: wind chimes, birdsong, and others, ones I knew I was only imagining. Washing-machine melody, satisfying shift of ice in the refrigerator, the unidentifiable metal *plink*—all the answers, every single *yes* I'd ever awaited, only now they were ringing from inside of me. I was my own house, my own oracle, and it was time I heeded the call.

I ran across the yard, tearing off my mask as I went, and then, just as Gabby's mouth opened in surprise, I kissed her. Softly at first, my lips a gentle brush to hers. When she drew in a breath, I pulled back slightly, heart thrumming, but the look in her eyes wasn't recoiling. It was amazement.

When we crashed together again, it was like the kisses I had only ever read about in books: lips meeting like this was where they were always supposed to fit, like we couldn't get enough. Her hand touched my neck. I buried mine under her shirt, brushing her shoulder blades, her spine, all the places I'd looked at for so long, certain I'd never know how they felt—warm and alive and safe, because it had to be. Nothing this good could be wrong.

"Cora . . ." Gabby pulled away, her face shaped into a question, but I shook my head. If this was going to kill me, then it was too late.

And then, just before I leaned back in, I felt it—a hot, itching feeling breaking over my skin.

If this was going to kill me . . .

"Cora?" Gabby asked, anxious now. "What's wrong?"

I tried to answer her, but the words wouldn't come. I reached my hand up to my throat as if to pull them out myself, but it only tightened. I couldn't breathe.

All around me, the house's silent keening: *Too late.*

"Oh my god." Gabby gripped my shoulders. "Cora, can you breathe?"

I shook my head, light dancing in my vision.

"Okay," Gabby said, and it sounded like she was underwater. "We're going to get you to a hospital, okay? Is there a car here?"

I nodded, a tiny bit of air slipping through the pin-wide opening in my throat.

"Mom's," I managed. "They took Dad's."

"Okay," Gabby said again. "I'll drive you. Just walk with me, okay?"

Into the house to get the keys. Door thrown open and then shut again, car unlocking. Head spinning, throat tight, blood rushing and roaring in my ears, raging. Car moving, world rolling past, all the things that I hadn't seen in over a decade, lost to my memory, grass and houses and road and sky until it stopped. Until we were there.

Gabby helped me out of the car, and my mask was on again. She must have put it there, but I still couldn't breathe, air trapped in the shell, hot and recycled.

White walls. Light. Sterile smell. Vaguely familiar, like somewhere I'd been in a dream or a nightmare—hall and light and hands and my name.

"Cora?"

A woman's voice, a doctor with a coat and a surgical mask. Her gloved hands brushed my shoulder.

"Can you hear me?"

Gabby was gone. I heard her voice before, frantic explanations, but now I was in this small room, just me and the doctor and silence.

"Yes," I said, surprised that the word made it out.

Heart slowing, invisible hands around my throat unclenching.

Maybe I was already dead.

"Breathe for me, Cora."

Cold pressed to my chest. Stethoscope, feeding my heart to her ears.

I breathed.

"Good," she said before removing the stethoscope. Above the mask, her eyes were brown and worried.

"Have you had panic attacks before?"

It wasn't the question I was expecting. The answer was instinctive, knee-jerk.

"I'm immunocompromised," I said. "I had a stem-cell transplant when I was two, but there were complications. I'm not supposed to be around people, but I messed up, and . . ." The hand tightened around my throat again, threatening, that same mournful moan in my ears: *Too late.* "Am I going to die?"

"No." The doctor said it so simply and calmly that for a moment, I was dumbfounded.

And then a new fear snaked its way inside.

"Did you call my parents?"

"Not yet."

"Do you have to?"

The doctor watched me for another moment, her forehead crinkling with something between concern and hesitation.

"Well, that depends," she said. "Are you under eighteen?"

I hesitated. Something shifted in the doctor's expression as she leaned forward in her chair, lowering her voice to a gentle hush.

"Would calling your parents make you feel unsafe?"

"No," I said automatically. "Just . . ."

The words died on my lips. I didn't know where they were going.

Still, the doctor nodded like she understood—like that question was tabled for now.

"You said you received a stem-cell transplant when you were two years old?"

I nodded back, uneasiness burying itself under my skin.

"I had leukemia," I said. "I think the transplant was at this hospital.

I'm pretty sure I had to come to this emergency room, too, for the complications."

The doctor watched me for a moment, a concerned line deepening between her eyebrows.

"That's the interesting thing," she said. "We did look at your records, Cora, but there is only one record of you ever visiting this hospital. You came into the emergency room with a high fever when you were five years old."

Suddenly, the white walls were too bright, the light burning my retinas. The time I'd gotten sick after the playgroup and had to be rushed to the hospital.

Dread pooled in my gut. The doctor had a strange look in her eyes—bewildered, but like an understanding was dawning—and even before she said it, some part of me already knew.

"In that file, there is no record of a stem-cell transplant or history of leukemia."

My breath stalled, a quiet rumble filling my ears. "What?"

"I'll want to run some more tests today to be sure. But as far as I can tell, Cora . . ." She took a small breath before saying, with all the care she'd use to deliver a fatal diagnosis, "You are perfectly healthy. You always have been."

PART THREE

HAPPILY EVER AFTER

23

AS SOON AS SHE STEPS onto the curb, I pull Aunt Mia into a hug.

"You made it!" I say excitedly. "How was the flight?"

"Good, good." She squeezes me tighter before pulling back with a little chuckle. "The engine worked, and all the doors stayed attached, so what more can you ask?"

I laugh. In addition to the many things of which my aunt is skeptical—self-driving cars, people who hate dogs—she's always been highly wary of air travel. In my four years of living in New York, she's only visited once, for Christmas, when I insisted on flying her out after getting the first payment from my book deal. We gawked at the big Rockefeller tree, wandered past the light displays downtown, and then decided that we were freezing our asses off and would much rather be back at the hotel watching the worst holiday movies we could find.

"Can I take that for you?" Liam swoops in, already reaching for Mia's bag.

"Oh, don't worry about it," she says instinctively, but Liam is already lifting her suitcase with one hand like it weighs nothing. My stomach does a little flip—not just because I find the gesture unbelievably hot, but also, I think, from the nerves. I've never introduced anyone I'm dating to my aunt before.

"It's so lovely to meet you, Ms. Harcourt," Liam says, extending his free hand.

For a moment, Mia looks at him with her usual skepticism, like she can't quite tell if he's legit or some kind of Hugh Grant–in-a-rom-com impersonator, and hesitation flickers in Liam's expression. It's not until now that I realize how nervous he is, too.

Then Mia smiles, taking Liam's hand. He visibly relaxes.

"Call me Mia," she says, giving him a firm shake. "It's nice to meet you, too." Then she spins around with a little jolt as she realizes the cab is gone. "Wait, where did he go? I didn't pay him."

"Already done," Liam says with a smile.

Mia and I both gape.

"Now when did you . . ."

"While you were saying hello to Ivy," he tells her with a little wink at me. "All part of my evil plan."

"You really didn't have to do that," I say.

Especially, I think, now that I know he's still looking for a job.

But Liam only smiles. "Nonsense. I'm happy to."

Warmth gushes through my chest, drowning out the worry.

"Well," Mia says, still a little stunned. "Then I'm at *least* buying you both dinner!"

Nerves squirm again as Liam leads us upstairs, still carrying Mia's bag. She was a little hesitant when I offered to have her stay with us at the town house instead of my apartment, but Liam had insisted, and when I explained that he has a whole guest bedroom just sitting unused, Mia gave in.

Now, as we step into Liam's unit, Mia's jaw drops.

"Wow," she says, in a way that makes my anxiety thrum.

Another thing Aunt Mia is suspicious of: the generationally wealthy.

With an enthusiastic bark, Frank bounds up the stairs and then immediately launches himself at Mia with an attack of slobbery kisses. A genuine laugh booms from her chest as she bends down to greet him.

Aunt Mia is *never* suspicious of dogs.

"Who's this?" she asks adoringly.

"That is Frank Lloyd Wright," I say, giving Liam a smile as he takes my aunt's suitcase deeper inside.

"Oh, he is just *perfect*," she croons, scratching him between the ears as his tongue lolls.

Once Frank has gotten sufficient attention, Liam and I lead Mia to the guest room; then we give her the full tour, ending up back in the kitchen, where Liam makes tea. As we sit in the living room with our mugs, my heart thrums again, nerves picking up now that there isn't business to distract us. There were times when I thought I'd never get the chance to introduce a partner to my family, and now that it's happening, I didn't realize it would make me so anxious.

Liam puts a hand on my knee, and all at once, the nerves dissipate.

"So, Mia," he starts, "Ivy tells me you're an artist?"

Her eyes light up the way they always do when she talks about her work.

"I am," she says. "I paint, mostly, and I also teach at a high school in LA. The one Ivy graduated from."

"I've never actually been to Los Angeles," Liam says. "I'd love to visit, though. I can't say I'm much of a beach man, but I'm of course eager to see anywhere that Ivy's called home."

The word pinches at something tender. *Home*. Technically, I spent seven years in LA—three years of high school plus college—and as much as I liked it there, and loved living with Mia, I never truly thought of it as home. Whenever anyone asked where I was from, my mind always wandered back to New York—not Manhattan, where I'd dreamed of living for years, but Tarrytown: the beautiful old house in its own little forest of green.

"We definitely need to set up a playdate for Frank and Frida," I say, smiling at the thought of Mia's Jack Russell terrier, named after her favorite artist, Frida Kahlo.

Mia jumps at the opportunity to pull out her phone's Frida album, and Liam leans excitedly in to see.

"Oh, she's precious," he gushes at a picture of Frida, paws covered in paint after a dip into Mia's supplies. "Now please tell me you've also got a treasure trove of vintage Ivy in there." He gives me a teasing grin. "I know it's cliché, but I'm quite keen to see the baby photos."

A tiny electric current runs through the space. Mia meets my eyes, and Liam tenses, no doubt noticing the uneasiness.

"I wish I had some," Mia says carefully, still watching me for my reaction. "But . . ."

"We lost most of them in the fire," I say, giving Liam's hand a gentle squeeze. "I never actually met Aunt Mia until I moved in with her. My family had always been pretty isolated, because of . . ."

"Of course." Liam squeezes my hand back, empathy flooding his expression. "I'm so sorry."

It hangs heavily in the air, the allusion like a physical weight. That photo flashes through my head again. Cora's smile, so carefree. So careless.

"But," Mia says, brightening, "I do have some of Ivy's early self-portraiture."

I groan playfully. "Please, spare him. I should *not* have been allowed access to art supplies, even in your classroom."

As Mia scrolls through her phone, a lightness returns to the room. I hold Liam's hand as if it will anchor me to the feeling. I am safe, and I am with people I love. For just this weekend, I won't think of Cora or Xander or the looming threat of those detectives at my door. They haven't been back since they left yesterday, which might be a good sign, but the dread slowly pooling in my gut knows otherwise. Even though I got rid of the rain gear from the video, it feels like it's only a matter of time before they find some other evidence—enough to come back with an arrest warrant.

Until then, I have no choice but to push it down. This weekend is about Dani's wedding—about family—and for now, I am safe.

For now, I am innocent.

ELEVEN YEARS AGO

CORA

THE MASK DANGLED LIMPLY FROM my wrist, the shell dented from where I mashed it in my hands.

"I don't understand," Gabby said, her voice just as mangled. We stood outside the hospital, the parking lot stretching ahead of us.

I didn't speak. I'd already explained it, and she did understand. It was just an expression people used when there was nothing else to say, a way to fill the silence when they felt useless.

"Why would your parents say you had cancer if you didn't?" she asked.

I took a slow breath. It should have felt wonderful, magical, this new safe air in my lungs, but it only felt thin and burning. I laughed.

"Cora?"

She took my hand, and I flinched. I might not have been sick, but the air around me felt more dangerous than ever, charged and volatile, and I didn't want to be touched. I hated that even this had been taken from me.

When I looked at Gabby now, I could see the uncertainty in her eyes—the hurt at my instinct to pull away. She let go of my hand.

"This is a good thing, right?" A smile flickered on Gabby's lips. "I know it's confusing, but you can live a real life now. We can do anything we want. You could even move with me to the city, or . . ."

Her voice faded, uncertain, and my chest tightened with an ache—an echo of only a few hours earlier, when I thought I was dying. I wanted so badly to believe her, but even stronger was the certainty that it wasn't true. I could never live a *real life*, because I didn't even know what that meant. My entire foundation was a lie, and nothing made sense anymore.

Nothing except for the rage stoking quietly inside of me, burning brighter with each breath.

"Whcrc did wc park?" I asked.

Gabby stared at me for a second, still with that mix of worry and hurt, but then she fumbled for the keys in her pocket.

"Do you want me to drive?" she asked.

"Obviously." My voice cut hard and cold, making Gabby shrink back. With a sting of regret, I added, only a few degrees warmer, "I never learned."

The drive home was practically silent, aside from the tires on the ground and Gabby's quiet, anxious breaths. She knew by now that I didn't want to talk. I couldn't. My mind was racing too quickly, digging into the doctor's words like a tender wound: *You are perfectly healthy. You always have been.* A theory proven by their tests, the blood work we had to wait two hours for the results ot—even though by that point, the mask was already crushed in my grip. From the moment the doctor told me, with that sad sympathy in her eyes, I believed her. I knew it down to my bones: Every time I'd gotten so sick in the past seventeen years, it was only because they'd kept me locked away. My immune system *had* weakened—just not from any illness.

And still, my parents kept up the lie. Either they genuinely believed, by some twisted logic, that I was sick, or . . .

I gripped the mask tighter in my lap, the shell crunching like bone.

Or they knew, and they chose to keep me prisoner.

It took me a moment to notice the car had stopped. My body was buzzing, my head still rushing like the highway we'd left behind. The house loomed above us, its turret and gable windows looking down like the eyes of a vengeful, crooked god.

"What do you want to do?" Gabby asked.

I didn't answer. Instead, I threw the door open and marched up the path, my blood thrumming. She followed me inside, and I shut the front door behind us, hard enough that the foundation seemed to shake in fear. A play, I thought. A performance. This house had never been afraid of me.

"It should be in the office," I told her.

"What?" Gabby jogged to keep up as I marched down the hall.

"Whatever medical records they have," I explained. "Ivy needed proof of vaccination for something once, and our mom came in here to get it."

Steps before I reached it, the office door creaked open. For a moment, I hesitated—it was only the air, the movement of the old hinges, but still, it chilled me. The house was in control again, inviting me inside. I pulled the door all the way open.

The office was big and old, like the rest of the house: creaking wood floors and bookshelves lining the walls, hulking desk and thick curtains. Mom always kept the door closed, but it was never locked. They'd had no reason not to trust me, just like I'd always trusted them.

I threw open the first desk drawer. Pens, office supplies, nothing of interest. The same in the next. Down the row, and still nothing.

I shoved it closed, hard enough to make the desk rattle.

"Cora?"

I whirled around, and Gabby stood behind me, her hands hovering like she wanted to touch me but was too afraid that she'd hurt me—or maybe that I'd hurt her.

"Maybe we should just talk to them," she said. "There could be some explanation for—"

"For why they lied to me for my entire life?" I snapped. Her jaw clicked shut. "I'm sure they *will* have an explanation, but I'm not believing a word they say."

Gabby chewed her lip, her brows furrowing in worry, and my chest stung with guilt. It wasn't fair how I was acting, like a wounded animal snapping its teeth at the hand that tried to heal me, but it wasn't fair, either, what they'd done to me. Someone had to feel the bite.

Her face darkened. "Maybe we should call the police."

I let out a breath, trying to keep my voice steady—to stop myself from lashing out. "I just want to find proof."

As I moved to the other side of the desk, panic quickened my heart. The house was eerily silent except for my opening and closing of drawers, like it, too, was lying in wait. And for what? The sound of a car pulling into the driveway, maybe. Police sirens. Before we left the hospital, I asked the doctor not to contact my parents, but she must have known from my records that I was still six months shy of eighteen. She probably had to report it, no matter how sorry she felt for me.

Maybe Gabby was right that we should have called the police. Maybe I should have gone upstairs, packed a bag, and turned away from this house forever.

As I reached for the final drawer, the framed photo on top of the desk caught my eye: the day my parents brought Ivy home from the hospital, her tiny body curled up in a blanket. At the edge of the frame, I stared down into her bassinet, fingers gripped tightly at the sides. On my eighteen-month-old face was not the proud look of a new big sister, or even the petty jealousy of one who was no longer an only child, but something more chilling: terror, cold and blank. Even then, before I fully understood it, I was scared that her life might be as fragile as my own.

But Ivy was never afraid. Even in this photo, she looked up at me in awe and adoration—just like how she looked at our parents.

I had always been the sister doomed to die, but for the first time, it struck me that I was not the one in danger. Learning the truth had awakened me, sharpened my anger to a lethal point. Whatever proof I found would only become ammunition.

I opened the final drawer, the creak like one more whispered *no*, but I didn't listen. I was done heeding the house's warnings.

Inside was a metal box, about the size of a small toolbox. I lifted it carefully out of the drawer, brushing a thin coating of dust onto my fingers as I touched the keyhole on the lid.

Locked. One final chance to step away, to stay in the darkness.

With shaky hands, I opened the first drawer again and pulled out a paper clip from the tangle inside.

"Can you pick it?" Gabby asked, noticing. In spite of everything, the awe in her voice made me smile.

"There's not a lot to do when you're a prisoner in your own house," I joked darkly. "I taught myself a lot of things online."

I straightened the paper clip so one side became a jagged line and then slipped it into the keyhole, where I jimmied it around until, finally, it clicked.

The box opened. My breath whooshed out in a quiet gust.

Carefully, I reached inside and removed a stack of papers. At the top was Ivy's birth certificate. Beneath that, a few smaller things: her Social Security card, some vaccination records. I set each one back in the box, moving almost mechanically.

And then I saw the first flash of me: a photo of me as a toddler, probably a little younger than I was in that photo with Ivy. I was standing in the backyard, sucking my thumb as I stared, wide-eyed, at the camera. My heart thumped. Something about the look in my eyes wasn't right. It reached up through time and grabbed around my throat, a wordless plea from my past self.

Setting the photo aside, I looked at the next paper: my birth certificate. I was about to put that aside, too, when something caught my attention.

Mother's maiden name: Emily Smith.

The father's name wasn't listed.

I stared at the page, my mind a dull hum of the same two words: *Too late.* There was only one more paper in the box, and then I would have it all—the truth that had been waiting here for me to find for nearly eighteen years.

When I took the final paper out of the box, my breath stalled.

Report of Adoption. I scanned the page, words and names coming into focus. *Information on Amended Birth Record. Adoptive Parents, Melanie and Arthur Parker.*

The hum in my head crescendoed to a piercing whine, the noise that rang in the movies when a bomb went off.

Something wasn't right. Something still didn't make sense. The pieces were scattered on the floor, in my lap, my quaking hands, and I was on the edge of putting them together, so close it burned.

"Cora?" Gabby's voice floated, muffled, through the ringing. Her hand found my shoulder. "I think—"

The door behind us creaked open.

24

THE WEDDING VENUE IS LIKE something out of a dream. As I walk into the outdoor courtyard for the rehearsal, I have no choice but to stop and gape.

Through the grass, a stone path leads to a white pergola draped in ivory flowers, the Long Island Sound captured in its frame, sapphire water dripping with golden light. Folding chairs line the aisle, every few rows punctuated by a bouquet bursting with those same white flowers. Lilies, I realize, now that I'm up close—just like Dani has had saved on her wedding Pinterest board since tenth grade. *Because roses are overdone*, she told me then, her eyebrow quirking in that self-assured way I always tried to emulate, desperate for a shred of her effortless taste.

Lilies also mean death, I remember, and I try to shake off the cold, eerie feeling it gives me. Or maybe that's just being back here in Westchester. We're still half an hour from Tarrytown, from the old house, but still, it's like I can feel it in the air, creeping under my skin.

I find Dani standing near the pergola with her parents, looking absolutely stunning in a short white dress with a feathered hem, bold and elegant and so effortlessly Dani. Jeremy stands with them in a crisp linen suit, looking at Dani like he can't believe he's lucky enough to be in her orbit.

Tears sting my eyes, surprising me with the sudden surge of sadness. Dani and I haven't talked since our fight on the phone—I've been too ashamed and overwhelmed by everything going on with Xander and Liam—and it isn't right. I'm supposed to spend this weekend bursting with joy and love for my best friend, not too afraid to step any deeper into her wedding rehearsal for fear that she doesn't want me here. That I've ruined everything.

"Ivy!"

The chipper greeting turns my attention to Taylor, Dani's sister, gorgeous in a summery orange maxidress and box braids.

"So glad you made it," she says.

I wonder if there's a dig behind her words, like it's very possible that I wouldn't have made it at all, but her smile is genuine. As Taylor consults her maid of honor binder, I let out a small breath, reminding myself to stop inventing things to worry about.

"The bridesmaids and groomsmen will go down the aisle in pairs," Taylor explains. "You'll be with John."

She points across the aisle to where Jeremy's childhood best friend stands, and I smile at the pairing—two people who've known the bride and groom longer than almost anyone but their families.

As I'm walking over to the lineup, I glance again at Dani, and this time, she's looking back.

I freeze, heart thudding. I can't read her expression. Every part of me wants to rush over and apologize, but I don't know if it's the right time. I'm about to turn and beeline for John when Dani rushes over to me, her feathered dress dancing around her, and crushes me into a hug.

"Hey," she says.

"Hey." It feels silly coming out of my mouth, that one word not at all enough to describe how I feel as I squeeze her back, my throat constricting with relief.

"Oh, you are *not* crying already," Dani teases, pulling back.

I wipe my eyes, laughing. "I'm a Cancer, we're emotional!"

She laughs, too, her eyes shining. All of her is shining, dewy and radiant in the fading sun.

"Well, then I guess I have to allow it."

For a moment, we're quiet, familiarity warming the air between us.

"Liam's here?" Dani asks. This time, there's nothing icy in her expression as she mentions him, only slightly hesitant.

"He'll be at dinner after this, if that's still okay," I say carefully. "For now, he's at home with Aunt Mia, probably sitting through a slideshow of my most embarrassing teenage moments."

Dani smiles. Guilt surges up in my chest.

"Dani . . ."

She stops me with a quick shake of her head.

"We can talk later," she says, seriousness dipping into her expression. "But for tonight, all I want is to look hot and have a good time with the people I care about the most."

Her eyebrows quirk in that familiar Dani way, and my smile widens to a grin.

"Deal," I say.

"All right, folks," Taylor calls in the commanding tone that reminds me she's head of about twelve different student groups at Georgetown. "Let's get this rehearsal started!"

With a quick squeeze of Dani's hand, I walk off to join the line of bridesmaids and groomsmen. Just as I'm settling into my spot, my phone buzzes. I reach to silence it but freeze when I see the notification: an Instagram DM from "Heathcliff."

Cold panic washes over me. I blocked the Heathcliff account, didn't I? Then I notice the account name: @heathcliff_2015, with an underscore added. This must be a new account.

Ignore it, I tell myself. *Delete it right now.*

But then, with a jolt of terror, I realize what this means: If there's a new Heathcliff account, then Xander wasn't my stalker. Whoever they are, they're still out there.

Hand shaking, I open the DM.

Hope you don't mind me
crashing

Attached to the message is a photo of Dani's wedding invitation—*my* invitation, fastened to my apartment fridge with my favorite magnet, which is printed with the Emily Brontë quote that inspired my book's title: *You said I killed you—haunt me, then! . . . Be with me always—take any form—drive me mad!*

My legs go weak. Heathcliff took this photo *in my apartment.* I spin around, glancing frantically at the friends and strangers in this sunny wedding venue. Whoever did this knows exactly where I am right now. They could be any one of these people.

Dani catches my eyes again, her head tilting in a quiet question. I silence my phone and shove it into my purse, giving her a smile and a thumbs-up as panic beats through me. Dani can't know about this. I won't ruin her wedding. If Heathcliff really is here, I'll have to find them on my own.

Until then, I'll do what I do best: Push down the darkness. Tell myself a better story until we all believe it.

ELEVEN YEARS AGO

CORA

FOR A BREATH, NO ONE moved. Gabby and I were crouched on the floor, heads whipped toward the door like cornered animals.

Ivy stood in the doorway, her hand frozen on the knob and her jaw dropped like she was even more afraid than we were.

I rose slowly, as if not to send her running. "Where are they?"

Somehow, I couldn't bring myself to say *Mom and Dad*. Ivy glanced behind her, her shoulders lifting with a breath, and I couldn't risk it—I darted across the room, shutting the door and pressing my back against it.

"Do not call them," I told her, sharp enough that she flinched.

"Who is she?" she asked, voice small as she stared at Gabby. "Why . . ."

"Where are they?" I demanded.

Ivy swallowed.

"Outside. We turned around because they got a call from the hospital saying you were there."

The blood rushed in my ears, adrenaline pumping. Ivy's eyes flicked toward Gabby again, and I grabbed my sister's hand. She jolted out of my grip, and that's when I noticed the white marks fading on her skin, the ghosts of my fingers. I tried my best to soften.

"That's Gabby. She lives down the road, and she's not going to hurt me."

Ivy blinked, her eyes muddy with confusion.

"I went to the doctor," I explained quickly, knowing with every passing second we were running out of time. "They told me that I never had cancer or a stem-cell transplant. I am not immunocompromised. There is nothing wrong with me at all."

Ivy made a small, stunned gasp.

"That's amazing," she breathed. "Do Mom and Dad know?"

The excitement on her face was so palpable that, for a moment, I couldn't speak.

That hesitation cost me everything.

Ivy turned, and before I fully understood what was happening, before I could stop it, she was rushing out into the hallway.

"Mom!" she called. "Dad!"

I raced after her, heart pounding. I was dimly aware of Gabby's footsteps behind me as I grabbed Ivy's arm in the hallway, trapping her in place, but it was too late.

They were already here. The man I called my father glanced between me, Ivy, and Gabby, his expression lit with panic. But *her* . . .

The woman I called my mother was icily calm, with something else thrumming just beneath her expression: disappointment.

"Cora," she said carefully, gaze flicking toward Gabby. "Who is this?"

In spite of myself, pure fear trickled through me, turning me into stone.

"I know," I managed through gritted teeth. "I know that you've been lying to me."

She barely even flinched. Instead, she told Gabby, without a hitch in her cool demeanor, "I'm afraid you need to leave right now. Cora is very sick, and your being here puts her in serious danger."

Gabby looked at me, and she seemed as petrified as I felt.

"Please," my mother insisted, calm but urgent. "I am a doctor, and this is very serious. I don't know what Cora has told you, but she's not well. You need to go. *Now.*"

At the sharpness of her voice, Gabby flinched, her expression turning hesitant—like maybe she was starting to believe her.

"You're lying," I argued, tears stinging my eyes. "I'm not sick. I've never—"

"It's Gabby, right?" Recognition dawned on my mother's face. "From down the street?"

Quietly, Gabby nodded. My mother's expression turned empathetic, but with something false glinting beneath it—something like victory.

"How is your mother doing?"

Gabby hesitated at the question, her shoulders tensing.

"Addiction can be such a tricky thing," my mother continued, and now Gabby went completely rigid.

My breath hitched. Gabby had never mentioned her mom struggling with addiction, but suddenly, I thought back to that day in the yard, gazing at the clouds. *That sounds really nice,* Gabby had said. *Running forever.*

Cold reached deep to my core.

"It was a shame to lose her from our nursing staff," my mother said, "but I heard she has a new job now. That's wonderful." She smiled, but it didn't reach her eyes. "Although, I do feel awful that I haven't been able to see her since she left. Maybe I should stop by for a visit."

Her smile faded, leaving only the threat that hung from each word like a pointed blade. One look at Gabby's face, and I understood: If Gabby's mom had ever gotten clean, that was over now, and my mother seemed to know it, too. One little *visit,* and she could ruin them.

Invisible claws reached inside of me and scraped me bare, leaving an empty, weightless husk.

"It's all right, Gabby," my father spoke up. His gaze was warm and kind, but fear simmered beneath it as he glanced back at my mother. "We just need to talk as a family."

Gabby's waiting eyes locked on mine, swimming with uncertainty—like if I just said the word, she'd stay or scream or call for help, whatever I needed. She'd risk it all.

My heart pounded, louder and louder as the understanding calcified. My whole life, I'd believed that other people were a danger to me, but now I knew the real danger was us. All of us: this family, this house. Anyone who walked through its doors was trapped, even if they managed to get out alive.

I forced myself to give Gabby a small, reassuring smile.

"It's okay," I said. When she still hesitated, I added, a little sharper, "Go. I'll call you later."

Gabby turned and sped away, sparing one more glance back at me before she disappeared.

For a few moments, we were all silent. I could feel Ivy's eyes darting between me and our parents, like they were strangers she didn't recognize.

But I recognized them. I knew them all too well. This cruel, vicious woman was not a stranger: She was only the logical extension of my overprotective mother, the brilliant doctor who held me captive, making me believe it was for my own safety—maybe even believing it herself. My father, too, was doing what he always did: keeping the peace, trying to make everyone happy, even if it meant burying terrible truths in the shadows.

We were all silent, like the room was doused in gasoline and the next word would ignite it.

And then my mother let out a sigh like she'd known this moment would come.

"Let's sit down," she said. "There are some things we need to explain."

25

BY THE TIME WE GET to dinner, I'm doing a pretty good job of forgetting. It doesn't hurt that, at least for now, Heathcliff is nowhere to be found—and, more importantly, Liam is by my side again.

"Mia didn't go too hard on you with the interrogation, did she?" I ask as we're finishing up the main course.

"Not at all. She's lovely." He smiles, his hand resting gently on my thigh. A bolt of electricity shoots up from where he touches me through the fabric, landing low in my stomach. I'm wondering how awful it would be to sneak him off to the bathroom or a coat closet in the middle of dinner when something in Liam's demeanor shifts, a little glint of hesitation.

"I wanted to apologize for earlier," he says, voice lowered. "Bringing up the baby photos, if it stirred up anything uncomfortable, or . . ."

The skin at the back of my neck prickles, and I grip Liam's hand, silencing him.

"It's okay," I say quickly, eager to move past it. "Really."

Liam's brow furrows, like he isn't convinced, but he says, "All right."

Champagne bubbles in a glass across the table, and I lick my lips, wishing I could drown this conversation in something stronger. I take a long sip of my soda instead.

Liam shifts, still unsettled. "Ivy . . ."

Three crystal-clear *tings* ring out as Taylor taps a knife to her glass, standing up from her spot next to Dani. I let out a small breath of relief for the interruption.

"I hope we're all enjoying dinner," Taylor says. "I just want to take a moment to celebrate our soon-to-be-married couple, Dani and Jeremy."

Taylor pauses as a round of applause rings out around the table, with a couple loud whoops and whistles from Jeremy's buddies, who have already had way too much to drink.

"Before we get to dessert, I thought now would be a good time to do some speeches, aka my big sister's least favorite part." Taylor gives Dani a sarcastic look: If there's one thing Dani loves, it's a well-crafted speech.

"Yeah, y'all better have whole sonnets written," Dani teases with a playful flip of her hair, earning a bubble of laughter.

"So," Taylor continues, "if anyone wants to—"

"I do!" My hand shoots up before I've fully thought about it, and every head at the table spins to me. Taylor lifts an eyebrow in a decidedly Dani-like way.

"See?" Dani says. "This is the kind of enthusiasm I'm expecting."

Dimly, I'm aware that I might have jumped at the speech opportunity as a way of avoiding whatever truth is waiting in Liam's eyes, but it's not only that. I haven't been the best friend to Dani lately, and I want her to know how much I value her—my big rom-com gesture, friendship edition.

"Hi," I start, letting out the rest of my nerves with a small laugh. "Sorry if that was a little impulsive. I just can't ever pass up an opportunity to sing the praises of the beautiful and talented Danica Hudson."

Dani puts a hand on her heart, smiling at me as the table throws more applause her way.

"For those of you who don't know me, I'm Ivy, and Dani and I go way back—like, all the way to the first week of sophomore year, when I was the terrified new girl who'd somehow been thrown into AP Chemistry, and I got lucky enough to be paired with this brilliant and impeccably dressed stranger for lab." I smile. "As you can imagine, she immediately started kicking my ass. My titration was *not* up to par."

Dani lets out a perfect snorting laugh as the crowd chuckles with her.

"But Dani made sure we got an A, and I made sure she cracked a smile every now and again," I continue, grinning. "From then on, we were inseparable—which is pretty much one of the best things that's ever happened to me." I look at Dani, tears misting my eyes as her lips curve downward with nostalgic tenderness. "I spent so much of my life feeling so lonely, and like things were so dark, but Dani changed all that." My chest tightens. "She's the smartest, most caring, and most badass woman I know, and every day, I feel so lucky to call her my best friend, even on the days when I don't deserve it."

I hesitate, my throat burning. A tear shimmers on Dani's cheek, and she wipes it away, laughing at her own sentimentality. Finally, my tears spill over, and I laugh with her.

"To Dani," I say, raising my glass, "who has always been my safe harbor. And to Jeremy: I am so, so happy that Dani has found someone who treasures her as much as I do, and I hope I get to be a part of your lives forever. Cheers!"

Everyone raises their glasses, and I keep my eyes on Dani, who's as radiant as the champagne bubbling around us, the sun sparkling through the windows. I take a sip of my soda as if I could drink down this moment, hold it inside me for just a while longer.

As I sit down, Liam gives my arm a loving squeeze. I smile at him, but I can't even convince myself. Already, the happy feeling is fizzling away, leaving an uneasy weight in my chest. It's familiar, but different—like how I feel whenever I wake up from a blackout, only instead of just me, it's this whole table of well-dressed, smiling people. There's something we're all forgetting, something lurking just at the dark edges of our memory.

But still we drink and laugh, pulled along in the current as whatever it is drifts away like the tail end of a nightmare, gone as soon as we know we're awake.

ELEVEN YEARS AGO

CORA

WE GATHERED IN THE LIVING room, a twisted picture of a family meeting: Ivy and me on the sofa, our parents facing us in the chairs. For once, the house was completely silent—like it, too, was holding its breath.

"You lied to me," I said, suddenly determined to be the first to speak. I said it again, a weapon held up to force them back. "You lied to me for my entire life."

Without looking at each other, they clasped hands, like they needed each other's strength—like this was *hard* for them—and fury rose up in me.

"Why?" I demanded.

My mother drew in a breath. "Ivy, honey," she said gently. "Why don't you go upstairs?"

Ivy's eyes widened, like she hadn't expected them to remember that she was here. Slowly, she started to get up.

"No," I snapped, stopping her with the word. "Explain this to both of us. Ivy deserves to know why you lied to her, too."

My mother's jaw set, frustration jolting through her. With one squeeze of her hand, my father melted it back into calm.

"When we first got married," he said gently, "we weren't sure if we planned on having kids."

I tensed. This wasn't what I was expecting, and it threw me off-balance.

"We were both so busy with our careers," my mother added, their words blending together, a story told from one mind. "Your dad was building his landscaping business, and all day, I worked with very sick children." Darkness flashed through her expression. "I wasn't sure if I was ready to bring another life into the world, especially when I knew how fragile they could be."

Quiet tension hummed between Ivy and me. I could feel it even without looking at her. Hearing her talk like this, the woman I thought was my mother, I had never felt so grown up and so young at the same time.

"And then," my father said, his voice brightening as his eyes met mine, "we found you."

The way he said that word scraped at me, some buried dread. *Found.*

He looked at my mother, both of them beaming like they were transported back to that moment.

"You were so tiny," she said, eyes glowing with tenderness. "You didn't even have a coat, and it was so cold."

"You were just wandering alone, this little girl barely even old enough to walk on her own."

My hands went numb, a coldness reaching out from within. Somewhere in my head, a gear ground forward, almost like I knew what was coming next.

"We tried to find your parents," she said. "But there was no one around, and you wouldn't speak. Just stuck your fingers in your mouth and looked up at us with this thousand-yard stare. I wasn't only worried as a human being—I was worried as a doctor." Darkness shrouded her features. "So, we took you inside, just to make sure we didn't need to bring you to the hospital, but then . . ."

"You stole me." It was an accusation, but it came out blank, limp. I'd thought the fake illness and concealed adoption were the worst of it, but now their lies twisted into something even bigger and more terrifying than I'd imagined.

"We planned to report it," he said, nodding like he understood how I felt. "We wanted to find your parents, but then we saw the bruises on your little arm, and signs of malnutrition, and . . ."

"You kidnapped me." Now my voice found its power again, sharpening. When I looked to Ivy for support, she'd shrunk back into the couch, face blank with disbelief.

Our supposed mother's stare was unrelenting.

"We saved you," she said. "Whoever your parents were, we would *not* let you go back to them. They didn't deserve you."

Nausea lurched in my stomach. I stood up as if to leave, but there was nowhere to go, nowhere to hide. It struck me like a stab in the heart, making my voice turn weak and pitiful.

"They didn't come looking for me?"

All my adult strength was gone. Now I was a lost and frightened child once more.

"The day after we found you, there was an amber alert for a missing girl." His eyes cast downward as he said it, unable to look at me.

"They were looking," I said, hope stirring. "They wanted to find me."

"No, they didn't." My mother's voice was so harsh and intent that I went silent. "Or if they did," she said, something haunting in her eyes, "it wasn't just to bring you home."

The haunted thing in her stretched across the room, burying itself under my skin.

"I'd seen this before," she continued, quieter. "There was another little girl, once. Millie. She was three years old, and I met her when I was on rotation in peds. Her mother brought her in for a fever and cough, but all the signs were there: obvious malnutrition, bruises that were inconsistent with the mother's explanation of them."

Her face warped with pain so unfamiliar and clear that, for a moment, I forgot everything but the urge to comfort her, even though I couldn't move. My father squeezed her hand, strengthening her, while my own stayed limply at my side.

"We went through all the proper channels," she continued. "The attending and I filed the report immediately, followed up several times. But the case was never investigated." She let out a shuddering breath. "CPS is often overwhelmed and understaffed. I don't know if they found the report uncredible, or it fell through the cracks. . . ."

Tears spilled onto her cheeks, but she didn't sob—almost like she just couldn't resist the overflow of grief.

"Three weeks later," she said, "Millie was dead. She'd been left alone in the garage, where she froze to death."

A quiet breath hissed from my lungs, pain cinching my ribs.

"Mom," Ivy whispered, a little sob rushing out of her.

"I wouldn't let that happen to you, Cora." She shook her head, insistent. "No matter what, I was going to keep you safe."

The room lurched around me, my body leaden. I fell back onto the couch.

"So you forged the adoption certificate." As the rest of it dawned on me, I nearly keened in despair. "You pretended I had cancer and then an immune deficiency so they'd never find me. So I'd . . ."

Her eyes flashed with what I could only describe as love—fierce and violent, piercing me to the bone.

"So you could be ours," she said, with a voice like an open wound. "So we could be a family."

A *family.* I wanted to laugh, but all that came out was a quiet, almost inaudible moan. A family. A prison. Maybe they were always the same.

"What about me?" Ivy's voice was small and frightened. "Am I . . ." Her voice hitched. "Am I adopted, too?"

A smile stretched on Mom's face, full of that same ferocious love.

"No, honey," she said. "You were our second miracle."

"We didn't know, when we found Cora, that you were already on your way," Dad added with his own wistful smile. "It's like you knew that we were always meant to be a family."

Ivy smiled, her fear melting away in the sunlight of their love.

That was all it took for the spell to break. I stood up again, dizzy as I veered toward the door.

"Where are you going?" my mother asked, her voice sharpening again with fear.

I whirled around to face them.

"Away," I snarled. "Anywhere but here."

"Wait." My father stood up, hands extended as if to stop me, and I flinched away. "Please, Cora. We can . . ."

He trailed away, looking back to my mother like she had all the answers. For a moment, I found myself waiting, too—hoping desperately that she did.

"We shouldn't have lied to you," she conceded softly. "It was with the best of intentions, but you're absolutely right to feel angry and misled. But now that you know the truth, things can change." Her eyes brightened. "You can go to college. You can live a full and healthy life."

They were the same promises Gabby had made me back at the hospital, just as hopeful, and this time, I felt them sticking—my heart opening slowly toward them like hands unfolding from prayer.

"You'll be eighteen in less than six months," she added. "If we can all promise to keep this story within the family, then Cora . . ." Her smile widened. "You can do anything."

It was subtle, the change: a prickle at the back of my neck, a little twist in my gut. *If we can all promise*, she said. If we can all uphold the lie.

A pit opened inside me, sucking away everything but a cold understanding. This was the same woman who'd just threatened Gabby with a smile, who'd promised to ruin her family without even having to say it. The so-called parents who had lied to me for as long as I could remember, watching me waste away with loneliness. No matter what, if I agreed to this bargain—if I stayed—then I would always be a prisoner.

If I didn't leave now, I never would.

I ran. Through the house and out the door, no longer caring about the noise that I made. Footsteps thundered behind me like the pounding of my heart, but I was fast. I was nearly there.

Outside, the cool air rushed up to meet me, and I gulped it down, pumping my legs even harder down the driveway.

"Cora!" His voice, close behind.

I fumbled for my phone, pulling up Gabby's number as I ran. The road grew closer, an inky strip winding through the trees. My thumb hovered over the Call button, but just before I pressed it, pain tore through my arm. The phone clattered to the ground as the man who called himself my father pinned me to his chest, my arm twisted behind my back.

"I'm sorry," he told me, like he really meant it.

I bucked and struggled, but he held me tighter. He was still so strong.

"I'm so sorry, Cora."

He dragged me back to the house, the door hanging open like a waiting mouth. Into the darkness, down the hall—all the way to the cellar door.

26

THE FIRST TIME I CRIED at a wedding, it was my parents'. As a child, I begged them over and over again to play the DVD, memorizing the sounds and movements the way I did with my favorite Disney movies—convinced, in fact, that my mother, in her beautiful white dress, must have been friends with Cinderella and Sleeping Beauty. I haven't watched the tape in years, but still, the details are carved into my heart: the veil that flowed behind Mom like a magic carpet; the church I'd assumed was a palace, with its towering stained glass and ceilings that seemed to stretch on forever; the tears in Dad's eyes when he saw her, like a prince at the happy ending.

I remember all this, but not the part they loved most to tell: When I was four, the very first time they showed me the video, I burst into tears. Surprised and worried, they'd asked me what was wrong, and through my sobs, I said, *You look so happy*—here, they'd pause for emphasis when they retold it—*and I wish I was there.*

Today, when Dani appears in the dress I watched her fall in love with last summer, it's no surprise that I'm immediately weeping. I'm not the only one, either—as he walks Dani down the aisle, Mr. Hudson beams with tears in his eyes, and even Mrs. Hudson, who instilled in her daughter her own stone-faced logic and realism, is dabbing at her eyes with a handkerchief. And Jeremy, standing at the altar, looks exactly like my father did in that video from thirty years ago: overjoyed and teary, like as soon as Dani meets him there, nothing will ever be wrong again.

I feel Liam's gaze before I meet it. He's sitting beside Aunt Mia, watching me with his lips curving into a tiny smile. *One day,* his eyes seem to say, *this will be us.*

I smile back, holding tighter to my bridesmaid's bouquet of lilies as a warm rush of feeling surges in my chest, somewhere between love and desperation. *Please,* I think, a plea without a specific aim—for this to be real. For it to last.

And for the other feeling, the guilty wrongness swirling in my chest, to wind itself back into the dark.

The rest of the ceremony is a blur of vows and tears. When Jeremy kisses Dani, we all erupt in cheers. Finally, the full bridal party processions back down the aisle to a soaring love song from the string quartet, and it's over: My best friend is married.

For the past year and a half since Dani got engaged, I've wondered how this would feel. Joyous, yes, but in the darkest parts of me, I've also feared that I'd only feel left behind. Now, though, as I pass Liam and Mia again, they cheer even harder, and my chest fills with a glow as bright and far-reaching as the sun that spills over the water, the cloudless blue of the sky.

Just as I pass them, I catch someone else watching me. She's standing at a distance from the wedding itself, back by the building where the reception will take place—far enough away that I can't immediately clock her features except for her blond hair and her dress, the same powder blue as my own. It's the same color as all the bridesmaids' dresses, but if she were a bridesmaid, then she should be up here, not all the way over there. The woman smiles at me, hands raised in applause.

Icy fingers scrape down my spine, turning my whole body cold with fear. I realize I've stopped walking when John, my partner in the procession, shoots me a confused look. I pick up my pace again, heart pounding.

When I turn to glance over my shoulder, the woman is gone.

ELEVEN YEARS AGO

CORA

I BANGED ON THE DOOR WITH the last of my strength, my voice too raw to scream any longer. Then, limp with exhaustion, I slumped against the wall and looked around at my prison.

The cellar was dark and windowless, with a cement floor and brick walls that had grown dusty white from lack of use. From the door, a set of unfinished wooden steps, where I now sat, led down into the cramped space, lit by the single bulb that hung from the ceiling. Besides the stacks of storage boxes, which had been kept down here since we'd turned the attic into a functional living space, the cellar was empty.

In the old days, my mother had said, this room was used to store food and coal, until refrigerators and gas made it useless. Now the cellar was a ghost of a space, haunted by its former purpose.

I pulled my knees closer to my chest, staring down the stairs and into the shadows. The bulb cast a halo of light in the center of the room below, but everything around it was darkness, the boxes turned into formless, hulking shapes.

I thought of Gabby waiting here, and a terrible pit of guilt yawned inside of me, threatening to suck me inside.

I understood, then, why she had disappeared after I'd locked her in this room two years ago. I didn't know how long I'd been down here, but already, I was overcome with the growing terror that I would never leave again—that the darkness might unhinge its jaws and swallow me whole.

But Gabby will come for me, I thought. *When I don't call her, she'll be worried. She'll tell someone.*

I waited, clinging to that hope like the soft shreds of light above me.

I waited and waited and waited.

Time passed strangely in the cellar. I wasn't sure how long it had been when, eventually, I could no longer ignore the urge for a bathroom. When a last attempt at desperate banging on the door proved useless, I winced and peered down the stairs into the darkness.

My entire body tensed in resistance, but I had no other choice. Slowly, holding my breath, I crept down the stairs. With the dim light of the bulb overhead, I could just make out the outline of an empty storage bin. I tried to turn off my brain as I used it and then shoved it to the farthest corner of the room.

After that, I sat in the single bulb's halo of light on the cement floor, curled slowly into myself, and waited.

I must have slept, because I jolted and found myself lying on my side, disoriented. Up at the top of the stairs, the cellar door was open.

"Gabby," I breathed, pushing myself up to sitting—but then the door started to close, the thin sliver of light from the hall illuminating a plate and a bottle of water. I had barely scrambled back to my feet before the door was locked again.

I collapsed back to the floor, a sob choking out of me. I should have run for the food and water, but it struck me, all at once, what this meant: My captors had no intention of letting me out anytime soon. They would keep me here as long as they wanted.

The light flickered above me. I looked up at the bulb, swinging down from its chain. It flickered again—and then sputtered out, plunging me into complete darkness.

I pulled myself into a tight ball, counting my breaths. Without the quiet buzz of the light, the silence seemed so heavy. The darkness around me deepened.

She'll come, I told myself. *They can't get away with this forever.*

I rocked back and forth, telling myself again and again, whispering the words out loud, "Gabby will come."

But she didn't. Every passing second was another crack in my heart until hope hurt as much as breathing with a broken rib—until I had no choice but to give it up altogether.

No one was coming to save me, and it was there, in the pitch-black darkness, that I began to really see.

When I was a child, I believed the house had spoken to me through signs and sounds. For the first time, in the cellar, I heard its true voice.

It was my own. Every question I'd asked was a boundary tested, from the first day I saw Gabby through the window to the day I met her on the street—even when, hours or maybe days ago, I kissed her.

I had always been inching toward escape. Now that I was truly trapped, I had the strange and thrilling understanding that freedom was closer than ever. I just had to take it.

But freedom requires a sacrifice, whispered the house—the quiet voice that had always lived inside of me.

"I know," I whispered back.

I was finally ready.

My eyes had adjusted to the darkness now. I could look more closely through the boxes around me. I searched, feeling my way through the shadows, until I found something that would suffice: an old rusted candlestick made of thick, heavy metal. It was cool in my hands as I pulled it out of the box and tightened my grip.

They would come back sooner or later; they'd have to feed me again sometime.

With the candlestick still firmly in my grasp, I climbed back up the darkened stairs and waited.

I didn't have to wait long—or maybe time had only sharpened to a fine point as I waited with a predator's focus, everything falling away except for the door above me.

The lock clicked.

I raised my weapon.

The knob turned, and just as the door began to open, a sliver of light widening into the cellar, I lunged.

27

THE WEDDING RECEPTION IS IN full swing—drinks are flowing, classic party hits are bumping through the speakers, and half the guests have ditched their shoes and updos, hair hanging loose around their shoulders.

Meanwhile, I'm sitting at a table on the edge of the room, scanning the crowd as panic mounts in my chest. I haven't seen the woman since the end of the ceremony, and I'm starting to believe she may not have been there at all. Still, I search for her specter—blue dress, swish of blond hair.

"Champagne?"

I startle at the catering server in front of me, a young woman with a tray of glasses, crisp and golden. For a moment, I feel my fingers flexing, my hand lifting almost on its own before I curl it into a fist.

"No, thank you," I manage with a tense smile.

The server breezes on.

Just then Liam reappears with two plates and a brilliant smile.

"They've started handing out cake," he says, setting a slice down in front of me—picture-perfect, heaped with frosting. "Thought I'd grab us some before the mob descends."

Shame clenches my stomach as I think of how close I got to drinking just now, and the concern that would no doubt be written all over Liam's face if he caught me. I take the cake with a smile and dip my fork into the frosting, forcing myself to take a bite. It's as delicious as the rest of the food, sweet and melting on my tongue.

"God," Liam mutters, lost in his own bite. "That's diabolical, isn't it?"

I smile genuinely this time, squeezing his leg. "And you just happened to appear right when I was in desperate need of sugar."

Worry flickers in his expression, like he can see right through me, and my nerves jump.

"You all right?" Liam asks.

"Of course," I lie. "Just a long day."

The song changes, and Whitney Houston's "I Wanna Dance with Somebody (Who Loves Me)" blares through the speakers. I swallow another bite of cake and then grab Liam's hand. His eyes widen, hesitant, and I grin.

"Come on," I urge, tugging him out of his chair. "Whitney demands it!"

Together, we join the dance-floor throng, and immediately, it's evident that Liam's buttoned-up English demeanor translates to his moves. I cackle with delight.

"What?" He grins back at me with an awkward shimmy. "I never claimed to be a dancer."

"And I wouldn't have it any other way," I say.

"As far as I can tell, *your* moves consist solely of jumping up and down and shaking your hair around."

I laugh, jumping with even more abandon. "That's how we do it in America!"

Suddenly, he reaches out and spins me around, my dress fluttering around my legs as a laugh bubbles out of me. Liam catches me against his chest, his hands on the small of my back and my arms flung around his shoulders. For a moment, I'm breathless, frozen in this re-creation of the first time I touched him, when I tripped on Frank's leash and tumbled into his arms.

"And that," Liam murmurs in my ear, "is how we do it in England."

His voice seems to travel down my body, vibrating in my chest before pooling low and hot in my stomach.

"Well, God save the Queen," I whisper back.

"There you are!"

At Dani's voice, I spin around, cheeks heating as I remember that Liam and I are not alone—but Dani only grins, pulling me into a hug.

"Is everything okay?" she asks. "I thought I saw you leaving with Mia earlier."

I pull back, a cold bolt piercing my center. "What?"

Dani frowns. "Was that not you? I thought I saw you walking her out. She looked a little woozy."

Panic grips me as I scan the room for my aunt, but I can't find her.

"No," I tell Dani, my own voice sounding faraway. "I should call her."

Without another word, I turn and push through the crowd, veering back to my table, where I left my phone. It's there beside my abandoned plate of cake, the screen already lit up with a notification. My breath catches when I see it.

A DM from @heathcliff_2015.

"Ivy?"

Liam is behind me, his hand on my shoulder. I spin around, lowering my phone so he can't see it.

"Everything all right?" he asks, worried.

"Yeah," I lie. "I just want to make sure Mia's okay. I'm going to step out and call her."

"Shall I come with you?"

"No." It's too quick, too certain. I take a breath and force my expression to soften. "I'll just be a few minutes, okay?"

He gives me a hesitant smile, gently rubbing my back. "Of course."

I grab my purse off the back of the chair and then make my way through the mass of bodies, my phone gripped tight. Just as I'm nearing the exit, the DJ comes over the microphone.

"All right, party people, we've got another request on deck," he announces. "This one goes out to Ivy!"

I freeze. Everything fades—the voices, the cheers, the clinking glasses—until all I can hear is the song beginning: the frenetic guitar, eerie synth floating above it. A drum hit, harsh and insistent. A roll of percussion, a cry, and then the familiar lyrics of Talking Heads' "Burning Down the House."

My gasp is trapped in my throat, head as light and dizzy as if I've just inhaled helium. I want to laugh. I want to scream. The crowd around me dances along, unaware, as I scan for the person who did this, but part of me knows they're already gone, like a ghost the moment you turn on the lights. The only person who sees me through the crowd is Dani, her worried eyes finding mine.

I turn and go, pushing through the doors and into the hall, where I practically sprint until, finally, I'm outside, sucking down the cool night air.

Once I can breathe again, I remember the DM on my phone. With quaking hands, I tap to view the message.

When I see it, my breath dies all over again.

It's a photo of Aunt Mia, gagged and bound in the trunk of a car, her eyes wide and terrified. Beneath it, Heathcliff has written out an address in Tarrytown, New York—the one I'll never forget, no matter how hard I try—along with a simple, three-word message that almost knocks me to the ground.

See you soon.

ELEVEN YEARS AGO

CORA

I FROZE WITH THE CANDLESTICK STILL lifted, adrenaline surging as I stared into my sister's frightened face.

"Cora?" Ivy whispered, almost like she didn't recognize me—and maybe she didn't. Something had happened to me down in the cellar: a sharpening, a hardening. I was as much of a weapon now as the candlestick brandished in my grip—maybe more.

I lowered it, heart racing.

"How long has it been?" I whispered, still standing at the top of the stairs.

Ivy swallowed, her terrified face darkening with guilt.

"Two days."

My knees weakened, and I gripped the doorframe. Two days, and Gabby hadn't come. I hadn't eaten or had any water, either, but somehow, that seemed less important.

"I'm sorry," Ivy whispered now, the words a rush of breath. "I didn't know they would do this to you. I would have come sooner, but I didn't know how to—"

I held a finger to my lips, silencing her. I looked down the hall, dark except for the moonlight filtering through the windows, and then whispered, "Where are they?"

"Asleep," Ivy said. "It's after midnight."

I nodded, my plan stitching slowly back together around my sister's unexpected presence. Then I noticed the metallic glint of the cellar key in her hand.

"Can I see that?" I asked.

Ivy hesitated, her grip instinctively tightening.

"Ivy," I demanded, and that was all it took. Her fingers uncurled and she held out her open palm.

I snatched the key, the metal warmed by her hand. When I looked at Ivy again, her eyes were wide, frightened moons in the dark.

"Do you have your phone?" I asked. I had no idea where mine was, but it was almost certainly somewhere close to my jailers, hidden away upstairs.

"They took it," she said nervously. "I think it's in their room. Yours, too." Then, after a breath, she asked, "What are you going to do?"

I knew from her sharp, quiet inhale that the answer was written all over my face.

"I'm sorry," I told her, and then, with one quick move, I shoved Ivy back into the cellar and then shut the door to trap her inside.

Ivy called my name, banging on the door, but the sounds were muffled by the thick wood and brick. I held the door closed with one hand as I locked it with the other, then slipped the key safely into my pocket.

I moved quickly—first, sneaking through the back door and into the yard. The fresh air landed like a splash of cool water to my skin, and I breathed deeply. It also reminded me how thirsty I was, but I didn't stop. Everything seemed so simple now, so clear. A *sacrifice*.

The grass was soft under my bare feet as I walked to the shed and opened the door, inhaling its scent: sawdust, soil. There, on the shelf above the lawnmower, were two canisters of gasoline.

I took them both and then sped back through the yard to the house's waiting arms. I pushed roughly inside, rejecting its embrace. I didn't want the house's answers anymore. Deep in the cellar, I'd arrived at my own.

As long as they remained—this house and my parents, the cancer rotting at its center—I would never be free.

I stopped in the living room to snatch the matchbox from beside Mom's favorite candle, slipping it into my pocket with the cellar key. Then I headed for the stairs. As I passed the hallway, I couldn't help looking down the hall to the cellar door. It shook quietly, Ivy no doubt banging against it on the other side.

Hesitation tugged at my gut, but I pushed it down and climbed up the stairs in a well-learned dance, my feet touching only the quiet parts of each step, so none of them creaked.

When I reached the second floor, I set down the gas canisters and then crept quietly toward their bedroom. I held my breath. Slowly, carefully, I opened the door.

It creaked. I froze, but neither one of them stirred—they were both fast asleep, Dad snoring loudly enough to drown out the sound. It was dark, but I'd grown used to the darkness. I could see everything. I crept to the nightstand, but our phones weren't there. Carefully, I reached toward the drawer.

"Cora?"

I snatched my hand away, terror gripping me at the sound of her sleepy voice. When I looked at her, though, her eyes were still closed. Asleep.

"Cora, come inside," she mumbled, before curling onto her side.

I let out a shuddering breath.

They both looked so fragile there, sleeping soundly, that it was impossible not to envision it: reaching for a pillow. Pressing with all my weight until they went still. I could practically see myself doing it, some shadow version of my arm stretching out toward the nearest cushion.

I balled my hands to fists, shutting off the vision. I'd never be able to do it to one of them without the other waking up, and part of me worried that if I really tried, I wouldn't be able to do it at all—that fear or familiarity or, worse, *love* would take over the moment I began. Because love can't just go away, can it? Not when it's been learned and practiced for the past sixteen years, even if it was stolen.

I pulled myself away. No time to look for the phones. There was still too much to do, and I needed to move.

I crept next to my bedroom, where I grabbed my backpack and then stuffed it with some essentials: clothes, toothbrush, the things I couldn't live without. I reached automatically for the bottle of immunosuppressants before I remembered that I didn't need them—that I never had.

A heady rush of laughter fought to break out of me as I wondered what I'd been taking for nearly my whole life: pills that actually suppressed my immune system or plain sugar placebo.

No time, I reminded myself. I set the bottle back down, swung my bag over my shoulders, and then hesitated. Before I could think too deeply about it, I rushed back to my bed and pulled out the box from underneath, unlatching the lid. I smiled up from Gabby's photo, happy and foolish. Quickly, I rolled it up, secured it with a hair tie, and slipped it carefully into my bag. Then, without sparing another glance at the room I'd called my own for my entire conscious life, I marched into the hallway and grabbed the gas canisters.

I opened the first one, the sharp smell rising up to greet me. I reared back, holding my breath. Suddenly, this was tangible. Real.

Simple, I corrected myself as I tipped the canister downward. *Mechanical.*

And it was: I splashed the gas easily over the stairs as I climbed to the attic floor, hesitating only when I reached the door to the turret—my reading nook, my haven. Part of me wished it could be spared, but I knew it couldn't. If I was going to be free, then everything had to burn.

I poured more gas onto the floor and then, just as I was about to douse the chair, I noticed a familiar book splayed open on the cushion: my treasured copy of *Wuthering Heights*, the one that I'd given to Ivy on her birthday. When I opened it up, her name was embossed on the inside cover with a pretty, flowery seal: FROM THE LIBRARY OF IVY PARKER.

She must have taken it up here to read sometime when I was trapped in the cellar, turning to our favorite book for comfort.

My heart wrenched, and I couldn't help myself. I grabbed the book and shoved it into my backpack with the essentials and Gabby's photo, the only other proof of my sentimentality.

Then I raced back down the stairs, my heart thumping like this, somehow, was the greatest wrong I'd committed.

Back on the second floor, the door to their bedroom was still cracked open. Emptying the last of the first gas canister on the stairs, I knew it was time. Quietly, I snuck back to their bedroom and closed the door, holding my breath as it let out a little creak—but when I pressed my ear to the door, I couldn't hear them moving.

Then my eyes darted around until they landed on the old armoire a few feet away from the bedroom door. I crept toward it and then, taking a deep breath, I pushed.

It slid to the left, toward the door. I pushed harder, sliding it farther.

It squeaked. I froze, heart racing, but after a few panicked breaths, no one stirred. I pushed the armoire again, more carefully, until it was blocking their door.

I let go, my chest heaving from the effort. My arms were jelly, but it was done. *Simple,* I thought again. *Mechanical.* Like I was just working through a series of impersonal instructions: gasoline, check; block the door, check.

I grabbed the second gas canister and took it back down to the first floor. I emptied the rest of it through the hallways until my throat burned with every inhale. Then, finally, I returned to the cellar door.

It had stopped shaking; Ivy must have given up far quicker than I had.

I set down the empty gas canister and then reached into my pocket for the reassurance of the matchbox. One strike. A flame. That's all it would take to turn my prison to ruins, to set me free.

The book sat like a stone in my backpack, weighing me down.

Ivy wasn't my sister, not in the way I used to believe, but none of this was her fault. She was always a prisoner, too.

I let go of the matchbox, digging instead for the key, which I pulled out as I inched toward the cellar door, certainty building with every step. Taking a breath that burned my lungs with gasoline, I slipped the key into the lock. Turned it.

And slowly, I opened the door.

28

I STARE AT THE MESSAGE, THE world pitching dizzily around me.

See you soon.

Heathcliff sent it ten minutes ago—barely a blink in the grand scheme of things, but long enough that anything could have happened. If Aunt Mia is still alive, she's alone and terrified. Dread deepens, turning my blood into lead. I'm about to call 911 when another DM flashes across my screen, almost like they've been waiting for the little notification that I've seen their first message.

If you tell anyone,
she dies.

This time, there's a video attached—the kind that disappears once you press play. Hands vibrating with terror, I press the button.

Mia is still in the trunk, bleary-eyed and terrified. She scoots away from the camera, her pleas garbled by the gag in her mouth, as a knife glints in the foreground, gripped by whoever's filming. The knife inches forward, and the video cuts out.

A desperate whimper escapes my lips as the message disappears. Then, like a flint struck, my fear sparks into something new: cold, sharpened rage.

"Ivy."

I whirl around just in time to see Dani stepping outside, her white skirt bunched in her hands.

"What's going on?" she asks. "Is everything okay?"

I'm about to argue on instinct that it's fine when I get another idea.

"Mia just called me. I think she's lost." I'm bending the truth, but the panic in my voice is real. "She's confused, and she needs me to pick her up, and . . ." I force myself to take a breath. "Is there any chance I can borrow a car? Jeremy's, or one of your parents', maybe?"

"Of course," Dani says, concern radiating from her face. "Here, I'll come with you."

"No." I hold out my hands to stop her, frantic. When she looks back at me in surprise, I force myself to relax my expression. "I'm not letting you leave your own wedding, Dani. I'll be okay, I promise. Mia just started a new medication, and it mixes badly with alcohol, and . . ."

I shrug, a little surprised by how easily the lies tumble out of me, even if I shouldn't be. I've been lying for over a decade now.

Dani sighs, relenting. "Okay, if you're sure."

I smile. "I am."

Convinced, Dani walks over to the valet and says something to him, gesturing back at me. He nods and then walks off.

"He'll be back with Jeremy's car in a minute," Dani says, coming back over. "Want me to wait?"

"Not for one second," I tell her, pulling her into another quick hug. "Thank you, Dani."

My voice tightens with gratitude, and for a moment, I'm gripped by a terrible fear that this is all a bad idea—that I should just tell her what's really going on and deal with the consequences.

But that would mean risking Mia's life, and I can't do that. I won't. All I can do is squeeze Dani tighter before letting go.

"Now get back in there!" I tell her. "The dance floor needs your moves."

Dani chuckles, doing a little shoulder wiggle.

"You'll let me know when you get back?" she asks, serious again.

Just then, the valet pulls up with Jeremy's car. I let out a breath.

"Promise," I say, smiling. And then, with a jolt of worry, I add, "Let Liam know I'll be back soon!"

With a nod, Dani goes, and I rush down the steps to take the keys. Adrenaline floods me as I climb into the driver's seat and plug the address into my maps app: a little over thirty minutes from here to Tarrytown. If I really try, I bet I could make it in closer to twenty. Thinking of Aunt Mia in that trunk, I know I have no choice.

I open Instagram and reply to Heathcliff's DM.

I'm on my way.

Then I drive out of the venue as calmly as I can manage, my foot itching to press down on the gas. Once the wedding is safely behind me, I take a breath, grip the wheel, and gun it onto the road.

New Rochelle blurs through the windows, suburban and green, until I'm up on the highway, the speedometer inching toward eighty. Another car honks at me as I pass into their lane a little too close for comfort, but I grit my teeth, focusing on the road.

I've never liked driving. Being behind the wheel should feel empowering, knowing that I can go anywhere I want, but I only ever feel out of control, like the world is moving faster than I can keep up with.

But tonight, I need fast. I press the pedal lower, my entire body tensing forward.

When the exit comes, I nearly miss it. I yank the wheel, earning a few more honks, but I make it safely into the turn, my heart thrumming out of my chest.

Living in LA, I always yearned to come back to New York, but in my three years here, I've never once returned to Tarrytown. One October, Dani and some of our friends wanted to take the Metro-North out to Sleepy Hollow, and I made up some excuse to get out of it. The quaint, Halloween-loving village is only a few miles from the house I grew up in, and it felt too close, like setting foot anywhere near there would open some irreversible portal to the past and welcome its ghosts to the present.

And now here I am, speeding straight into the monster's open mouth.

I'm forced to slow down once I reach the residential streets, and now, thirty miles per hour feels like crawling. Trees curl and sway around me, the dark, empty road punctuated by houses that grow bigger and more spread out as I drive on. Compared to the light and noise of the wedding venue, the quiet here is oppressive, like invisible hands pressed to the car windows.

Finally, I turn onto the first road that strikes me as truly familiar. This one feels even more deserted and dark, lit only by the beam of my headlights, but suddenly, I'm gripped with the certainty that I could find my way even with my eyes closed.

When my app instructs me to turn, I'm already spinning the wheel.

Our little private road curls through the trees, twisting at intervals that I still remember even without thinking, as much a part of me as the veins beneath my skin. Then, like curtains parting, the trees open up to our driveway—to the house rising at the top of the low hill.

Or what's left of it. As the car crawls up the drive, my heart is in my throat, a grief so powerful I nearly moan.

What used to be a home is now a blackened husk. Parts of the roof and porch have caved in, exposed beams reaching like the ribs of a creature picked clean. I follow them up to the turret, and my breath catches. It still stretches up to the inky sky, but even in the shadows, I can tell it didn't survive the blaze: Black crawls up the side like a sickness, and the glass from the windows has all blown out.

I pull the car to a stop, the high beams ghosting over the decaying porch.

Technically, after everything, the house is mine. I could have sold it, or battled with the home-insurance company after the investigation went unsolved, but my parents' savings and life insurance were enough to keep me afloat, even after my own astronomical medical bills. When the dust settled and Aunt Mia stepped up to take me in, it seemed easiest just to leave this house in the past—like if I didn't have to see it, I wouldn't remember that it was still there, rotting.

But death always has a smell. Even thousands of miles away, I felt it clinging to my skin: the burning, the decay.

Now it hits me all over again. Maybe it's only my imagination, but smoke and ash seem to hang in the air, reaching deeper as I climb out of the car on unsteady legs.

For a moment, I stand there, looking up at the ruined skeleton. When I breathe in again, it's like I've swallowed a wave with it: burning and overpowering, a feeling I can't name even as it chokes me.

And then, through the empty socket of the front door, something moves.

I tense, gripping my phone tighter.

"Hello?" I call out, my voice carried into the breeze.

I wait, heart thrumming, but nothing answers.

My whole body is shuddering now, my teeth chattering, but my feet pull me forward as if I've been nudged by an invisible hand. I slip off my heels and then test the first porch step under my foot. It creaks, but my weight holds. I step up, and then onto the next, telling myself I have no other choice, not if Mia is here. I'm running out of time.

Still, as I climb onto the porch, sidestepping a hole where the planks have caved in, there's another voice in my head—a quiet, familiar whisper that says I've never had a choice. Somehow, I was always going to end up back here, called home to the ruins of my childhood.

When I step through the threshold, it's not quite peace that settles over me, but something close: the quiet surrender to inevitability.

My breath stalls, heart clenching.

The house is a body turned inside out. Paint peels from the walls in blackened strips, its pieces littering the floor with the other broken things: wooden planks, furniture, and even a few bits of trash and empty bottles, left over from the brave few who must have ventured into this haunted house for the thrill, or maybe out of desperation for shelter. Somehow, the grand staircase remains intact, except for the blackened wood and the gaps where the banister was eaten away. Moonlight spills through the busted windows, glowing over the carnage.

I feel almost numb, like I'm walking through a dream space where nothing is real. And maybe, I think, that's all this is—a blackout, a nightmare.

I turn like a sleepwalker down the hallway that leads to the cellar door. I don't know how, but I know that this is where I'm meant to go. The door is open now, hanging off the hinges like a broken jaw inviting me to be swallowed.

I step toward it, but I don't feel any fear—only a strange sort of relief. The cool, quiet welcome of an open grave.

ELEVEN YEARS AGO

CORA

AS THE DOOR OPENED, Ivy rose to her feet. Moonlight slipped in through the hallway to illuminate her red-rimmed eyes, catching the tearstains on her cheeks, but when I looked back at her, it wasn't just guilt that cinched my chest.

It was fear.

My sister hadn't shrunken. Just like me, she'd grown in the cellar, her anger sharpening to a lethal point, one that I could almost feel pressed to my neck.

"I'm sorry," I whispered—the same two words I'd told her before slamming the door in her face, but now it was my turn to feel helpless as her gaze swept over me, landing on the backpack slung over my shoulders.

"You're leaving," she said, like it didn't surprise her.

I nodded. "Do you want to come?"

I hadn't fully understood that this was what I wanted until the words were leaving my mouth, but now it made perfect sense, the picture growing clearer with every urgent word.

"We'll find Gabby, and then we'll go—to the city, maybe, wherever we want. We'll find my real parents, or if we can't, then . . ." I shook my head, breathless. "Then we'll have each other."

Ivy's face softened. I could see it: a door creaking open in her expression as she started to picture it, too. But then, like that same door slammed shut, Ivy tensed.

"What is that?" she asked, sniffing. She stepped out of the cellar, and then, before I could stop it, Ivy's stare landed on the empty gas canister I'd left in the hall.

She turned to me, bewildered.

"What are you doing? What . . ."

Ivy went silent. Because now she saw the matches I held out in my hand, and her confusion morphed into bare betrayal.

"I doused the whole house," I told her, fighting to keep my grip steady. It was a warning, but also a plea. A promise. "One match, and it all burns."

Fresh tears sprang to Ivy's eyes, but they weren't broken—they were angry.

"You'll kill them," she spat.

And then, in my silence, Ivy read the answer.

"Oh my god." She backed away, toward the stairs. "That's what you're doing. You're going to—"

I pulled out a match and struck it, holding out the little flame like a gun. Ivy froze. I walked carefully over to the stairs, blocking her path.

"Go get your things," I told her, surprised by the calmness of my own voice, even as the flame wavered. "And then we're leaving."

Fear flickered over her expression like firelight. "Cora . . ."

"We don't have another choice." The desperation squeezed my chest so tight, I could almost hear the ribs cracking. When I spoke again, my voice was as thin as smoke. "As long as they're alive, we're prisoners. We don't have anyone but each other now."

Her fear melted into devastation.

"You don't have to do this," Ivy pleaded. "You can still leave. *We* can leave together, but we don't have to hurt them. You'll be eighteen soon, and then they can't stop you. Just don't do this." Tears spilled onto her cheeks, her face crumpling. "Please, Cora."

Something reached out from the broken place inside me, a tendril of hesitation snaking through. Ivy was right. This wasn't the only way. I could go to the police and tell them what happened, send them banging down our door. I could still be free if my captors were alive and in custody.

But Ivy . . .

"Please," she begged. "They're still my parents."

With a sharp intake of breath, the gas making me dizzy, I understood. It wasn't me who needed them gone.

It was *her.* As long as Ivy's parents were breathing, she would never escape this prison, even if the door was wide open. She would never even know it was a prison.

And burning beneath that thought was another one, as volatile and undeniable as the gasoline splashed all over this house: I might not have needed them to die, but I wanted them to burn.

Like she could read my mind, Ivy drew in a breath.

It happened as quickly as the match's strike, both of us understanding what was about to happen. Ivy lunged around me, running for the stairs—and just as she called out for them, I freed us both.

With a flick of my hand, I threw the lit match to the ground, and the fire roared to life.

29

IT RUSHES BACK FROM ELEVEN years in the past, as clear and vibrant as if I were there again: that millisecond of suspension before the match hit the ground, and then, fire. Crackling, climbing with a force that fed on itself until, in a blink, it was everywhere, the heat breathing into my face.

I can almost smell it now: the smoke curling into my lungs, rancid and all-consuming, the kind that will never let go once it has you.

It still hasn't.

I step through the cellar door, my feet moving as if on their own, a ghost caught replaying the final moments of its life. Shockingly, the stairs remain intact. Someone must have closed the door before the fire started—maybe even me. I don't remember now. It's another detail lost to the blaze of that night, everything twisted and confused.

I walk onto the first step, the little creak echoing into the silence. Then it's easy: down and down, my hand trailing the brick wall for balance, until I'm at the bottom in the darkness. My breath comes tighter now, frightened, but this is just a place. *Just a place*, I tell myself, as I feel for the pull cord that will turn on the light.

I'm moving toward the center of the room, hands searching, when I hear it: a quiet intake of breath.

Not mine.

My heart jumps, a terrified *thumpthumpthump* as I scramble for the light cord, dropping my phone in the process, but before I find it, there's a click. The dim bulb flickers to life overhead, and I gasp.

I am not alone in the cellar.

A ghost smiles back at me, like she's been waiting so patiently for me to arrive.

ELEVEN YEARS AGO

CORA

FOR A MOMENT, WE WERE both stunned—frozen and powerless in the face of the blaze as if standing at the feet of some unstoppable monster.

Then Ivy bolted for the stairs.

I followed, panic seizing my body.

"Ivy!" I shouted as her feet pounded up the steps, the banister already burning.

Something snapped—a beam right beside her. The plank fell to the ground, and Ivy stumbled. My stomach lurched, but then Ivy caught herself, turning back to me with a look that made my breath hitch. It wasn't rage or betrayal in her eyes. It was fear, pure and childlike—a girl looking for her big sister to save her.

I extended my hand.

"We have to go." My voice scraped, but it didn't waver. "Ivy, it's going to collapse."

Carefully, she reached for my hand.

Then, just before it clasped mine, something banged upstairs. Our eyes both snapped upward as, behind the burning armoire, the bedroom door began to shake.

Ivy's shoulders tensed, her jaw set as her fear hardened into bravery. And then, before I could shout a warning, she ran.

30

SHE'S WEARING THE SAME POWDER-BLUE dress I saw at the wedding, a mirror of my own, only this time, I know for a fact she's flesh and blood—no hazy, disappearing figment of my imagination.

My breath whooshes out of me.

She looks different now. Her hair is darker, duller than the honey blond of her childhood, cut at her shoulders instead of spilling down her back like it used to. Her face has thinned out, and despite her youth, the years have etched themselves on her skin: fine lines on her forehead, little crinkles around her eyes when she smiles at me—a twisted smile that chills me to the bone, cruel in a way she never was.

For all those differences, though, her sharp blue eyes are exactly the same.

I would know my sister anywhere.

"You're alive," I breathe, stepping toward her as if she might dissipate into smoke, but she doesn't move at all.

She just smiles, her lips stretching into a snarl as she says, "It's good to see you, Cora."

ELEVEN YEARS AGO

CORA

I LUNGED FOR IVY, catching her hand.

What happened next would haunt me for eleven years.

It was supposed to be a gentle tug, pulling her back toward safety, but maybe I pulled too hard, too fueled by adrenaline or maybe by anger. Maybe I *wanted* it, because even then, in the moment she ran for them, Ivy had made her choice. She'd chosen them.

I caught her hand. I pulled.

And Ivy's feet slipped out from under her.

She tumbled down the burning staircase, her head slamming into the wall with a horrible crack before she rolled limply onto the landing.

For a breath, I stood on the staircase, petrified. Then I snapped back into my body and ran after her.

"Ivy," I cried, shaking her limp shoulders. Her head tilted to the side, but she didn't open her eyes.

That was when I saw the blood spilling from the back of her head, wetting my fingers. Nausea surged up in me, and I shook my head as if my own refusal would prove it wrong.

"Ivy." I grasped her shoulders again, tears blurring my vision. "Ivy, we have to go."

She didn't move. I grabbed her wrist and pressed my fingers to her warm skin, but I couldn't feel a pulse. When I leaned down to hold my ear to her chest, there was no telltale beat, at least not one I could hear over my own.

A sob ripped through me as another beam snapped from the staircase, falling to the floor in a shower of embers. All around us, the fire raged. It had grown so much bigger than I'd expected, even in my wild, reckless fury.

Something popped overhead. The house moaned.

I knew, as I looked at my sister's motionless body, that it was too late for her. If I didn't move, it would be too late for me, too: The fire was creeping toward the front door. Any closer, and there would be no escape.

But I couldn't leave her. Even if she was already gone, I couldn't let her burn.

I curled my hands under her lifeless shoulders, pulling her up, and then dragged her down one step, her limp feet thumping over it. I sobbed again, my chest clenching. Still, I pulled. *Thump* again on the next step. *Thump-thump.*

When I tried to take a breath, smoke stung my lungs. I coughed, my grip on Ivy's shoulders slipping, but I tightened my hold and pulled her the rest of the way. I stumbled toward the front door, planks snapping and falling around us, embers scattering. It was so hot. The smoke was getting too thick to see.

Then, through the blackness, a halo of moonlight. A door.

I gasped with relief, but it was a mistake—more smoke flooded in, and I choked, nearly dropping Ivy in the process. I caught her just in time and kept moving. One step and then another, the light growing brighter, nearer, as the fist in my chest closed tighter.

Then, with a gasp, we were through. The relief of clean night air was so great that I nearly fell to my knees, but I had to get us farther away from the house. It crackled behind us, a dragon spitting smoke and flame.

I carried Ivy into the yard and then laid her out on the grass, hacking as I fell beside her. The coughs turned into gagging, bile heaving out of me. When I could finally breathe again, I turned to look at Ivy. Still motionless. Limp.

Grief pierced through my heart. This was all my fault, I knew. I thought I was saving us, and now . . .

I looked back at the house. Everything was fire: the windows, both floors, even all the way up to the attic, where my turret burned like a terrible crown.

I sobbed again, tears and smoke blurring my vision.

I had to get help. Smoothing Ivy's hair away from her damp, cooling forehead, I scrambled to my feet and then ran down the drive, just like I had two years ago, when I was so full of hope and rebellion. Now the night pitched around me, tilting under my feet. Still, I pressed on, fighting the tightness in my chest, the weakness in my legs—keeping my eyes on the road.

"Help," I tried to shout, but it only came out as another hacking cough, like knives slashing my throat.

I was still watching the road when my feet wouldn't move any longer, and the dark grass rushed up to welcome me home.

31

HER WORDS CURL TOWARD ME, spreading and reaching like smoke.

It's good to see you, Cora.

The name I buried along with that night—with my family—but now here she is: a ghost, my sister, the real Ivy, digging it up with hands that were supposed to be dead.

Cora. No one has called me my real name in eleven years. Not since before I woke up in that hospital bed, an unfamiliar voice at my side.

Ivy, the woman said. *Can you hear me?*

Confusion as I heard my sister's name in her mouth.

Where am I? I asked her. *What happened?*

The memories tumbled back in a breathless wave: the fire. Ivy crumpled on the grass, lifeless, the blood in her matted hair.

Grief stole my words, emptying me. The woman introduced herself as a social worker, her name forgotten as soon as she said it.

I have to tell you something that will be very difficult to hear, she said, and already, I knew.

They were gone. All of them. I'd killed them.

But what she said next changed everything.

I'm so sorry, Ivy. There was a fire. Your parents and Cora . . . they didn't make it out.

Even now, I can't be sure why I did it—only that in that moment, when I was so broken and alone, it felt like the only answer, a weight lifted. Ivy hadn't died in that fire after all, because I was Ivy. Cora had tried to kill her, but Cora was dead, and I remained.

Ivy Parker, alive and free.

"I had your book in my bag," I say now, finding my voice through the shock. "*Wuthering Heights*, with your name embossed. There wasn't any other identification on me, and they just assumed it was mine, and . . ."

The words die, useless once more.

"You let them," Ivy says simply, her eyes never leaving mine.

It was easy. That's the strangest part of it all: Despite our lack of shared genes, Ivy and I had always looked alike, aside from my paler skin and hair, white-blond before I dyed it. Not that it really even mattered, when I became her: We'd been so isolated that no one even knew what I looked like, except for the doctor who'd treated me the last time I went to the emergency room—but she wasn't on shift that night, and so she never saw me before I was transferred to ongoing care. The hospital didn't have access to any of Ivy's picture IDs, either. At the beginning, when I was still unconscious, they kept everyone but the staff out of my room, since there was no family to visit. Then, once I was awake, I asked visitors to be kept away, insisting that it was too painful. Eventually, Ivy's friends and their families gave up on seeing her—seeing *me*.

There was the problem of our grandparents, still down in Florida and both too frail to travel, but that was solved with a simple phone call: In my best Ivy impression, I told them that I was okay, and that they didn't need to worry. By then, the hospital had already contacted my estranged aunt Mia, the only relative who could feasibly take me in, and despite never having met me or my sister, she had already booked the next flight out to New York.

The only threat posed to my new identity, then, was Gabby. Every day, I kept waiting for her to appear, or to run to the nearest news outlet and tell them what my parents had done. At the very least, I hoped, in my most tender, bruised moments, that Gabby would reach out to Ivy—to *me*—to express her grief.

But she never did. It wasn't until later that I learned she'd run off, packing a bag and splitting in the middle of the night. She was eighteen, so they couldn't report her missing—not when she'd so clearly planned to leave. I already knew she wanted to move to the city, but I still couldn't believe it at first, until I thought back to that threat my mother had made, Gabby's mother's addiction, and the darkness in Gabby's eyes that day in the yard. *Sounds nice, running forever.*

So I left, too. I bundled up my grief and heartache and shoved them in the darkest corners of myself, along with Gabby and the girl who had loved her, in whatever way I had—because I'm not sure, even now, if it was love or just desperation, grasping greedily at the first real connection I ever had in whatever form would keep her with me. It felt like love. It was, I think.

But I wasn't Cora anymore. Cora died in that fire, because I killed her. Because it was the only way to survive.

It was my sister's final gift to me: a new life. I knew just how precious it was when I was finally strong enough to talk to the police, and they asked me who started the fire. If it was my sister, Cora.

I told them I didn't know. I'm not sure if they believed me, but they had no other choice. The investigation wrapped up. I moved to LA.

I became Ivy Harcourt, two weeks shy of sixteen with a whole life in front of her. Grieving, but not broken. A girl who could see the best in the world, even after all the pain—who would grow into the brilliant, beautiful woman that my sister should have become.

Only now that she stands before me—still beautiful, still undoubtedly brilliant—I know she is not Ivy Harcourt or even Ivy Parker. My sister is a woman who has died already, whose beauty conceals a hunger that will never be sated. A woman who could sink her teeth into me, tear me apart, and still never lose that blank, broken smile.

"Where is Aunt Mia?" I demand, glancing around the dark, empty room with a new surge of fear.

"She's fine," Ivy says, like I'm overreacting. "Probably not happy with me for ditching her on the side of the road somewhere outside of New Rochelle, but she'll live."

Relief spikes through me for one beautiful moment before the rage gathers to replace it.

"You were dead," I growl, like the words could make it true again. "They found your body."

Ivy smiles, but something changes behind it, sadness seeping in.

My stomach plummets. Just like I did that day with the social worker, I know already, some innate sense attuned to the truth.

"Now that," Ivy says, the cruel mask slipping back on, "is where the story gets good."

I don't want to hear it—not when I think I know how this ends—but I don't have a choice. Ivy is practically shuddering with anticipation, like she's kept this inside of her for so long, dreaming of this very moment: her story and the perfect audience. I can't take that from her, not after all I've already done.

"I don't remember much," she starts. "When I woke up on the grass right in front of the house, I was alone. Everything was burning. Everything hurt. I thought, for a minute, that I was already dead."

Pain cinches my heart as I think of her lying there motionless. I thought she was dead. She *was* dead, or else I never would have left her.

Would I?

"And then," she says, eyes widening slightly, "I heard her."

The ache digs deeper. She hasn't said her name, but already, I know.

"Gabby came back," I breathe, ribs tightening.

"She must have been trying to reach you for days," Ivy says with a shrug, almost detached. "She had a backpack, too, like she was ready to run away with you. I assume that's why she came. To *save* you."

Those words are a blade, digging deep into a still-bleeding wound. *Gabby came back.* All that time in the darkness, thinking she'd forgotten me . . .

"We didn't get a chance to talk about it, though. Because when I woke up to find her kneeling over me, the first thing I said was your name."

No. I want to cover my ears like a child, scream that this isn't true.

"I was groggy," Ivy says. "My head was all messed up. I didn't remember how the fire started, but I knew my sister was in danger. I thought you were still in there."

Tears sting my eyes, my throat squeezing tight.

"Gabby told me to stay outside and call for help." Ivy's lip twitches—a smile or a twinge of sadness, I can't be sure. "And then she ran back into the house."

I break. The tears stream down my face, a sob scraping out with them. Ivy just watches me, cold and a little disappointed—like she thought she'd enjoy this, but now it only disgusts her.

"They said they found your body inside," I manage. "I always wondered why you went back into the house. I thought . . ."

"You thought I went back to save them," Ivy finishes, a dark little smile curling on her lips. "Maybe I would have, if I hadn't been so focused on saving you."

When I draw another breath, it burns. I press my hands to my chest like that could hold me together. All this time, I consoled myself—or at least I tried—with the knowledge that I did everything I could to save my sister. She chose our parents one final time, and that cost Ivy her life.

None of it was true. My sister chose me, and look how I've repaid her.

"By the time Gabby was gone," Ivy continues, "I realized I didn't have a phone, and I didn't know what to do. I couldn't call for help, but I was terrified to go back into the house. I wasn't sure if you were still inside, but I knew I needed to do something, and I panicked."

For a moment, her eyes flicker with the ghost of her teenage self: young, afraid.

"I ran. It was so dark, but I ran, and as I was running . . ." Another smile twists on her lips. "I stumbled over you, lying unconscious at the end of the drive, in that little ditch at the bottom of the hill. Gabby must have run right past you when she saw the fire and not even realized it."

I can't bear it anymore. My legs go weak, and I lower myself onto the ground, knees pulled tight to my chest. I'd been so close, and I still couldn't save her.

"I tried to wake you up," Ivy says, voice sharpening like she's angry with me all over again. "Shook you, called your name, but you wouldn't move. I thought you might be dead. I searched through your pockets for a phone, but you didn't have yours, and I didn't know what else to do, so I ran. I ran and I ran down the road, but it was dark, and I was terrified. My head was still messed up from the fall, and I didn't know which way I was going. I was still running when a car swerved around the bend."

My stomach clenches.

"I waved at them," she says. "Yelled for them to help, but they were going so fast. One second, they were down the road, and the next . . ."

I can almost feel the collision in my own body, a memory that isn't even mine.

Ivy's voice gets quieter. "I don't remember it, but apparently, the asshole who hit me just kept driving. It was a full day before someone found me in a ditch on the side of the road, barely breathing. That's what they told me after. All I remember is waking up in the hospital. Someone was asking my name, and I was terrified because I didn't know the answer." She smiles, almost amused. "It's funny. We must have been in the same exact hospital, and no one had any idea. When they found a third body all burned up in the fire, they just assumed it was you. You had already become me, and I . . ." Her smile stretches wider, teeth glinting in the moonlight. "I was no one."

"I didn't know." My voice comes out small and pitiful, a useless defense.

"No," she snarls. "You didn't."

I force myself to look her in the eye. "What happened?"

She crouches to my level, leaning closer as if to tell a secret.

"I was in a coma for almost six months, and when I woke up, I didn't remember a thing. Apparently, I'd cracked my skull when the car hit me, around the same place I'd hit it falling down the stairs." Her hand creeps up to her head, fingers running over what I imagine are the scars. "I had no identifying information, no memory, and no one looking for me. That was the part that confused them the most: a teenage girl must have *somebody* looking for her after six months, but not me. Not when 'Ivy Parker' had already moved to Los Angeles and changed her last name."

The guilt works through me like a poison. "Ivy, I'm . . ."

She silences me by reaching out to tuck a piece of hair behind my ear, making me shiver. For a moment, Ivy holds the strand between her fingers, examining the color. It's her own. I kept dyeing it after that first time, even if I didn't really need to—no one ever figured out my secret—but it was a ritual, a tether. A reminder of who I'd become.

"They tried everything," she says, dropping my hair. "Fingerprinting me, bringing in law enforcement to try to see if I was in the system. When that didn't work, they were talking about going to the media with a photo of me, but by that point, I knew no one was coming, and I didn't know if I could handle it—if it would be worse to find my family and not remember them or to have no one come for me at all. So, I left."

She sits all the way down in front of me, crossing her legs like we might play some sort of clapping game, but her eyes are haunted.

"I slept on the street for a while. Found whatever work would pay me cash and not ask too many questions. When people would ask my name, I started to say Catherine."

Recognition sparks in my chest. She smiles.

"I guess *Wuthering Heights* was still there in the back of my mind, even if I didn't know that's where it came from."

"When did you remember?" I ask, suddenly afraid of her answer.

She bites her lip, like she's savoring my fear.

"I remembered," Ivy says slowly, "when I saw your book."

My breath stalls, catching in my throat.

"Actually," she adds, grinning, "I saw it on your own social media. You'd posted a video a few months before it came out, letting people know it was available for preorder, and when it came up on my feed, it was like a switch flipped."

Her eyes brighten. My chest caves.

"Imagine me just scrolling through my phone," Ivy says, awed, "trying to numb my brain, when all of a sudden, there you were: a woman with my own name—my own *face*—and a book about a historic house in Westchester. It came back so quickly, it made me dizzy. I remembered *everything*."

At that last word, her awe sharpens into anger. I don't realize I'm crying again until she swipes a tear from my cheek with her finger, and I flinch.

"Still so afraid," she murmurs, "when you're the one who took everything."

"Ivy . . ." My voice breaks. I don't know what to say. There is nothing that will make any of this right again.

"Of course, I didn't have any real proof," Ivy continues. "I couldn't even be sure this wasn't just a brain injury–induced delusion. So, I followed you online. I tracked down an advance copy of your book, and I read it in one night. Then I read it again. It's good, you know." She smirks, one eye narrowing in an almost-wink. "Just a little fluffy for my taste."

Cold spills through my veins. All those stories Ivy scrawled so excitedly in the notebooks I lent her, her grin when I read them and told her, honestly, that they were good . . . *Haunt Me Then* is entirely my own work, but still, this feels like another thing I've stolen from her.

And then I remember: *Ivy Harcourt is a fraud.* That defaced book, those angry messages like threats from beyond the grave.

"You were Heathcliff," I say, even though it's been obvious from the moment I got here.

Ivy chuckles. "'I am Heathcliff,'" she quotes from the book, mockingly grandiose. "A little on the nose, maybe, but I'd already started calling myself Catherine, so I figured I'd keep working with the theme."

It lands like a zap of electricity.

"Oh my god," I breathe. "*Catherine.* You were Cat."

Now she grins.

"It was shockingly easy to track Xander down," Ivy says. "You tagged him on Instagram plenty of times, and the bar where he worked was all over his profile. So I just happened to find myself there one night."

My head spins, but she only gives an exaggerated shrug, performing innocence.

"I only wanted to meet him," Ivy says, "to learn some more about you—but then, when he was so clearly interested, I couldn't resist."

My stomach plummets. All those messages, the burn of betrayal as I read them . . .

"At first, it was mostly just an experiment. It thrilled me, being with him—like I was taking back what I should have had. Like I was trying on your skin." Ivy runs a cold finger over the curve of my cheek, and I shudder. She smiles. "He never even mentioned you. As far as he knew, I was blissfully unaware of his secret girlfriend, until one night, when he got drunk and started telling me his secrets."

She shapes the word into a hiss, and another tiny shiver rocks through me as I remember Xander's desperation at the bookstore. *I know what really happened to—*

"His secrets?" I repeat when Ivy still hasn't spoken. She wants me to prompt her—wants to draw this out, build the suspense.

She leans closer.

"He told me he had an older sister who ran away from home when she was eighteen." Ivy smiles, reading the terrible understanding all over my face, savoring it for another breath before she says, "Her name was Gabby."

32

"NO." IT RUSHES OUT OF me in a quiet moan, involuntary.

Ivy smiles like it delights her.

"Unlike the rest of his family," she says, "Xander never believed that Gabby ran away. She wouldn't have left for the city without at least telling him where she was going. And then there was the other weird thing." Ivy's eyes glimmer with intrigue. "A few days before Gabby disappeared, Xander overheard her on the phone with someone named Cora."

A chill races down my spine. My own name, and even now, it feels haunted, dangerous.

"Xander recognized the name, of course," she continues. "It was their neighborhood ghost. The girl who lived in the creepy old house and couldn't go outside."

It tumbles back from my memory as quickly as if it had been only days: Gabby's little brother, Alex—or Alexander, I assume, rebranding to just Xander as an adult. He was the boy who had looked through our window all those years ago, his hands cupped to the leaded glass. *I heard she's already dead.*

I let those same hands roam all over my body, let myself trust him—convincing myself that he might have loved me. Now my skin feels contaminated, itching.

"Then," Ivy says, like she's enjoying every second, "on the very night Gabby went missing, that same old house burned down, killing everyone but the youngest daughter. Xander knew the two things were connected, even if no one would believe him. He was just a fifteen-year-old boy, they thought, who was hurt that his sister left him behind and looking for an explanation. Eventually, he almost started to believe it."

Gabby. The grief guts me anew as I think of her running into that burning house for me, not knowing I was just a little farther down the driveway, hidden in the dark. Xander was right: Gabby never would have left him, and she didn't leave me. I can't believe I ever let myself think that she had.

Ivy wipes another tear from my cheek, and this time, I don't even flinch. Besides the heavy weight pushing against my ribs like it could crack them, everything else is numb.

"But then," she whispers, "Xander found you."

Something snaps into place inside me, the night we met at that Halloween party lit up in a new, warped light.

"You seemed so familiar to him." Ivy taps my chin. "When you mentioned that you were from LA, but that you spent some time in Westchester, it all came together: You were Ivy Parker, the sister who'd survived the fire and then moved to LA to live with some distant aunt. He'd never met you, but after the fire, Xander had done his research."

That flash drive, those articles . . . *Oh god.* The whole time, I thought I was falling in love with him, but he was only keeping me close so that he could probe me—probe *Ivy*—for information. If only he'd known who was really sleeping beside him.

And then, with a jolt, I realize.

"That photo," I say. "The one Gabby took of me. Xander had it. How did he . . ."

Ivy smiles like she knows the answer, and it thrills her to keep me in suspense—but I already know, too.

"He found it in my room," I guess.

After the fire, the only things I kept were what I managed to stuff into my bag that night: some clothes, essentials, and the only two sentimental items I couldn't leave behind—that photo and the copy of *Wuthering Heights* I'd given to Ivy. Even after I became her, I couldn't get rid of them. Neither was proof of my real identity, I told myself: The book was technically mine, as "Ivy," and the photo didn't give anything away. Ivy or Cora, it didn't matter—she was just a girl, smiling and free. I'd kept it hidden away under my bed, along with the book, a secret graveyard of my old life that came with me wherever I lived.

"Actually," Ivy says, "he found it in mine." She chuckles at my shocked expression. "You never grew out of hiding things under your mattress, did you?"

All at once, I understand. That candle blazing, almost lighting my apartment on fire. The email to my publisher. My old name scrawled all over the mirror . . . it was never Xander, or Liam, or even me losing my grip on my own sanity. It was Ivy. Maybe that should be a relief, but all I feel is cold.

"You stole the photo," I say, but it comes out weak, barely even an accusation. What is one little violation of my privacy, one petty theft, when I've stolen her entire life?

"He found it in my room one night." She lets out a laugh that's more like a huff. "*Cat's* room, technically. I guess he recognized it as a photo Gabby had taken, because that's when he started putting everything together. Or, at least, he thought he did."

Electricity hums under my skin, volatile and dangerous. Now I understand the look in Xander's eyes at the bookstore. I was afraid he'd figured out my secret, but I'd had it completely wrong.

I know. I know what really happened to—

"He thought *you* were Cora," I say, my stomach churning. "He was trying to warn me that you were still alive. That it had been Gabby in the fire." And then I remember, my hand lifting to my own neck. "Those bruises . . ."

"He went totally wild." She shakes her head, haunted. "Screaming at me, accusing me of killing his sister. When he lunged at me, I managed to knock him with a bottle. That threw him off-balance enough that I could get on top of him, put my hands around his neck."

I know it's true, but still, my jaw drops. I can't picture it—sweet ballerina Ivy strangling a grown man. But Ivy isn't the teenage girl I knew, not anymore, and I'm certain, from that vicious look in her eyes, that she is more than capable. The thought winds fresh fear around my ribs, pulling tight.

"Of course, that didn't work as well as I'd hoped." She gives a dark laugh. "When he passed out, I assumed I'd killed him, and I got the hell out of there. You can imagine my surprise when, later that night, I got a bunch of texts from him telling me that he'd tried to confront you at your author event, and he was going to go to the police if one of us didn't come clean. So, I paid him another visit." A smile curls on her lips. "You're welcome, by the way."

My heart seizes, turning to stone. Already, I knew that she'd killed him, but still, hearing it aloud—seeing her callous expression—is like one final blow.

And then I remember something else.

"You were wearing my clothes." I rise, backing away from her. "You tried to frame me. Why?"

Ivy rises to meet me, her expression eerily calm—almost sad.

"You stole my life," she says simply. "And I want it back."

Her hand slips out of her pocket in one smooth motion, something glinting in her fist: a knife, the same one from the videos of Mia. Dread pools in my gut as Ivy lets out a manic chuckle.

"I thought about just bringing some strawberry extract," she says. "But then I thought, been there, done that."

Confusion thrums under my wild heart. Ivy's eyes widen, delighted.

"Wait, did you never put it together? Oh my god." Now her glee takes on an edge of macabre fascination. Her face looks, for a moment, like a teenage girl's. "That's how I made you sick after Gabby came to the house. I swiped some strawberry extract from a friend's house and put it in your dinner. Mom figured it out and gave you the EpiPen as soon as you went into shock, but she never called me out. I think we all knew that you needed a reminder of how much danger you'd put yourself in by bringing someone inside." Her face warps into desperation. "How much you needed us."

I stumble back, my spine jutting into the wall. It's like she's carved me down the middle, gutted me clean.

A cold mask hardens Ivy's face once more. She traces a thumb over the knife's sharp tip before her eyes snap back to mine.

"This time," she says, "I want to see you bleed."

Fury spills into the hollow space between my ribs. With a growl, I rush at Ivy, knocking her to the ground. The knife falls from her hand and clatters into the detritus on the floor. She reaches for it, but I stop her, grabbing at her wrist.

Pain rockets through my face as Ivy's other fist cracks into my nose, stunning me enough that she rolls out from under me. Blood runs thick and hot into my throat as Ivy grabs the knife again and flashes the gleaming blade. I scramble backward on the ground like a crab, terror pulsing through me as broken boards and other debris jut into my palms, catching at my skirt. I cough, and blood spills from the side of my mouth.

Ivy stalks toward me, breathing hard.

"I'm sorry, Cora," she says. "There's no way out."

She lifts the knife.

I close my hand around the nearest broken beam and swing up, the wood connecting with Ivy's chin with a sickening slap. She stumbles, and I'm already running up the cellar stairs, but something catches my skirt—

Ivy's hand. I hurtle forward, pain screaming through my wrists as I catch myself on the steps. She claws at me, but I buck my legs, my foot landing hard enough in her chest that she releases me.

I sprint up the stairs and into the hallway, but already, I hear Ivy racing after me, feet thundering over the cellar stairs. I spin around to slam the door in her face before I remember that it's broken off of its hinges. The extra moment costs me. Before I can run, Ivy slams into me again, shoving me back against the wall, one arm braced against my throat and the knife poised overhead.

Her eyes are wild, gleaming in the moonlight. Blood is smeared over her bared teeth, and I can't be sure if it's hers or mine.

"Please," I beg, the word no more than a wheeze as her weight presses into my throat.

Maybe it's the desperation in my voice or on my face, or maybe she just wants to hear what I have to say for myself—either way, Ivy pulls back slightly, enough that I can still talk while the blade waits inches from my neck.

My breath catches. It's just a flash, but in this moment, beneath the bloodthirsty woman pinning me to the wall, I see my little sister, eager to hear what I think.

Tears spill onto my cheeks, mingling with the blood so that my whole mouth tastes of salt and brine. I blink them away, clearing my vision, and my eyes focus on hers. Waiting. Hesitant.

"I'm so sorry, Ivy," I tell her, chest burning. "Not just for stealing your life, but for leaving you behind. Even when I thought you were dead, I . . ." Pain cinches my throat, even without her pressing into it. "You're my sister, and I should have been there."

No matter what we've done to ourselves or each other, it's the truth—one I've carried with me for eleven years, its sharp corners pressing into my heart with every breath I've taken since that night.

"Everything I've done," I say, "everything I've written . . . it's all been for you, even if I couldn't say it—couldn't make myself tell the truth." I take a shuddering breath, reaching up to brush Ivy's forearm. At my touch, her grip on the knife loosens. She lowers her arm, and hope pulses through me. We're still there, buried beneath the selves we've created: Ivy and Cora Parker, sisters who've spent the past decade searching for each other, even when we couldn't admit it—when the pull home felt less like gravity and more like a curse.

"We're the same, Ivy. We always have been. No matter where we came from, we're family. We were both trapped, and we've both been doing what we can to survive." I reach for her hand, the one with the knife, and softly close my own around it. "But now we don't have to do it alone."

Tears shimmer in Ivy's eyes, pricking my own heart all over again. She looks so young. They say that grief can freeze you in time, and maybe we're both still there, still burning in this house—children who were burdened with so much more than they should have been, trying and failing to protect each other. To free ourselves.

No matter how far we run, or who we become, we've never really left.

"I'm sorry," she whispers, a darkness dipping into her eyes that fills me with dread.

Before I can ask her what she means, I hear another voice.

"Ivy?"

My skin tingles with familiarity. I know, even before I see him walk through the door. *Liam.* Relief rushes through me, love crushing my chest. Dani must have told him I was gone. I don't know how he figured out I was here, but he found me. *He came for me.*

I'm about to call out to him when my sister screams.

My head snaps back to her just in time to see her swing the knife downward. It squelches, plunging through skin, and I gasp.

Ivy turns to Liam as he rushes into the burned, rotted house, his eyes widening in confusion when he sees us—my hand still touching the handle of the blade that's stuck in my sister's side.

She stumbles back.

"Help," she whispers, moving desperately toward Liam.

And then she crumples to the ground. We both rush to her, but she's already fading, the light in her fluttering eyes going dull.

"Who is this?" Liam asks. "What did you do?"

He's talking to me, but I barely hear him. I'm focused on Ivy's face—on the smile that flickers on her lips, a little secret between sisters, before she shuts her eyes for good.

ONE MONTH LATER

THE SUN BEAMS DOWN OVER the Village. Midsummer now, nearly too hot to brave the sticky subway or the baking concrete, but New York is not deterred: Washington Square Park is full of life. People lounge on benches or in the grass, books and blankets splayed around them, iced drinks melting quickly in the heat. Couples stroll by, hand in hand, laughing or talking or simply listening to the music around them, booming from distant speakers or even into the headphones they split like a shared head, one partner with the left ear, the other with the right.

I sit across from the dog run, a notebook open in my lap. For now, I've paused my scrawling ink to look up at the dogs zipping through the park, tongues lolling, their owners looking on from the shade.

I watch, and I wait for him.

He's already late—only five minutes, but part of me is afraid he won't show. More minutes tick by, and just as I'm starting to lose hope, he appears. He's wearing a familiar crisp button-down and slacks, a messenger bag slung over his shoulder, and he's breathless as he approaches, like he's been walking fast—or maybe he's just nervous.

"Sorry," Liam says. "I got caught up at work."

"That's okay." I close my notebook, setting it beside me. "How's the new job?"

He hovers over me for a moment, like he isn't sure how to greet me. There's a hesitation between us, an icy wall that's yet to melt. Finally, he settles for no greeting at all, simply sitting beside me on the bench and setting the messenger bag between us. A barrier, I think. Protection.

"It's good," Liam says earnestly. "I really like it."

"Good," I say.

"And how's the, er . . ." Liam hesitates, glancing down at my notebook. "You're working on a book, right?"

I smile, a warm tendril snaking through my chest. "Actually, that's what I wanted to talk to you about."

Liam tenses, adjusting his glasses.

"Oh," he says. "How so?"

Across from us, two owners untangle their dogs' leashes, laughing nervously as they do. The man says something, and the woman chuckles, her cheeks turning pink. A *meet-cute*, I think with a little smile. I wonder how many of them happen every day in this city, with all its different lives splitting and rejoining, shifting like so many rivers.

When I answer Liam, I keep my voice casual, light.

"I was wondering if you'd give me an interview."

Now he turns to look at me straight on.

"Just about the time you spent with her," I say. "To provide a little context. Another shade, so to speak, since I spent so many years without her. I'll be talking to Mia and Dani, too."

He frowns, uncomfortable. "But I didn't really . . ."

I take his hand, and he flinches, stopping short.

"I think she would want someone else who loved her to be a part of the story. I'm trying to paint as full of a picture as possible, because I know how easy it will be for people to villainize her."

Liam looks down at our hands, still stunned, and I let go.

"There's plenty of time for you to think it over," I say, fixing my eyes back on the dog run. "But I'd really appreciate it." I glance back at him. "I think Cora would, too."

Liam tenses at the sound of your name. He still hasn't said it out loud, at least not that I've heard. I've caught him almost calling you Ivy a few times, still so used to your stolen identity, but he always catches himself, settling for some other name instead—*she, her, your sister.*

"Have you talked to her?" he asks, with a little twitch in his throat, like he's not sure he wants the answer.

I shake my head, apologetic. "I'm not supposed to. Not until the trial is over."

I'm also not supposed to speak publicly about your crimes, which means that technically, this book isn't allowed to exist yet. But it will—I've already had a few literary agents poking into my inbox, even a handful of publishers, all inquiring whether I'd be interested in writing a memoir about my years in the shadows and, ultimately, my triumphant reclamation of my stolen life.

I haven't officially accepted any offers yet, of course, but the ideas have been humming, spilling eagerly onto the pages. My veins fill with sunlight every time I think of it: my name, Ivy Parker, printed on the cover.

"Me neither," Liam says sadly. As the witness to my stabbing, he also isn't supposed to be communicating with you, the defendant.

For a few moments, Liam is silent, staring out at the dog run like he's suddenly deeply interested.

"We talked for a few minutes, though," he says without looking back at me. "That night, before the paramedics arrived."

My heart thumps. "What did she say?"

I can't hide the eagerness in my voice, no matter how hard I try. Since getting out of the hospital, my stab wound freshly stitched and bandaged, the only information I've gotten about you has been through the news, the brutal headlines.

ROMANCE TURNED HORROR: BESTSELLING AUTHOR "IVY HARCOURT" ACCUSED OF MURDERING HER PARENTS IN A 2015 HOUSE FIRE AND THEN STEALING HER SISTER'S IDENTITY.

READERS STUNNED AS AUTHOR IS ARRESTED FOR KILLING PARENTS, NEIGHBOR AND EX-BOYFRIEND IN STRANGER-THAN-FICTION TWIST.

Finally, Liam looks at me. Behind his glasses, his eyes are devastated.

"She admitted to the fire and taking your name," he says. "But she swears she didn't kill Xander."

He swallows, face twitching like he's trying to ward off tears. When he speaks again, it's so quiet I can barely hear.

"She says she didn't stab you."

I flinch back, heart jumping.

"You saw it," I argue. "You watched her do it."

"I know," he says. "But . . ."

I bring a hand to my bandaged side as if his doubt makes it physically hurt. Maybe it does. There is, after all, a dull throb of pain there, one that never seems to go away.

This time, it's Liam who touches me, his hand falling gently onto my knee.

"I'm sorry, Ivy," he says. "It's just a lot for me to take in."

My lips twitch into a soft smile. "Me too."

Liam nods, a smile ghosting over his own lips. I turn away, back to the dog run. The meet-cute couple is gone now, and I feel a little pang of loss.

"My sister is a very disturbed person," I say. "But she's been through a lot—we both have—and I still love her."

"Yeah," Liam says, stopping short of a *me too*, but I can feel it in the way his arm twitches, his hand about to lift from my leg.

I stop him with my own hand, threading our fingers together. Liam's breath hitches, his eyes meeting mine.

"Thank you," I say. "For meeting with me today. You really didn't have to."

"Of course." I don't think I imagine the little squeeze he gives me before letting go. "I'm happy to."

"And seriously, no rush on the interview," I add with a little smile. "Like I said, there's time."

Liam nods, rubbing at his nose with the back of his hand as he blinks away the tears in his eyes.

"Right," he says. "Yeah, I'll let you know." He hesitates for a moment before glancing down at his bag. "Listen, I should probably . . ."

"Of course." I smile brighter. "No problem at all. It was really good to see you, Liam."

He hesitates again as he stands, still unsure how to handle the space between us. This time, it's me who decides. I stand up and pull him into a hug, and he tenses at first, but then, after a breath, he relaxes into me, his strong hands pressing into my back.

"Good to see you, too," he says, his breath warm on my cheek as he pulls away. "I'll be in touch."

With another little wave, Liam goes. I watch him as I settle back onto the bench, desire pooling low in my gut as he swings his bag over his broad shoulders.

It's not hard to see what you saw in him, Cora. I know I won't get to read your second book anytime soon, since it was pulled indefinitely from publication, but I can imagine it perfectly. It almost writes itself.

Liam glances back over his shoulder, cheeks turning pink when he realizes I'm still watching. I give him a wave, and he returns it shyly before turning around again, walking deeper into the stream of people. As he goes, my open hand curls into a fist, as if catching a firefly. I press it to my heart.

He may not be mine, Cora, but give it time. I've already reclaimed so much of what you stole from me: my name, my life. *My story.* Maybe you've been punished enough, locked away for the crimes you committed and the ones you didn't, but you said it yourself: We have both been prisoners. We're doing what we can to survive.

And maybe, I think, as Liam disappears, I deserve him, too. You've taken so many things that weren't yours, after all. I'd simply be returning the favor.

The truth is, you couldn't stop me if you tried. The pen is in my hand now. It's finally my turn to tell our story—and I'm only just beginning.

ACKNOWLEDGMENTS

Making it to the acknowledgments of a book always feels like such a gift and a celebration, especially for this one—because there was a brief time when I truly thought I might not get here. Of all my books, *Man of My Dreams* has been the hardest to crack, and I couldn't have done it without my phenomenal editor, Alex Sehulster. Thank you for being so willing to dig into this story with me, with all the lengthy, occasionally frantic calls and emails that entailed. I'm endlessly grateful for your wisdom and talent!

Speaking of gratitude, I'm forever pinching myself that I have an agent as wonderful as Claire Friedman. Five books in (five??!), I can't thank you enough for not only believing in my work but making it better. I am so, so lucky to have you in my corner.

Another huge thank-you to the team at Minotaur: Jen Enderlin, Kelley Ragland, Allison Ziegler, Kayla Janas, Ashley Quintana, Paul Hochman, David Baldeosingh Rotstein, Devan Norman, Alisa Trager, Melanie Sanders, Diane Dilluvio, MaryAnn Johanson, and all the other amazing people who have touched this book. I'm so thankful for your support and enthusiasm for my twisted love stories—working with y'all is a dream!

Thanks also to the full team at Inkwell Management for all your support; to Florence Hare, Vanessa Phan, and Jemima Forrester for championing this book in the UK; and to Debbie Deuble Hill at IAG for your support in the film world. I'm so glad to have y'all on board!

As always, one of the deepest, most heartfelt thank-yous goes to my family and friends. Mom, Dad, Grayson, and Eugenie—I wouldn't be here without your support and encouragement. Thank y'all for always cheering me on (and being the best marketing team around). And to my friends—y'all are the best hype squad and support system a girl could ask for. I'm so grateful every time you've checked in, come to an event, recommended my books to friends and strangers (and the occasional Hinge match), or even just sent me a picture of my books in the wild. I love y'all so much!

And to Mitchell—thank you for always being there to talk through plot holes, listen to me rant and rave, and pick me up when I'm in the throes of an existential crisis. (Also for accidentally inspiring this book!) I love you, and I'm very glad you're real.

Finally, from the bottom of my heart, I want to thank the readers. It means so much that I get to share my books with you, and I truly can't thank you enough for giving them a chance. Every review, recommendation, post, and kind word is so appreciated, and I'm so grateful to all the booksellers, creators, authors, and book lovers who've helped my books find new readers. You are all a dream come true.

ABOUT THE AUTHOR

Sub/Urban Photography

Olivia Worley is an author born and raised in New Orleans. A graduate of Northwestern University, she now lives in New York City, where she spends her time writing thrillers, overanalyzing reality TV, and hoping someone will romanticize her for reading on the subway. She is also the author of *So Happy Together*, *People to Follow*, *The Debutantes*, and *Final Cut*.